THE BATTLE FOR YGGDRASIL

VOLUME TWO OF THE VÖRÐUR OF YGGDRASIL

KARI ROBINS

FOWLER INK, LLC.

A NOTE FROM THE

I write within the dark fantasy genre. Some themes I write may not be suitable for all readers. If you are new to dark fantasy/romance, please read the possible triggers below.

All my books are spicy. Some are sweet spicy while others bring darker elements into the bedroom. If there's ever a question or you find something that I don't have listed, feel free to contact me through email or social media.

The Battle for Yggdrasill is slightly darker than The Rise of the Vörður so I wanted to give a warning to all my readers.

- Blood, fighting, violence, and war.

- A few of the characters are cursed with a magic that forces them into self-mutilation.

- A few of the characters are victims of childhood neglect and trauma.

- There is a magically created sex scene that could be viewed as non-consensual or cheating but don't worry... nothing ACTUALLY happens between them she just makes it seem like it does.

- There is also a VERY dark sex scene.

- PTSD

- Parental abuse of adult child

- Mental & physical abuse

- On a more enjoyable note... There will be a lot of detailed sex.

To the best friends an author could ask for.
Julia, Lianona, Amanda, & Marissa.
Without you this book would have had a different ending.

ALSO BY

Glossary

Names:

Jörð /Jey ö ar ð/—Goddess of earth

Njörðr /Nj ö ar Ð ar/—God of Fertility

Surt /Sir-t/—God of War and Fire

Skadi /Skahd-ee/—Goddess of Ice

Aric Hvit Eik /ærɪk ʋiːt æjk/—Fae Prince

Byrnjar Alm /Brin-Yar Alm/

Places:

Asgard /'æsgɑrd/—Home and fortress of the Aesir

Midgard /'mɪdgɑrd/—Earth

Alfheim /ALF-heim/—Home of the Light Elves

Vanaheim /van-a-heim/—Home of the Vanir gods

Jotunheim /yaw-toon-heym/—Home of the Giants

Niflheim /nɪfəlˌhaɪm/—Home of primordial darkness, cold, mist, and ice.

Svartalfheim /SVART-half-hame/—Home of the dark Elves

Helheim /hell-heim/—Home of the Dead

Muspelheim /muh-spell-hame/—Home of the Fire Giants

Things:

Flygeblad /flyːgəblɑːd/—winged warriors

Kompis /kumpɪs/—Bonded Mate

Yggdrasil /ɪgdrəsəl/—The World Tree and the Gateway into the Nine Realms

Vörður /Veeöarðer/—Protector/Guardian

contents

PLAYLIST

This book was a struggle to finish. Not because it was difficult to write but because impostor syndrome is a b!tch. Listening to music helped to clear my mind and keep me motivated.

CHAPTER 1

Emma

D arkness surrounded me, making me temporally blind. Slowly, my eyes adjusted to reveal the cold damp cell. The stale, icy air burned my lungs as I sat up, gripping the iron bars that caged me in. My palms sizzled at the iron and I cried out, and sank back down into the hard earth. The pungent aroma of my own burning flesh made me retch.

My mind went fuzzy leaving blank spots in my memory. The last thing I could recall seeing before waking here was King Herrick striding out toward me, grinning wildly. Flashes of the battle exploded behind my eyes, and I doubled over in agony. My back and shoulders ached. The cause of my pain was just out of reach in my memory.

Mother's armies had been sent to ambush him, but my father was waiting for us. How had we not seen it coming? We had a god of war on our side and were utterly defeated.

The cold, dark rocks were unforgiving as I leaned into the wall for support. *This has to be Svartalfheim*. My father had to have stolen me in the chaos of the battle. Rubbing at my temples, I tried to put the pieces together. It was the only explanation that made sense. After all, I was his prize, the one thing he wanted most—right next to total domination of Yggdrasil and the Nine Realms.

My chest tightened as I paced the little cell. *There's got to be a way out!* He had taken me away from my home, my love, my family... Silent tears streamed down my cheeks as I thought of my mate's face. Getting free and back to Brynjar was my only thought. Father had some nefarious plan for me but I couldn't allow him to use me like that.

"You will destroy my floor if you pace much longer, my daughter," he hissed from behind me.

His voice in the silence caused me to jump, turning in midair to face him. The tall, thin man stood there, smiling at me. His pale skin and ice-blue eyes sent a shiver down my spine.

In some ways, I could see Aric in him. They had the same ears and coal black wings that nearly dragged the ground. But while Aric wore the baggy clothing of an 80s grunge band, my father wore tight black pants, a red button-up shirt with a black jacket. I could imagine him being considered handsome in the human realm.

Pain radiated down my back as I slammed into the wall behind me. My hand reached back, grasping the feathery limbs when the realization came crashing to the forefront of my mind. Wings. A vision of bones and feathers tearing through my skin flashed in my mind. How had I forgotten that painful memory?

My eyes widened. "What?"

"Lovely fresh addition, darling. We will have to help you learn to use them. Dragging them like that will cause you harm."

Sweat beaded on my forehead. My body tensed, not daring to speak a word. King Herrick shifted into mist and walked right through the iron bars, his fiery breath inches away from me.

"Wha-what do you want?" My voice came out hoarse.

"My darling daughter. All I have ever wanted was you, don't you see that? Those miserable Alfheim faeries left you for dead.

If I would have known about you sooner, I would have saved you myself." He raised his clammy hand and stroked my cheek. "I love you and want you to reign at my side."

"What about Aric? Is he safe? We are both your children. Why not have him as well?"

"You are far more powerful than he is. Besides, he already believes me evil. You have no idea the struggles I face." He took my hand, tracing the scars on my arms. "You don't remember what happened, do you?"

Tearing my arm from his grasp, I yelled, "You kidnapped me! That's what happened."

"Oh Daughter, you are far smarter than that. Look again and remember."

My face hardened, glaring at my father. Disjointed images flashed in my mind making me want to remember, but also fearing what I'd see if I did. Blood and death. So many bodies. My mother laying lifeless with a spear jutting from her chest. My own hands coated in white blood.

White blood? Not the blood of the dark fae?

Questions rang through my mind. Flames shot from my hands at my allies, my friends. When I saw Thyra stand between me and my brother, I pushed out of the memory, refusing to watch anymore of his lies.

"That... that didn't happen like that!" Tears fell from my eyes as I spoke. "What have you done to me?"

"Nothing that wouldn't have happened naturally, I only unleashed you, allowed you to become what the Gods meant you to be." He knelt beside me and lifted my chin. "They wanted to chain you down. They wanted you caged!" Anger rose in his voice.

"Aren't we sitting in a cage? How are you much better?"

"You are only here until you decide where you want to be. Your power is strong, you can't deny that. You have known it for a long time. If only you let me release you fully, you will see. You are not just some fae princess. The gods bestowed their gifts on you so that someday you can become a goddess of the entire Nine Realms." He brushed my hair away from my eyes. "Are you still in pain, my dear?"

He ran a finger down my arms and the memories of the battle blurred together.

Scars tore through my flesh, both new and old. A cold anger washed over me out of nowhere. The face of my mate Brynjar that I had so longed to be with again now brought me to the brink of rage. *No, this is my Kompis.* My attempts to push away the hurt was thwarted when my father gripped my wrist, sending fresh hatred into my heart.

I had taken this curse for Brynjar. Why had my mate not stopped me from taking it? Where is he now? Did he let me do those things I saw, or did he fight me?

My father's cold eyes softened.

"Yes," I whispered. "It still hurts."

"If you'd like, I can take that away for you." He stood. "But you have to make the choice. Fight for me, daughter, and you will have all my powers on top of your own and so much more." He offered a hand to me. "Join me and together we will right all the wrongs this world has done us."

It was pointless fighting his control. My body sagged against my father, and I let go of all the hurt and confusion. Anger radiated through me at all those that stood by for years and did nothing to help me. Even at Brynjar, who allowed me to take the curse from him. He never saw how much pain I was in. If he did, he said nothing, never asked to take it back, never offered to help me.

They all sensed the power lurking beneath my skin and cowered from me anytime I showed the slightest hint of it. My father was right: they wanted me muzzled like a dog.

I raised my head toward my father, giving in to his power, and took his hand. Relief settled over me and it washed away the scars over my arms. When I stood next to him, ice flowed throughout my body, cooling my anger. We strode up to the bars and together, we shifted into mist and walked through.

CHAPTER 2

Aric

Mother's chair consumed me, even for my large frame. In an attempt to relax, I shifted from side to side before settling on resting my head in my hand, grateful for this rare moment of silence in the empty Throne Room. My world had crashed around me, yet my people needed my help. Mother was dead. Bodies littered the battlefield. The room felt empty without Emma ruling at my side. Her fear surrounded me even now but... she'd killed so many of our people and I couldn't see them welcoming her back. Brynjar had yet to speak to me. I hadn't wanted to speak to him either, but I knew we couldn't avoid each other forever. And Thyra... She lay in the infirmary, frozen until the healers could repair the injuries my sister had caused.

"Your majesty?" a gruff voice asked, bringing me out of my trance.

Slowly raising my head, I saw my mother's High Chancellor standing before me fiddling with his hands. "Please, High Chancellor Tavis, don't call me that. Aric will be just fine." Dark circles lined the chancellor's red-ringed eyes.

The fae bowed. "But that is what you are. With your mother..." Tavis wiped his eyes. "You are all we have left. We need you to help us pick up the pieces and move on."

Tears trickled down my cheeks. "Move on?" I scoffed.

"Our people need to see strong leadership," he said.

My feet moved as I bolted out of the throne and stood toe to toe with my High Chancellor. "Strong leadership died on that battlefield. My world died out there, and there is nothing left for me!"

High Chancellor Tavis stumbled backwards. "Please, Sire," he whimpered.

My knees hit the ground, sobbing. "I don't know how to lead. How to move on, Tavis. My... everything is gone."

The thin fae hesitated before resting a hand on my shoulder. "My King, I lost a great deal on that battlefield as well. We all did. We can only survive this if we do so together. We are all hurting, but you mustn't show this to our people. Please let me help you and we can help the others."

Nodding in my hands, High Chancellor Tavis let his magic flow. Warmth wrapped around me, shaking off the despair.

"This is only a temporary fix, Majesty. You will still grieve, but my magic can keep you from hitting rock bottom."

Feeling better than I had in days, I stood. Not happy, but also not weighed down with sorrow. "Thank you, Tavis. I fear I will need your magic more than you know."

"I'm here anytime you need me, Sire." He bowed.

Tears filled my eyes. "I'm hurting enough. When it is just us, please be less formal."

"Yes... Aric."

"Thank you. Now, what can I do for you?"

"The memorial service." Tavis averted his eyes. "It is about to start."

The purple haze of the setting sun welcomed me as I stepped out into the light. Silence echoed throughout the land. Even the birds were quiet.

My dark wings trailed behind me. My body shook as each row of faces bowed as I walked through the sea of white-robed fae. Every single one of my people and our allies stood watching me. From the very young to the old. Their grief consumed me as much as my own had and it took all my strength to focus on my steps.

The tears flowed freely down my cheeks by the time I reached my seat at the front of my people. Clasping my hands in front of me, my eyes locked on the massive funeral pyre. Hundreds of my people lay upon the wooden tree trunks.

The very earth had cried out and shook violently when the army returned with so many dead. Trees had fallen of their own accord giving their lives for each fallen fae.

No words needed be spoken. None could calm the sorrow that radiated through my people.

We stood there in reverence until the sun sank behind the earth.

A small fae approached the pyre and knelt before it, bowing his head, he spoke a prayer of peace before touching the wood. Flames licked away at the pyre until the fire spread over everything.

Sobs of the people surrounded me, pulling me under the veil of grief with them. My knees gave out pulling me to the ground and I wept.

The heavens opened up and mourned with us as the fire burned on through the rain, devouring death.

My knees sank into the mud, watching the flames die out. My people had retreated long ago, but it was my duty to see the dead to the next life. Only the two guards that rarely left my side stood far in the distance.

A voice behind me shook with rage. "Who the Hel do you think you are to deserve the honor of watching over our dead?"

Brynjar's presence brought the fight I'd been waiting for to me. Spinning around to face him, I clamped my jaw tight. "Don't you dare to question my pain! My grief is far deeper than yours."

Brynjar stood in the rain, wings spread wide, sword in hand. Blood dripped down his arms from fresh cuts. "She is my mate. My *bonded* mate. Not my lover. Not my sister." He scratched at his arms with the blades edge. "That damned curse is back. My arms burn with the need of cold steel. We're still connected." He raised his sword. "She is scared and completely on her own and you have left her to her fate!"

Flicking my wrist, I conjured a sword of my own. "You think I can't feel her too? She is my twin. Her pain has always been mine."

Brynjar shot into the sky and clashed into my sword, pinning me to the ground. "She is my love, and I will not sit here and do nothing!"

Shoving him off, I jumped to my feet, and thrust the tip of my sword toward Brynjar's throat. I spat, "And what of my love? She lay all but dead at the hands of my sister. Even if we could find Emma, Herrick might have claimed her already."

Brynjar batted away my sword and stood. "You heard her. She left to keep us safe!" He swiped at my chest, grazing the surface of my flesh.

"Damn you, Brynjar," I winced at the pain and clutched the wound. "I love her too and will do what I can to save her. But this will not help!" I didn't break eye contact with Brynjar as my guards approached. "No!" I called to them. "Stay back, I'll handle this." Vanishing my sword, I raised my palms to the sky speaking to my brother once again. "You're our best chance to save her, my friend. I need your help. Please."

Brynjar gripped his sword tighter and locked his jaw but made no move against me.

"Please, Brynjar. No one else can do this. We should be fighting side by side, my brother."

He faltered, discarding his sword, he dropped to his knees, burying his face in his hands and wailed. "I need her. I can't breathe without her."

Kneeling beside him, I wrapped my arm around him. "I know, brother. We will find her." We sat together as our grief overtook us.

CHAPTER 3

Emma

S hadows swayed on the floor from the torchlight as I paced my new home. Father had relocated me to one of the largest rooms in the mountain.

Leaning against the cool rock wall, I slid to the floor and I licked salty tears from my lips. The *drip*, *drip*, *drip* of water leaking through the crack in the cave ceiling echoed in the cathedral room. My vision blurred as I thought back to the battlefield. Memories flashed behind my eyes.

That wasn't me. No, I couldn't have done those things.

Bile rose in my throat.

The white blood of the light fae stained my hands and I moved frantically to wipe them, but the ivory still clung to them. Father hadn't lied to me. I had killed for him. I knelt, retching on the floor, then curled up into a ball and sobbed.

What have I done?

My skin grew cold laying on the rocky floor before the pounding on my door pulled me out of my haze.

The door opened before I could speak. His warm hands grasped my arm, helping me to my feet. He brushed my hair from my eyes, his face contorted in an almost fatherly concern.

"Daughter? Are you all right?" he asked.

"I remember e-everything. How... how could I have done those things, Father?"

"They stood in your way. You are my child, and nothing will ever stand in your way again." He pulled me into an awkward hug.

Ice trickled through my veins at his touch and the fear and disgust at what I had done faded the longer he held me.

"Now." He broke the hug and looked me in the eye. "How are you feeling?"

"Better. Thank you." The crisp tone of my voice was almost unrecognizable.

"Good because I have a surprise for you." He offered me his arm. "If you want to come see?"

My fears vanished and a devious joy overflowed me. Grinning wildly, I took his hand and nearly skipped out of my room.

Father led the way deeper into the earth and the cold tunnels narrowed in on me. My heart quickened as the darkness engulfed us. A vision of being locked in a closet flashed through my mind. *Breathe, just breathe.* Snapping my fingers, flames licked my palms before light blossomed in the darkness.

"Beautifully done, daughter." Father faced me, watching the flames flicker on my palm.

"Th-thank you."

We reached a thick metal door, and Father opened it for me, ushering me inside. A shiver ran down my spine as I stepped into the large room. The black walls curved upward, towering overhead. Iron bars lined the walls to my left and right, leaving a small path between the cages. Emaciated creatures huddled in the corners of every cell, not daring to move as he walked past.

"Don't mind them. They won't hurt you."

"Who are they?" I whispered.

My stomach was in knots. *This isn't right.* Deep down, I knew something was very wrong, but I couldn't pull my thoughts away from Father.

"Some are humans. Some are fae. All are enemies." Turning his back to me, he walked on. "Now, for your surprise."

We passed dozens of cells filled with filthy beings before he finally stopped in front of one. Standing beside Father, I faced the tiny room. My eyes widened as the people inside came into focus.

"E-Emma?" a hoarse voice asked, so foreign I hardly recognized it.

"Drew?"

The tall, thin man cowered in the corner, shielding his mother. It had been years since I had seen them, but I'd never forgotten the family that had tormented me.

"Wh-what's going on? Where are we?" he stammered. "What is that behind you?"

Shaking, I turned to Father. "What are they doing here?"

"They plagued you as a child and I thought it was only fair that you got to repay them. Happy birthday, my daughter." He beamed at me.

"It... it's not my birthday."

"No, but I have missed twenty-two of them. Family shouldn't treat you the way they did. They take care of you, not harm you."

Nausea gripped my stomach. Placing my hand over my mouth, I turned from them. Father's influence over me broke at the sight of their terrified faces. Hatred filled me for these people, but I would not do what my father wanted, so I ran for the door and didn't slow until I found my way back to my room.

My throat was raw by the time I stopped screaming into the darkness of my room. My head and the lingering, icy touch of his magic had cleared the moment I stepped away from Father. *I'm still his prisoner.* Crawling onto the bed, I buried my head in the pillow.

The sulfurous smell that emanated from the fabric gagged me as the wall of the large foreign room closed in. Clutching at my neck, I willed myself to take a breath.

Vomit crawled up my throat as I ran to the bathroom and spewed into the cold stone sink. It was all I could do just to breath as I leaned against the wall, trying to calm myself.

Snapping my fingers, I stripped myself of clothing and stepped into the shower, catching my wings on the edge of the door.

Damn.

A cascade of warm water flowed over the rock the moment I stepped in and I turned my back to the shower head, letting the heat soothe my sore wings and back as I rested my head on the cool stones. The tears flowed freely.

"I should have jumped," I said to no one. My life changed irrevocably the day I decided to end it all. If I had gone through with my plans, I wouldn't be in this living hell. But then Aric would have died that day too, trapped in the bottle.

Wrapping my arms around my chest, I sunk to the floor and accidentally sat on my wings. "Shit!" I cried out as the pain ripped through me. Bryn would've tucked his wings behind his back, so I stood and tried to mimic his movements. Groaning at their weight, I tried again until I managed to move them and was able to sit without harming them.

The water rushed over me again, helping to slow my heart rate. Lifting my palm, I twirled the water into a tornado and smiled as it spun around and around like a top.

The faint whispers of my name from the only men who ever really loved me echoed in my ears. Was that really them or my own desires to hear their voices one last time? Either way, a warmth spread throughout my body at the thought of my brother and mate's faces. Memories of all the love I held for them flooded me. My cheeks ached from my smile. I needed to get back home to them.

Standing, I sent the water-nado to the floor, and stepped out onto the cool rocks. I attempted to shake out my wings and whimpered at the effort. Instead, I simply snapped my fingers and dried my body, wrapping it in clothing.

The thin, feathery dresses of Alfheim would have left me shivering here, but the weather was warmer back home. In the coolness of Svartalfheim, I was grateful for the warmer, long-sleeved, floor-length cotton dress as it wrapped around my chilled skin.

The room was dark as I walked across the stone floor. The rocks crept up to the ceiling leaving black walls with no decoration making the space as cold as the air. Even the wood that made up the four-poster bed was blackened as if it had survived a fire. The cold and the dark made me miss the warmth and brightness of Alfheim. Crawling up under the flannel blankets of my bed, I fell asleep instantly.

A sharp pain in my back forced me awake. My wing twisted under my body, pulling at my back. With great effort and care, I rolled off the bed and stood. Walking to the bathroom proved difficult when my long wings I dragged behind me caught on something, sending me tumbling to the hard floor.

"Fuck!" I shouted. Pain seared down my back as I rolled to my side. Blood trickled from my nose where my face had connected with the hard floor.

The door creaked open, drawing my attention to it as Father strode through. His smug smile faded as he saw me. "What are you doing on the floor, daughter?"

Scrambling to my feet, gazing downward. "I tripped," I said, glancing behind me at my new wings before wiping at the blood under my nose and struggled to hide the bitterness in my voice. "What are you doing here, anyway?"

"I came to wake you for the day but when I heard you scream, I let myself in."

Great, just one more freedom he was taking.

He flicked his eyes behind me and I could only imagine the mess my wings were. "I can help you with that. It will take some getting used to and a lot of hard work. Normally, winged fae grew into their wings when they are very young. Your mother's antics seem to have delayed your development. You won't be able to fly anytime soon, but at least we can help you not hurt yourself." He stretched out his hand toward me.

Glaring at him only made him smile again. After a moment I gave in and accepted and walked out into the hall with him. The icy tingle of his magic flowed into me and tried to pull away, but he gripped me tighter.

"Where are we going?" I asked stiffly.

"To the training room. We will get those wings in proper shape."

My mind fought his pull, but my body gave in and relaxed the longer we walked and I edged closer to Father, feeling more and more comfortable around him.

"How long will it be before I'm able to fly?"

"It will be a while yet. The human body is not born equipped to fly. Even though you are pure fae, your time in the human realm has weakened you. If you would have grown up here, you could fly right now. As it is, we have to work at it so you can even use them." He patted my hand. "Don't worry. We'll get you there."

"Thank you, Father." Something snapped into place and I gave in completely, smiling at him.

We walked until we entered a large room filled with dark fae. Their red eyes reminded me of those that snuck into Alfheim. My heart sank at the memory of killing them. They were family. *Right?* Shaking my head did little to clear the confusion.

The scent of week-old socks invaded my nose before I entered the vast room. My eyes followed the curvature of the walls until I couldn't find the top. The clashing of metal weapons echoed all around me. The fae parted for us, bowing before they turned and left the space as we walked into the center of the room.

"Let's get started."

"Who are they?" I asked, pointing to the fae filing past me as they watched their feet.

An odd shiver ran down my spine. Their fear of Father seeped into my emotions. My brain couldn't process why they couldn't be in the same room as their king.

"They are my warriors."

They were tall and muscular with skin as soft as the surrounding rocks. Some were just as dark as the obsidian walls but I halted, gaping at the ones with sandstone tones.

"Just like in Alfheim, daughter, the fae come in all sizes and colors." Father spoke pulling me back to my task and I kept walking.

"I assume your mother had you doing some kind of training." He raised an eyebrow. "Martial arts of some sort?"

I could only nod.

"So mundane of her. Here I will teach you how to actually fight, but for now, we need to condition your body for your new wings." He turned to face me. "Shrug your shoulders." I did. "That's the movement I want you to do with your wings. It'll take you a bit to understand what muscles you need to use to do this. Close your eyes and try to feel where they connect with your back."

Doing as he asked, I pictured my new wings, focusing on my shoulder blades where my wings connected to my back. Grunting, I forced the muscles to move. It was only a fraction of an inch, but I could move them. Grinning I thought of my mate and wished I could tell Brynjar before my smile faded.

"Well done. Now do that about a thousand times."

I laughed at Father.

"That wasn't a joke. You need to build up strength. Also, don't move your shoulders when you do it. When you are back in your room, do it in front of a mirror," he said.

Up, down. Up, down. I raised and lowered my wings repeatedly until the pain seared through my spine and I could take no more. After what felt like hours, he told me I could stop.

"That's the easy part of today." He sighed. "To use them properly, you have to strengthen your core. I'm surprised you haven't fallen over at the weight of them to begin with."

"I... I worked out a lot in Midgard," I said, feeling a little defensive. "I worked in a dojo," I half whispered at his stone face.

He smiled. "That explains that. Very well, but we still need to work on strengthening your core more. It will be different from lying flat on your back doing crunches. You have to take care of your wings and laying on them won't help them. And until you get used to them, you'll need to stand to work out."

We trained for hours before he walked me back to my room and I collapsed into bed without bothering to undress.

CHAPTER 4

Aric

T he massive room closed in on me with so many fae jammed in it. The giant, red oak table stretched out before me as I sat shifting in my chair and pulled at the collar of my tunic. The surrounding fae blurred in my vision, their voices muffled. I rubbed at my ears trying to clear the noise.

Wobbling to my feet, I sent my chair crashing to the floor. Every eye turned to their king in silence.

High Chancellor Tavis gently stood. "King Aric Rødt Tre? Are you feeling well?"

Flinching at the use of my new title, I stammered, "I... I'm fine. Just need some air." Turning my attention to the crowd, I bowed slightly before ducking out the door. Once out of the eyesight of the Council, my pace quickened and was all but running by the time I reached the castle gardens.

Yanking the buttons of my shirt free, I gasped for breath. The evening air was cool, yet my skin was on fire. Falling to my knees, I dug my fingers into the soft earth, trying to connect to the one thing I loved more than anything else.

"Having others depend on you is a fucking bitch, isn't it?" Brynjar's voice echoed behind me.

My rattled mind couldn't take another argument with him today. I tried to block him out.

Brynjar knelt in front of me, placing his hands on my shoulders. "I've trained so many soldiers. That day, I watched my students fall and die before me and there was nothing I could do to save them." His voice broke. "It's never easy knowing your actions will affect other's lives." His arm draped around my back in a half hug before he stood offering me a hand. "It will do no one any good to see you on your knees. Come, let's walk. There's something I think we both need to see."

Gripping Brynjar's offered arm by the elbow, I stood and brushed the dirt from my knees. "Tha..." My voice trailed off, unable to complete the thought.

"You are my brother first, then my king." He led the way without looking at me. We walked in silence for a long while.

The trees gave way to the open training field. One solitary tree stood in the center. The day Emma had created that tree was ingrained in my memory like it was yesterday. Thyra and I had been training in the air and I was falling when she had grown that tree out of nothing to save me.

Almost forgetting I wasn't alone, I continued walking. My sister was gone, but her tree remained tall. When we stood before it, I pressed my palm into the rough bark and inhaled deeply. The rich nutty scent washed over me. Tucking my wings in tight behind me, I reached for the lowest branch and climbed. The tree rustled below me reminding me of Brynjar's presence. Ignoring the thin trickle of blood in my hand, I didn't stop until the branches thinned.

"Coming here makes me feel closer to her." Brynjar sat beside me. "She's still here." He turned. "She's not lost to us Aric. She is struggling, still fighting."

The laugh that I released warmed my heart. "That sounds like our Emma," I said as I wiped a tear from my cheek then tore my eyes from my friend. "The others want me to forget what happened. They don't want me to save her. They only want me to go about like everything is business as usual."

"They believe her lost," Brynjar replied. "But I saw what happened. Hel, she threw me halfway home. I can't blame them for what they feel. But if anyone knows the truth, it's us." He gently shoved my shoulder. Turning back to my friend, I noticed Brynjar's outstretched hand. "Maybe, just maybe, here in this tree where her energy is strongest, we could reach her. Will you help me try?"

My eyes found my sister's mate's before I tentatively took his hand.

"I've only caught brief glimpses of her, but I think we can find her," Brynjar continued. "Close your eyes and focus all your energy on her."

Doing what he asked only surrounded me in sorrow. My heart broke as the battle replayed in my head. Thyra bleeding and gasping for air. Emma standing before me, shaking with fury. The bodies, dead by her hand, lying in the dust.

Tears streamed down my face.

"Happy memories, Aric," Brynjar reminded me.

Shoving the recent trauma aside, I pulled at the memories I cherished. We were mere children the first time I found her. She was playing in her yard in Midgard and her smile lit up my world. Sneaking across the realms for just a moment to watch her play was something I'd willingly risk getting in trouble for as a child. She had many sad memories, but every time she caught the smallest hint of me, warmth radiated off her. Then not that long ago, I brought her into my world.

My smile grew hearing her laugh echo in my head. Fresh tears flowed, tears of joy. My life was whole with her in it.

Gasping at the sudden pain searing in my arms, I looked over at Brynjar.

"Hold on. You are feeling my pain. Hold on, we are almost there. Keep thinking about her."

Taking a deep breath, I pushed past the pain. Emma and Brynjar stood before the great tree, Yggdrasil. She beamed ear to ear at the leather tying her to her mate. Pride erupted from me at that memory. I had treated them horribly, but the gods blessed them, and I could not have been happier for them.

Screams pounded my ears. Brynjar gripped my hand tighter.

"Emma," Her mate sighed.

Turning my energy to the sound sent an icy chill washing over my flesh. Clutching my stomach with my free hand at the scent of sulfur, I choked down the urge to hurl. The cold rocks beneath her feet soaked through our worlds, sending a shiver up my spine. An eerie silence echoed around the room our minds occupied.

I should have jumped. Her voice rang out as if she were beside us. Water washed over her body, tickling my own skin.

"Emma," we whispered together.

"We are here for you, sister. Hold on, we are coming for you!"

"We love you. My Kompis, we will save you." Brynjar told her. A warmth rushed through our bodies.

Emma looked up and smiled. It was a small smile, but that was enough.

Her image faded, and we sat in the quiet, high in the treetop.

After a long moment, I said, "We can't leave her there."

"She felt us." Brynjar laughed, wiping his eyes. "She really felt us."

"We need to leave soon. We need to save her," I said.

Brynjar dropped his hand at last. "We will but you are our king, Aric. You cannot go anywhere."

"Like Hel I can't!" I unfurled my wings and shot into the sky, not caring about the branches tearing at my feathers.

"Damn you!" Brynjar bolted up in the air to meet me.

"She is my twin," I spat.

"And you are the king. If something happens to you, we are all lost."

Guilt settled into my stomach. He was right, so I bowed my chin, slowly lowering myself to the ground, and sat in the grass fighting back the tears.

"She is my sister. It is my fault she left with him."

"She is my mate. Send me to retrieve her. I will bring her back and keep you both safe." Brynjar knelt, wrapping me in a warm embrace. "It's my fault as well."

When he pulled away, I laid flat on my back, watching the clouds dance and slowed my breathing to match the sway of the tree. The plan formed in my mind with little effort. My heart ached to join the fight for my sister's life, but my mind knew Brynjar was right. Staying in Alfheim and leading my people was now my sole duty, but a part of me could go with my friend. I smiled and sat up.

Brynjar cocked his head at the look on my face. "What?"

"Are you willing to be bound to me as well, brother?"

"Excuse me?" he asked.

"You're right, I can't go with you, but I will not send you without a way to communicate with me. Will you blood bond with me? If we do this, I will be able to connect with you. We know that together we can connect to Emma. This way you can pull on me when you find her. We can save her together without me having to go with you."

"That hasn't been done in generations. How do you even know it will work?"

"I have to try. Please."

Brynjar hesitated before he nodded. I pulled a knife from a sheath around my ankle, wincing as I dragged the blade across my palm, opening a deep cut then handed the knife to Brynjar, who did the same.

Dropping the blade in the grass, Brynjar looked at me. "Now what?"

Clasping our wounded hands together, I spoke reverently. "We have been friends a long time, Brynjar. Your mating with my sister made you family. Our blood makes us brothers. Wherever you go, I will sense you. Wherever I am, you will feel me. From this day forth we will never be alone." The tiny hairs all over my body stood on end, sending shivers down my spine.

Brynjar smiled. "I think it worked."

"I agree."

"Now when you say you can sense me... does that mean..."

My raised palm stopped him, "Only when I look for you or you for me," I laughed. "Trust me, I wouldn't have done this if it couldn't be turned off. Once you save her, I'll want nothing to do with your mind."

"Good." He stood and offered his hand to help me to my feet. "Now what?"

"Go get her, brother." Smiling, I slowly walked back to the castle. The fight was far from over and I was now the sole leader of my people. My sister was lost, gone somewhere I couldn't follow. A new battle was raging, but with my new brother and Thyra grasping onto life, I suddenly had the courage to face the challenges that lie ahead.

CHAPTER 5

Emma

Bolting upright in the king-size, four-poster bed, I scanned the room, remembering where I was. The cool, damp room sent shivers down my spine as my eyes quickly adjusted to the darkness surrounding me. Fear permeated my skin, creating goosebumps over my arms. The memory of the last few days flooded in. Moments where I seemed to be watching myself from a far with no control over my actions mixed with the times I tried to fight Father's magic.

My body didn't want to get up and I groaned, knowing if I had any chance of getting out of here, I needed to strengthen my wings. Crawling out of the bed, I stood and stared at my reflection, trying to raise my wings. Pain seared down my spine, causing me to bite the inside of my cheek. Focusing my energy on my massive wings sent the warmth of my magic down my back, healing the muscles.

After a few minutes of my magic strengthening my back, I tried again. By the end of the day yesterday, I had been able to lift them up an inch, but to my surprise, I now managed to raise my wings to over the top of my head. I had to root my feet in place to keep from jumping with joy. Stretching my wings wide, I thought of Aric's wings, of Brynjar's wings and I smiled, knowing that someday I would be able to fly with them. If I ever broke free.

"Impressive daughter." Father's voice broke my peace.

Wiping the happy tears from my face before I turned to greet him.

"Good morning, Father," I said, wrapping him in a hug before I could stop myself.

"Good morning." His chest rumbled with laughter as he hugged me back.

"What will we be doing today?"

"We are going to continue your training." He smiled. "We will be working on your magic. You did beautifully on the battlefield, but that was in the heat of the moment, and we need to make sure you can replicate it on command. Come, I have someone to introduce you to."

With a snap of my fingers, I dressed for the day.

He led the way to a smaller room I'd never been in before, with a round table in the center. One seat had already been occupied as we entered the room. The man sitting at the table was not one of Father's dark fae, nor was he of the light fae, but something altogether different. His skin shimmered an iridescent green and gold. But his dark eyes held me transfixed.

Father sat and gestured for me to join them. "We can't have you training on an empty stomach."

Standing behind the chair next to him, I stared at the stranger's face across from me. He lifted the corner of his bow-shaped lips and brushed a lock of mocha hair from his eyes.

"This is Damion, Emma. He will be working with you. He's been excited to meet you."

Damion stood slowly and strode around the table, offering me his hand but I hesitated a moment before I took it. He brought it to his lips. "It is my pleasure to meet you." He breathed on to my hand before gently kissing it.

I blushed before responding, "Th-thank you." My insides twisted at the emotions stirring within me when I remembered my true mate.

Fae fled the training room as the three of us entered. Damion offered me his hand and led me to the center of the floor. He spun around to face me and shrugged off his navy wool coat.

His form fitting shirt and pants left little to the imagination. My breath caught in my throat and a strange heat rushed through my core.

"You're a skilled fighter, I saw you on the battlefield." His smooth voice rolled over me. "I know you have already discovered your talents. We are here to further push those boundaries. You can control the elements, correct?"

I could only nod.

"Let's see."

Raising my palms, I pulled at my powers. One hand ignited in flames and the other in ice.

"Good. That's two."

I glared at him. Focusing my energy, I swirled the air around him and shook the ground at his feet. He staggered backwards before falling to the floor. His laughter only fueled my rage.

Once recovered, he said, "Very good. Now, can you do that to the King?"

Glancing at Father standing at the edge of the vast room, I tried to move the air around him. Nothing happened.

Grunting, I slammed my foot to the ground, sending a wave through the floor. Father faltered slightly before steadying himself. Damion laughed.

"What the fuck is so funny?" I demanded.

"Sorry, Highness." He bowed. "You're cute when you're frustrated."

Blasting him to the floor with ice only made his laughter grow.

Father cleared his throat behind us, snapping Damion's attention back to the lesson.

"Sorry," he said to Father before he stood and glanced at me. "It takes some practice to project your magic. You have excellent control up close, but to really master your powers, you need to be able to use it anywhere." He gripped me by the shoulders and turned my back to him. "Close your eyes. What do I look like? What color are my eyes? My hair? Pull that image up in your mind. When you see me as if I were in front of you, attack again."

A trickle of ice flowed through my veins as I closed my eyes and pictured those eyes. His oval face came into view. Attraction for him invaded my mind and I reached out a hand, running it through his smooth hair. He gripped my hips and pulled me closer. My heart thumbed in my ears as his lips gently brushed mine.

'Emmy.' Brynjar's voice whispered in my ear, making my gut churn.

Slamming down my mental shield, I pushed the image of Damion out and thrust flames in his direction. His yelp snapped my eyes open and I turned around quickly to face him. Smoke rose from his shirt, revealing an angry red welt on his chest.

Running to his side, I stammered. "I'm so sorry!" Placing my hands on his warm skin, I poured my magic to his wound returning it to its natural glow. A burning desire kept my hands on his soft flesh. The feel of his touch in my mind lingered.

As he wobbled to his feet, I nearly dropped at the weight of him but caught him around the waist just in time. My fingers slipped under his shirt, grazing his skin and I inhaled the salty breeze of him. The sensation pulled me back to the one and only time I'd been to the beach, squishing sand between my toes.

"Are you... Are you okay?" I stammered. My world spun between the images of my mate and Damion so fast I couldn't see straight. *Brynjar is my Kompis.* The words repeated over in my head. But Damion was... What was Damion? Studying his features again only brought up more questions. Not human, but not fae. *What other mythical creatures are based on facts?* Shaking the feelings from my mind, I asked again. "You okay?"

"Yeah..." He straightened in my grasp. "I'm fine." He brushed his fingers against my cheek. "You're unexpected, Highness."

Gripping him tighter, I corrected him. "Just Emma, please." My smiled widened. "But I think we should take a break."

He bowed his head. "You're right. Can I escort you back to your room?"

I nodded, turning to his side.

We walked in silence, arm in arm, back to my room. When we reached my door, I turned to him and again he raised my hand to his lips, kissing it gently.

"I'm so glad to have met you today, Emma. I look forward to seeing more of you."

Heat flooded me at the lingering scent of the ocean and before I could stop myself, I grasped the tattered remains of his shirt, pulling him closer. His heart raced against my chest. My hands wrapped around his hair at the nape of his neck as I pressed my mouth to his. He parted his lips, and I tasted the salt on his tongue.

My hand reached behind me, grasping the door handle. The moment I touched the brass I was back in Alfheim, my lips pressed against Brynjar's, tasting the sweetness of him.

My eyes flew open. The man standing before me was not my Kompis, not my mate. Shoving Damion off me, I slapped him hard. My palm burned as it connected with his face, but the pain was nothing to what warred inside. My body wanted this man like I'd never wanted Brynjar. My mind hardly knew the man, but my body ached to feel him against me. But he was not my mate. And what would Bryn think of me kissing another? My stomach soured at the thought of telling him. Slamming the door behind me I dropped to the floor and sobbed at what had just happened.

A cool breeze flowed over me as his face swam in my mind. "What have I done? I am so sorry, Bryn," I whispered into the darkness.

The warmth of his arms wrapped around me. *'I'm coming for you, my Kompis. I love you. No matter what. Remember that. Always.'*

And he was gone. My sobs renewed. But he had brought me hope.

Chapter 6

Damion

The imprint of her hand left a burn on my cheek as my desire raged on even after she slammed the door in my face. Resting my head on the wooden doorframe, I dragged my mind back to the present. Her scent lingered in the hall, engulfing me. With a heavy sigh, I pulled away from the door, trudged down the hall and to my room.

My fingers traced over my lips where hers had just been. The taste of her sank into me. My body needed more. As I meandered through the halls, images of her pressed against me took up every inch of space.

Sulking as I walked through my room, I plopped into my large leather chair. Her beauty had stolen my breath the moment she walked into the room. Air was less precious than this woman.

And then the training room... Her skin on my skin. She wanted me just as much, despite her slap a few minutes ago.

She *will* be mine.

Snapping my fingers, I removed my clothes. My mind wondered as I crawled into my bed and the warm sheets wrapped around me, pulling me in as sleep called to me.

The scent of saltwater filled my nose as I rolled over, burying my face in my pillow. Emma had drawn the memory of home from my mind, but raiders had destroyed it years ago and my family long since dead. My mind wouldn't let me push the thoughts away.

My lungs burned as the frigid water pulled me under. I attempted to claw my way to the surface, but the hand around my ankle dragged me deeper into the ocean. When I looked down at the creature, she smiled with sharp teeth, sending a shiver down my spine. Her tawny hair flowed in the water and her green eyes stared back up at me. My chest constricted as we descended further and further into the darkness.

Once we reached the bottom, she released my leg. When I kicked out it was not with a foot, but a dark green, scaly tail and fin had replaced my legs. Gasping in a lungful of water didn't choke me like I'd expected and I tried to push away from the woman but the unfamiliar tail wouldn't work properly and it kept me close to her.

She reached out. My eyes searched for an escape. For a way up. But everything was dark as night. The woman touched my cheek and my vision cleared as if I were standing in the sunlight.

I was sure I had to be losing my mind but after rubbing at my eyes, time stopped. Had I been here a moment or a lifetime?

The woman swam closer with her own scaly tail. Matching green dorsal fins grew out of the side of her arms and her hair draped over her shoulders, covering her chest.

"Who are you?" My strong voice surprised me.

"Remember who you are, son."

I rubbed my still very human arm and shook my head.

"No." I practically shouted at the woman. "No... no...."

My own shouting woke me. My sheets were soaking wet so I sat up, throwing the blanket from my body to make sure it was all a nightmare.

I exhaled. Legs. Pale and strong legs.

"It was just a dream." I slumped back into the bed, covering my face with my arms.

My body ached all over. It was pointless to try and go back to sleep, so I crawled out of my bed and dragged myself to the bathroom, flicking on the shower with a simple thought then stepped under the water to let it flow down my back.

I tried to pull up the images of my dream tail again but what I saw was different somehow. Smaller maybe. I shut my eyes and willed the thoughts from my head.

"It was just a dream," I kept saying over and over, but I could still feel the tail. There was more to this than a dream. Wasn't there?

A cloud settled over my mind, and a sharp pain in my arm zapped me like a rat in a cage bringing me back to the bathroom. Something felt off but what, I wasn't sure; the pain vanished and with it, whatever thoughts that were floating around my consciousness. Flicking the water off, I stepped from the shower and with a snap, I dressed and walked from my room.

My fingertips ran over the cold stone as I walked, lost in my own thoughts. A splash of water at my feet grabbed my attention, but when I looked, there was nothing. A strong sulfurous scent flooded my senses and grounded me. This was my home but as I continued walking, a green flick of a tail caught my eyes, but the name Herrick pounded my ears. Herrick was my family; my parents were dead. I halted my steps and shook my head. Right?

"Good morning, son." Herrick's booming voice called to me.

Straightening, I gazed up at the man who had been my father since I was young.

"It's morning already?" I asked.

"Near enough." Herrick grinned. "How'd your night go?"

"It was... complicated. She kissed me, then slapped me. Then..." I scratched at my temple. "I had the strangest dream..." I stared off at nothing.

Herrick clasped me on the back, sending me forward a step. "It was just a dream, my boy."

A strange cold seeped into my skin causing a shiver to run down my spine.

"Just a dream," I responded robotically.

"Come. Let's have some breakfast." He wrapped his arm around my shoulders and led me forward.

Chapter 7

Aric

The sterile room enclosed me as I stood clasping her cold hand. The electric buzz of the magic keeping her alive made the hairs on the back of my neck stand up. My eyes refused to leave the center of her white gown. The thin fabric did little to hide the three holes in her middle. Hitting my knees beside her bed, I prayed the gods wouldn't take her from me.

"Please, Thyra. Don't leave me." I leaned in, kissing her cheek, inhaling in the trace amounts of rose lingering on her skin. "Don't leave me," I sobbed.

"Excuse me, Your Majesty."

Wiping my eyes, I stood and nodded a curt greeting to the newcomer.

"I'm Healer Dawson." He bowed low. "We are doing all we can for her, Sire. We don't know why her wound isn't closing. We have tried everything we know of, but nothing is working. The good news, though, is the spell we have placed over her is keeping her stable." He turned to look at his patient. "It's all we can do for her right now."

My eyes refused to look away from her. "Can... Can she hear me?"

"We aren't sure, but it couldn't hurt to talk to her." He clasped me on the shoulder before ducking back into the office.

Pulling a chair to her side, I sat stroking her hair.

"I'm so sorry," I said, laying my face next to hers. "I have been so stubborn. I should have mated you years ago. I swear to you the second you wake up, I will tie myself to you forever." I gazed at her unmoving face. "Please, just wake up."

'You better keep your promise, Aric.' Thyra's voice rang out in my head.

I jumped, knocking my chair to the floor. *'Can you hear me?'* My heart pounded as I waited for the response.

'Yes... But...'

'But what? What's wrong?'

'Things are muddled.' Her thoughts came in a rush.

'How are we speaking mind to mind? I can only do this with Emma.' I straightened the chair and sat looking at her.

'I... I don't know. I have been screaming at everyone. Maybe you heard me because...'

'Because you are my Kompis.' I brought her cold hand to my lips. *'I'm sorry I refused to see what was right in front of me. I love you.'*

Her smile ran through my mind. *'I love you too, Aric.'* After a pause. *'Where is Emma? I don't blame her for this.'*

'Herrick took her. Brynjar and I were able to connect to her. She is fighting his hold.'

'Good. You have to go after her.'

'Brynjar is preparing to head out as we speak. He would have gone, no matter what I said.'

'And what about you?'

'I have to stay here.' The words came out bitter.

'I know it's hard, my love. Are you sulking?' Even in her frozen state, she was chiding me.

My grin widened. *'I am not, thank you very much.'*

'You are.' She laughed. *'You must move forward. You need to keep our people together or more deaths will come. Let Brynjar bring her back. She might be the only one to save me, to save us all. She's more powerful than she knows.'*

I leaned in, kissing her cool skin. *'You're amazing. I love you so much.'*

'And I you. Now stop shirking your duty and let me rest.'

Kissing her hand once more, I stood. She lay there in perfect slumber. She was safe. For now. That was all that mattered. Tearing my eyes from her I walked toward the disaster I knew was waiting for me in the war room.

Brynjar

The image of my mate's lips on another man ignited a fire in me. Rushing about my home high in the trees, I threw all I would need in a small pack before strapping my blades to my thighs. Her father had stolen the Emma I loved from me, and if I didn't hurry, his plans might actually kill her.

My arms itched to be cut. The moment she had turned dark, Herrick's curse that had plagued us both returned with a vengeance. Physical pain I could handle. Knowing she was by herself fighting her father's mind-control had become more than I could take.

Stepping into the evening light, I spread my wings and launched into the air. My heart rate increased as I flew high above the treetops. Thoughts raced through my head. *Would I be too late? Would she refuse me?* I couldn't think like that and pushed my emotions down.

I landed on the training field, decked out for war. My fighting leathers pulled tight on my chest, weapons on my hips, and my pack around my lower back.

Eyes followed me to the center of the field, but I ignored them. My hands rested on Emma's tree. "Please stay with me, Emma," I whispered in a silent prayer. Reaching up, I snapped a small twig from the tree and tucked it into an empty sheath.

"Master Alm."

Turning, I saw two fae had approached me.

"You're going after her, aren't you?" Rajnish, the taller of the two, asked.

"Alone," I said.

"You cannot go without us. Please, let us help you." Mayank bit his lower lip but held my gaze.

The pair of them were just as prepared for battle as I was. Each wore their own fighting leathers and weapons.

"We fully understand the risks and are prepared to fight and die if need be."

"Rajnish, Mayank, why would you risk your lives for someone you don't even know?"

"She is our queen. Even if she doesn't know it, she is. We were here the day she did that." Rajnish pointed toward the tree. "She can heal our lands and bring us together. We need her home."

Mayank clapped me on the shoulder. "Besides, you can't do this by yourself. Your emotions are all over the place.

Examining the warriors like a general going into battle, I smiled. Mayank stood nearly a foot shorter than me, but twice as wide. Muscles rippled under the leather. The light wings behind him were sharp and featherless but just as fierce as my own. Rajnish, on the other hand, stood as tall and thin as I was, and I knew he was just as deadly in a fight. Magic tugged on me as I gave in. *Damn it, Mayank.* Few fae could control emotions, and of course Aric would send the one he knew I couldn't resist.

"Fine but if you get in my way, I will send you home." I pushed past them. "And stay out of my emotions, Mayank."

"Yes, sir."

They were quick on my heels as I walked away from the training field and headed for the ancient tree, Yggdrasil, on the edge of town. Once we reached the outer ring, we took to the air.

Aric was already waiting for us at the base of Yggdrasil. His stoic face grinned slightly as we landed.

"Glad to see you couldn't stop them from joining you." He nodded to my companions. "They came to me earlier and asked to help."

"Thanks," I quipped. "They'll come in handy. And three can still be stealthy." I clasped Aric in an embrace.

"Bring her back safe," Aric whispered.

The dry bark rubbed against my flesh as I gently placed my hand on its trunk and heat radiated off it. Turning to Aric I spoke so only he and I could hear, "It's dying." Tears welled up in my eyes.

"We need Emma back home. Thyra said she might be the only one who could save us."

Snapping my full attention to Aric, I asked, "Is she—"

"No, she is not awake."

"Then?"

Aric tapped his skull.

"But how?" A smile spread over Aric's face and I laughed. "She is your Kompis? How long have you known?"

"I have always enjoyed her company, but I let my damn pride get in the way. The moment Emma..." He gazed down at his feet. "The moment I thought I lost her."

"You know it's not Emma's fault, don't you?"

"I... Yes. Part of me wants to hate her, but I know it's all Herrick's fault. Bring Emma home. But if you can bring me his head, I wouldn't complain."

My smiled widened. "I will do my best." I bowed low to my King, then turned back to Yggdrasil. Placing my hand on a low knot, I waited for the pull.

The icy chill that crept over my skin through the transition stayed with me. Dark clouds loomed over head; thunder crashed all around me.

"Is this Svartalfheim?" Mayank asked as they joined me.

"This is the way to Svartalfheim. That is the entrance." I pointed toward the enormous mountain ahead of us. The basalt cone stood larger than the Great Tree itself. The size of it hid the true span of land between it and us.

Mayank sighed. "How do we get in, then?"

"See that on top?" My finger moved along the silhouette of the rocky edge that formed a giant ring atop the cone shape. "It's the caldera of the dormant volcano. That is how we enter Svartalfheim." Flicking my wrists, I conjured three long black leather coats. Throwing mine around my back, I said, "And we can't fly. The electricity in the air will shred our wings. It's not too late to turn back and go home, boys."

Pride rippled through me as the fae stood at attention, clapping their fists to their chest.

CHAPTER 8

Emma

Images of Brynjar and Damion fighting in the training room haunted me all night. My fear poured out of me as I slept and soaked into my blankets. Pulling myself out of the bed, I stretched my arms. My wings automatically followed. A sigh escaped my mouth as I gazed at myself in the mirror.

Testing out my wings, I moved them. Up, down. Stretching wide, then pulling them back in close. I grinned, dressing with a snap before running out the door. My brain couldn't focus on mundane things like eating. Instead, I headed straight to the training room.

Thankfully it was empty. *Good, I want to try this without anyone watching.*

Extending my wings out as far as they would go, I moved them every which way I could. I pictured the way Brynjar would move just before taking flight and I did my best to mimic his wings.

"I'm impressed, daughter."

Father's voice behind me made me jump.

"Brynjar said I was a quick study." I smiled at hearing his name on my own lips.

"Ah, that boy again." He sneered.

A growl rumbled low in my chest as I pulled myself into a spirit and reappeared in front of Father, hand raised, prepared to strike.

Clasping my wrist, he chided, "Daughter, when will you learn? I'm here to help you. The sooner you forget that life, the more I can."

I bowed my head. "I'm sorry, Father, I don't know what came over me." I wrapped my arms around him, glanced up, and asked in a sing-song voice, "What are we learning today?"

"You have brilliant control over your magic. Today, we will work on other uses for your talent." He nodded toward the door. The slender form of Damion walked into the light. But he was not alone. He held a thick chain attached to a collar around a tiny human being dragged behind him.

The human slumped to the floor when they approached. "P-p-please, Sire." The man's eyes pleaded with Father and sobbed.

Father and Damion never glanced at the man, but I couldn't tear my eyes away. He wore a filthy white shirt and torn jeans. Soot freckled his skin. Tear streaks ran down his cheeks, revealing the fair color below.

"He was one of my informants until he turned on me. Now he is my enemy." Father cupped my face in his hands, pulling my gaze away from the human. "He is your enemy as well."

"Yes, Father. He is my enemy," I repeated.

He reached out to Damion who handed him the chain. "Good. Now, shall we begin?"

"Come, Emma." Damion said.

Damion interlaced his fingers with mine and squeezed. "I'm glad you are not still angry with me after yesterday."

"Of course not." I squeezed him back. My steps halted, pulling him toward me and before I knew what I was doing, I cupped his cheek in my hand, thumb grazing his lips. "It's just..." Something pulled at me making me struggle to find the face of my mate.

"It's alright, Emma." Damion's cool voice called me back. "I know what it's like to lose someone you thought you loved. It'll all work in the end. I'm not going anywhere." He smiled and pulled me in front of him. "Now, you want to learn what else you can do with your magic?" he asked.

I nodded.

"There are two things we want to show you today. I'll help you with projecting your magic but King Herrick—" He nodded to where Father still stood several feet away with the man. "—I will help you with mental control. You have some of our king's abilities to control others' minds, which means you can make anyone think anything you want."

"Really? That's pretty awesome!" I laughed.

"Yeah, I guess it is," he said.

"What's the other thing you want to show me?"

Shaking his head, he continued. "One of the easiest ways to get information from someone is to use their needs against them. What is our greatest basic need?"

"Um... food?"

He shook his head.

I thought, resting my hands on my stomach, watching them rise and fall before it clicked. "Air? Breathing?"

"Yes. Air. Everything needs air to survive. Even here, we have tunnels up to the surface to bring fresh air down. Since you can control the elements, you can manipulate air as well."

I nodded my understanding but unsure of where this was going.

"So far, you have merely pushed air around, but what if you could take it away?"

Looking from Damion to Father, it took me a long moment before I finally understood as my eyes fell upon the human.

"You mean? That man?" My lungs froze.

Damion nodded. "He refuses to tell us what he told our enemies, but we need to know. So, we... Herrick, thought it would be beneficial if I taught you some techniques to help him remember."

I couldn't look at the man. "So, how do I take air away?"

"You have to push the air away from him. I know you can do that, but you have to keep more air from moving in. If you make a shield around him to block the air from returning, you can then push the air inside of it out." Damion stepped behind me placing his hand on my shoulder. "I will be right here if you need me."

Closing my eyes, I formed a shield around him. The man clutched at his throat as I took his air away. Pushing the air through the shield took more effort than expected and I fell back into Damion's arms. He wrapped his arm around my middle, slipping his hand under my shirt, just grazing my side, and pulling a sigh from my lips.

"I gotcha," he whispered in my ear, sending heat to my core.

The man dropped to the ground, gasping as the air returned to him.

Father leaned down, eyes boring into the man. "I will let this continue until there is nothing left. Save yourself the pain."

"I... I..." he choked out.

Damion held onto me as I sagged into him, unable to keep hold over the bubble, dropping the shield.

"I'm sorry, Father," I collapsed to the ground, unable to breathe myself.

Father gazed down at me. "Have you eaten yet?"

I shook my head, looking up at Father.

"That is why, then. I will be right back." Father snapped and chained the man to the wall. Then with a pop, he vanished.

Damion sat in front of me, pulling me into him. "Are you alright, Emma?"

"I… I couldn't breathe," I gasped.

"Magic costs. It will drain you of energy. If you use magic against someone and you aren't prepared, it will turn on you. You took air from him, but you took it from yourself as well."

Peering up at him sent a wave of heat throughout my body and I pulled him against me. His hands ran down my spine as he pulled me tighter. All thoughts of another life fled as his lips met mine and I lay flat on my back, pulling him down on top of me. His hardness pressed into me.

"Emma," he said.

My hands fumbled with the edge of his pants.

The fog cleared from my brain and I jerked my hands away and pushed from Damion.

This is not my Bryn. I gasped, wrapping my shaking hands to my chest and closed my eyes. *This is not my home.* The words repeated like a battle cry in my head to fight Father's magic before it consumed me.

A small pop caught my attention, and I jumped to my feet and spun around to where Father stood by the door watching us and holding two plates in his arms. The icy touch of his magic reached out for me.

This is not my home. This is not my home.

His cold settled over me, and I relaxed, straightening, and smiled at Father.

"I'm sorry, Father," I said with strength I didn't know I had.

Father laughed. "No, my daughter. I'm sorry for interrupting. I can leave again, if you wish?"

He started for the door.

"No!" I shouted, grateful for the distraction. "Sorry. I'm hungry." Damion's face flushed as his eyes were glued to the floor.

"Very well." Father handed me the food he brought. I sat and ate. Damion sat next to me, just barely brushing my knee. "You have the idea of how to pull the air from an area. I'll explain how the mind control works." Father spoke as Damion and I continued to eat.

"You are going to train me?" I asked between bites.

"Yes. I'm the only one here that understands that. Damion can also control the elements, though not as impressively as you can." He looked to Damion. "No offence."

"None taken, sir. You aren't wrong: she is amazing." He smiled at me.

"But I'm the only one who knows how to control the mind. It's not impossible to control a complete stranger, but it is harder to do it to someone you are not familiar with. So, we'll start small. If you figure out something that matters to them, you can use that to get past their shields. Then you can make them see whatever you want. Did your mother show you how to build a mental shield?" I nodded. "Good. Put one up."

I closed my eyes and pictured that wall in my mind. I fortified it, strengthening it more than before. Opening my eyes, I nodded again.

In a flash, the training room vanished and a lush field stretched out before us. A small cottage sat beside us and I rested against Damion's chest.

A tiny creature jumped onto my lap, pushing us down to the ground.

"Give your mother some peace, will you?" Damion's voice called. I rolled over to see the smiling face of a small child. The girl pounced on Damion. The three of us rolled around in the grass, laughing until we were crying.

A cool breeze fell over me and I was sitting back in the training room with Father and Damion.

My breath caught in my throat. "Wh-what was that?"

"It was a picture of what your life could be." Father spoke. "The future isn't set in stone. You can have whatever life you choose. Damion is a higher fae. He can give you a life that that lesser fae can't. You can have a life here. You can have a family."

I smiled at the warmth that lingered on my skin. Turning to Damion, his grin told me he had been there in that field as well. Damion reached out to me and my heart raced as I interlaced my fingers with his. The thought of children made my heart light.

'Emmy.' My mate's voice sobbed in my head. *'It's a lie, Emma. Please stay with me. I'm coming.'*

Giving into a life I never knew possible, I threw a wall at the sound in my mind and snapped my attention to Father.

"He is coming, Father. Brynjar is coming to try to 'save' me."

CHAPTER 9

Brynjar

I nvisible hands barreled into my chest causing me to hit my knees, gasping for breath and rubbing my chest at the force of her thrust. Tears pushed their way to the surface.

Shrugging off my coat, I spoke to my companions without looking at them.

"Go home." I barked.

"No, sir. We are with you until the end," Rajnish spoke.

"Thank you for helping me get this far, but go home." My voice sounded even rougher than normal, even to my ears.

"S-Sir?"

My vision blurred as I turned to them. "Don't follow me. She is in the grips of that monster and I won't risk anyone else's life in there." Turning back to the mountain looming ahead, I barked one last order. "Warn Aric."

Unfurling my dark wings, I bolted to the sky. Sparks rippled through my wings and penetrated into my back. I clenched my jaw as a thousand tiny knives dug into my body. The scent of burning flesh and feathers drowned out the sulfur in the air. It only made me fly faster.

The ring of the caldera ahead grew larger until I hung in the air above it. Unsheathing two long swords, I landed with the grace of a bull ready to fight. Kneeling to take a moment to catch my breath, I peered into the heart of the volcano.

'I'm on my way, Emma. Hang on just a little longer.'

In one swift motion I stood, tucked my wings behind me, and dove. Wind rushed past my ears, deafening me. Flattening my body out and spreading my wings wide, the feathers caught the air, slowing my descent. Not caring who heard me, I slammed to the ground. The fragile webbing of my wings stung from the storm clouds but my body was quickly healing it.

I straightened, raising my swords; one behind my head, the other blocking my face. The dark fae hissed around me, eyes glowing red as the sickly-looking beings crouched low and circled me. I stood tall and massive among them.

Slicing through the nearest one with ease, I laughed. The others charged me at once. Twirling the twin blades, I danced around the dark fae, drenching the ground with thick, dark blood.

When the fight ended, I knelt, panting among a dozen oozing bodies. Flicking the blood from my swords as I stood and strode over my kills, I reached out my mind to my mate. *'Where are you, Emma?'*

Rushing off down the only hall, I ran deeper into the earth. Sweat poured down my face, mixing with the blood clinging to my flesh. One by one, more dark fae fell under my blades. I ran until I reached a large, open cave.

The red eyes surrounding me numbered in the dozens.

Too many.

Inhaling deeply, her face flashed in my mind. It was all for her. Gripping the hilts of my swords tighter, I prepared for the fight ahead of myself. My head swiveled, searching for a plan.

The first flew at me, razor sharp talons clawing the air. I swiped, cutting off the fae's hands in one fluid motion. Flipping around to face those at my back, I stabbed through another. Pulling my blade from the body, I twirled, slicing across the chest of one more.

My heart pounded in my ears as I cut down another two in a series of quick movements. Licking the salt from my lips, I sized up my next prey.

An icy chill crept over my body, freezing me in place. Forcing my breath to slow, I put all my energy into a slight movement, then stepped closer to another fae.

'Stop fighting it, my love.' Her voice rushed through me like a cold rain.

'Emma, please stop this, I beg you. Come home with me.'

'I am home, Brynjar.'

My eyes searched for her in desperation. Through the crowd of snarling faces, I found the only one that mattered to me.

She stood beside Herrick at the edge of the room wearing a long red dress that clung to her body. The ivory liquid that ran down her arms and dripped to the floor fueled the fire within me.

"Father. Release him. Please." Her icy stare never left me.

Warmth returned to my body and I was able to move, but a sea of red eyes stood between us.

"Please, Emma." I let the tears fall.

She only stared back.

My blood boiled at the man responsible for her coldness. Turning my gaze towards the dark fae, I sliced through another dozen figures before invisible icy hands clasped around my wrist. I jabbed at the hand, but a force blocked my path. Punching at the shield, I roared.

"It is too late, Brynjar." She strode through the dark fae as they bowed to her. My chest tightened at the sight of her. Her former radiant vine tattoos that snaked up her arms were faded into a muddy water shade. My breath left me as I hit my knees, sobbing.

"Emma." I put my hand to my chest, middle and ring finger tucked in tight. Our secret love sign. Her face slacked; eyes went wide.

"Bryn," she breathed.

'Emmy. Fight it. Fight for me. For us'. I spoke in her mind. *'Remember... No matter what!'*

'I... I'm trying.' Her hand moved discreetly to return my love.

"Let's end this," Herrick said. "Emma, take him to the cell we prepared for him. Get him out of my sight." Herrick touched her shoulder, and I felt the cold grip of his magic take hold of her and her expression flattened.

Emma nodded, walking over to me but I didn't fight her when she gripped me by the wrist and pulled me into a spirit and emerged in a dark dungeon. Iron bars surrounded me.

Tears streamed down her face as she turned to me and reached up to lightly touch my cheek.

"I... I'm sorry," she said, spiriting out of the cage.

"Emma! Please!" My voice stopped her from leaving. She turned, looking at me. My hands wrapped around the bars. Searing pain crawled up my arms as smoke rose from my hands, but I couldn't let go.

Her stone face softened as she rushed to the bars. "Bryn! Stop! That's iron! It will kill you if you don't let go!"

"I'm dead already if you are lost to me."

"But..."

"The burning in my arms returned the moment you left with him. I can stand the pain of the iron if only to see your face." My arms shook and I collapsed, still holding the bars.

"Bryn!" She knelt before me, loosened my grip on the iron placing her hands over mine and a cool breeze washed over my skin as the flesh stitched back together, healing the burns.

"Emma, he has you under his spell. You can't see what he is doing to you, can you?" She cocked her head. I turned over her arms. "Look, Emma. Look at your arms."

Her eyes fell and rose back at me. "What?"

"Look again. Really look, Emma. Push past what you think you see and really look." I brought her hand to my lips, kissing softly. "Please Emma, see the truth."

She looked down again and stared for a long moment. She gasped at the sight. Raising her head to me, her eyes wide. "He... no, it can't be true."

A dozen fresh cuts stretched across the underside of her arms. White blood dripped to her dress.

"He is using you, Emma. Please break his hold." I kissed her wrists. "Please, my Kompis."

A pop sounded, and Emma jumped to her feet. She wiped the tears from her face and nodded at Herrick's approach.

"I see I cannot trust you with this one, daughter. What lies has he fed you?" His gaze moved from Emma to me. I locked eyes with him. "Never mind. To your room." King Herrick never looked back to his daughter, but bored his gaze into me. Only when Emma slunk away did my eyes move to my mate. Her middle and ring finger tucked into her palm as she walked gave me hope.

"And as for you," he shifted into mist and walked through the bars, "you will never have her. She is far too important to my plans for you to destroy her."

Grinning ear to ear, I stood in defiance.

Herrick shook, eyes glowing. A laugh rumbled from deep within me. The King of Svartalfheim struck my face hard, sending me crashing into the rocky floor.

I sat up, spitting blood, still laughing as the Dark King walked away.

CHAPTER 10

Emma

T he room spun about me, my vision blurred, and the air vanished from my lungs. I dropped to my knees as the pain tore through me like a bolt of lightning. His pleading words echoed in my head. Acid burned in my throat, sending me straight to the bathroom.

Flipping on the shower minutes later, I scrubbed the filth from my arms and sank to the floor, letting the water wash over my body and wings as silent tears continued to fall.

I reached for the face I loved so much and had just cut so deep. My mate, my Kompis—Brynjar. My heart fluttered as he strode through the gardens back in Alfheim. His perfect grin made my heart light.

The warmth of his coat around me and his smooth lips brushed against mine.

But my actions had him locked away.

'I'm so sorry, my Kompis.' I grasped out to his mind. Praying he heard me, doubting he would.

'I love you, Emma. No matter what. Remember that, always.' His raspy voice shook with every word.

I stood so fast my head spun and I had to brace myself on the wall. His image flooded my mind. He stood in the furthest corner of his cell; arms propping himself up against the stones. Fresh welts covered his now bare chest.

His voice never broke when he spoke. "Hurt me all you want, Damion. You won't stop me from loving her." He silently crashed to the ground, a new burn appearing across his flesh.

I stood in a cold shower, boiling with rage. I had to help my mate.

Stepping out from the shower, I snapped my fingers, drying and dressing myself in an instant. Rage moved me forward towards my bedroom door, yanking it open with my magic.

Before I could step through it, I slammed into an invisible wall inside and staggered back into the room. Herrick must have placed a ward, locking me inside. I tried to pull myself into a spirit, but nothing happened.

An icy voice spoke, "Where d'ya think yur going, *Princess*?"

The creature that stepped up to the doorway was even more terrifying than my nightmares. His green-black leathery skin draped loosely over his massive frame. He had to arch his back to peer into the room, glaring at me with those glowing blood-red eyes. Crimson dripped from his fangs, jutting from his lips. I didn't dare to guess what creature's blood he'd consumed.

I gulped hard before I lied, "I-I want to see... Father."

"Oh, don't chya worry, love. He will be here shortly." The creature reached through the barrier and closed the door.

I paced the room, pouring my anger into every step. Nothing could rein in the thumping of my heart. A sharp pain burning through my skin, sending me running back to the bathroom. I pulled the shirt from my chest and saw the fresh welt that stretch from shoulder to shoulder.

My breath caught in my throat. '*The gods bound us together. You are mine and I am yours.*' I pushed the words to his mind through the pain.

Seeing his strength shattered all control Herrick once held over me. I clasped my hand to the burn and focused. Not on my own body, but on my mate's and I was pulled into his vision.

The dark eyes of Damion stared back at me as if he stood in front of me. The cool comfort of my magic rushed into my mate's body until the burning welts retreated.

Fire burned in Damion's eyes.

"See," I heard Brynjar say. "We are one. No one could destroy that, least of all you."

A grin spread across his face.

Damion stormed off to find Herrick, I assumed, so I lingered there just to feel the warmth of my mate's touch, even if it was through his eyes, I still connected to him in a way I'd longed to for weeks.

'*I love you so much. You amaze me every day. We will fight him together.*' He spoke to the empty cell.

"I love you too. We will find a way."

A sudden crash pulled me from my mate. Opening my eyes, I watched as Damion charged into my room, grip me tightly by the arms, and lifted me off my feet. I kicked out wildly but never made contact with him. His magic flowed into me, freezing me in place.

Swallowing the fear that froze my veins, I focused on one solid truth. *My arms.* The scars from the words, 'I'M COMING FOR YOU,' that my own father had etched in my skin, barely visible under the fresh cuts I hadn't known I'd done. My eyes moved from my arms to the man holding tight to me and gasped at the new version of him I now saw.

The same scars that ran across my forearms snaked all over his body. Straight cuts, mixed with jagged cuts. One phrase carved into my flesh, but hundreds marked his skin.

You are not free.

You are my servant.

Without me, you're nothing.

You cannot think on your own.

You made me do it.

I tell you what to do.

I will kill you if you try to leave.

Tears flowed down my face. Damion released me and I slumped to the floor, clenching my stomach. Damion was my father's prisoner as much as I was, if not more so.

"Oh, Damion," I whispered. "Can you not see what he is doing?"

His eyes softened. "He... he saved me."

I placed a hand on his cheek. "How long have you been here, Damion?"

"Since I was a child. Raiders killed my parents."

Raiders. I scoffed to myself.

"Damion." Clasping his wrist, I pulled him to my mirror. "Look at yourself."

He cocked his head at his reflection. "I see myself. What do you see?"

"I can't tell you. You won't believe me unless you see for yourself. Please, Damion. You need to see it."

"What a picture of beauty." Herrick's bitter voice stabbed through my chest.

Damion spun around to face his master. "Sir. I... this isn't—"

"Whatever it is, I'm glad you are here. Both of you. I think we need to break the bond between Emma and that monster in the dungeon. Until we break it, we will get nothing from him. And you, my daughter, can never move on."

My heart shattered at the words. My knees gave out as I turned to face Herrick, but Damion's hands were quick to catch me and hold me against his body.

Looking into Herrick's cold eyes, I fortified the wall in my mind, keeping my true plans to help my mate a secret and partitioned a small area that he couldn't see past, and poured out every nauseating ounce of love I could for the man in front of me.

Steadying my voice, I asked, "How do we do that?"

His eyes turned to Damion. "Give in to the desires you share. I will leave you now to make your choice, Emma. But choose wisely. I'll know either way." He grinned and slid out the door, closing it behind him.

I turned in Damion's grip, looking into those sad eyes as he reached a shaking hand to the ribbon in my hair, pulling it free. My long curls fell around my face.

"Emma, I want this. Not because he wants us to be together, but because I think you are amazing." He tucked my hair behind my pointed ears, tracing their outline with his fingers. I shivered at the sensation. "But I won't force you to feel anything for me."

Acid burned my throat. I froze for a moment as his lips pressed into mine, but I knew what must be done and I moved my mouth against his.

Pulling away, I said, "I want this too." I swallowed the vomit that crawled its way up before plastering a smile to my face.

He grinned at me as I pushed him down to the bed and stepped between his legs.

'Stay strong, my Kompis.' Brynjar spoke to my mind as I reached for him. My mate lay before me in his massive bed, back in Alfheim

and I smiled at the memory. *'There you are, my love. Don't let him win.'*

Looking back at the scene before me, I focused on my task ignoring the nausea that rumbled in my gut. Damion's length pressed against his tight pants. He reached out a hand to me, making my skin crawl, but I refused to shiver. Taking it, I climbed on top of him, closed my eyes again, and reached for his mind.

I pictured the family he so longed for and the life Herrick had stolen from him. I moved through the dark history that was his life to find this moment.

The dream he desired played out before me. We lay there, kissing parts only we could see as our bodies melded as one. I rocked on his hips, gasping at his touch. I filled his mind with joyful moans. I held on long enough to make sure he climaxed in order to seal the false memory before peeling out of his head. I snapped my fingers, removing our clothing, and mussed up my hair before he opened his eyes.

"Emma," he gasped. "That was even more amazing than I thought it would be." He brushed his lips over my cheeks.

I looked down at his naked body—semen coated his stomach—and clasped a hand to my mouth. "I... I'll be right back." I bolted for the bath, retching into the sink, then dropped to the floor, shaking.

'Emma.' Brynjar's raspy voice enveloped my mind. *'I am so sorry you had to do that, my love. You are so brave. We will find a way out. I'm not a fool. I... I know what will happen next, Emma. Play the part. Do what you must. We can only put the pieces back together once we are free. Don't worry about me. I can take it.'* Invisible arms wrapped around me tightly. *'Go, sleep, you will need the rest. Never forget or doubt my love.'*

I stood, silently walking back to my bed, and crawled under the sheets. Damion's arms tucked me in close, but I still sensed the presence of my true mate. I lay there, wide-eyed, all night. Every movement from the man at my back brought up fresh tears.

CHAPTER 11

Brynjar

The cold, hard floor was unrelenting under my back. My eyes were closed, but sleep eluded me. Instead, images flashed through my head. The curve of her hips fit so perfectly into Damion's. The way his hands lingered up the bow of her spine. I crawled to the corner of my cage, retching bile.

I sat and leaned against the wall. "It's not real. It was a fake. It's not real." I hugged my knees and rocked back and forth, reminding myself that Emma hadn't given in to Herrick's control completely.

Heat boiled deep in my gut and my vision slid into a red haze. Clutching fistfuls of hair, I pulled it at the roots as a soft growl rumbled up my body.

Standing rapidly, I barked, "No!"

I dug my nails into the flesh of my palms, so full of rage I hardly registered when hot liquid dripped from my fists. Panic rose in my chest, looking down at the pink droplets at my feet.

No! No! No! This can't be happening. Not now. I'm not my father. I'm fae. I paced the tiny cell in two giant steps, breath ragged as I walked.

'Settle my love.' Emma's voice rang out in my mind. *'Panic will only make it worse.'* I could hear the tears in her voice. *'We are coming. I'm sorry my Kompis. I-I can't stop him.'*

I stood back against the wall, clutching my chest. *'Emma, my Kompis, I know.'* I swallowed hard. *'I assume you aren't coming to free me.'* I attempted to smile.

'No, my love, we aren't. It will... if I refuse, Father will do it and he will take pleasure in it. I think I know how to do it without causing permanent damage. Brynjar,' she went silent for a long moment. *'This won't be easy for either of us. Let me in but... show him you are fighting me. Do you understand me?'*

'Emmy, remember. I love you always. No matter what.' A creak from down the hallway signaled their arrival. Flames fluttered on the wet stone walls as they drew closer.

The three of them stood in front of my cell. Emma stood between King Herrick and the man who wanted to steal my mate. I bit down at the rage that flowed through me. Bracing myself for the pain that I knew was coming, I smiled at the group.

"Ah, how nice to have visitors. Here I was just thinking you had forgotten me," I said with an air of calm.

"Last chance, mongrel." The king glared at me. "Do you wish to speak to me, or do you want your former mate to make you talk?"

My eyes locked on my mates. "Let her do her worst. I have seen what she is capable of. I'm not worried." I leaned back, crossing my arms, my heart breaking at the shine in Emma's eyes.

"Very well, beast." The king stepped back, pulling Damion with him. "He's all yours, daughter."

"Yes, yes, he is." Her voice was ice, but the wink she threw me told another story.

The corners of my mouth curled into a smile. My mate closed her eyes, tilting her head to one side and a tingle fluttered through my mind where she probed. Lowering my wall, I invited her in but screwed up my face as if to fight her off.

"No," I murmured.

Flames licked over my legs, climbing higher, and then gen-uine pain tore through me, sending me to my knees. My jaw clinched as a scream erupted from me at the fire burning in my chest. Flames engulfed me. I looked back at Emma, scratching my throat. Her eyes still closed; mouth turned down. I begged her to stop, but it was Herrick who spoke.

"Tell me what you know, and we will make your death quick."

My voice came out harsh. "Never."

As my eyes found my Kompis', tears flowed down my face, her concentrated scowl turned to a grin. The flames lessened as another image flooded into my mind. I closed my eyes, holding to the images of her tightly.

We were no longer in the dungeons but back in her massive room in Alfheim. I lay back in her soft warm bed with her straddling me. My hands moved to the thin silky dress she wore that showed every curve of her.

I winced as the flames licked my leg again.

'Shhh,' she whispered.

Focusing on her body, I placed my hands on her ass, pulling her to me. Her soft kisses along my jawline brought me to full attention.

'My Kompis,' she purred in my ear.

I roared as a burn rippled up my spine.

'Shh, my love, stay here with me. Don't think about the pain. Tell me, what do you want to do with me?' Slowing my breathing, I looked up at her. Those brilliant eyes held my gaze. *'Tell me?'*

'I-I want to feel you.'

Still in the vision she'd gifted me, my hand slipped under the silky fabric and rested on her breasts, flicking the bud of her nipple, and she rocked her hips on mine. Gently, I pulled the scrap of clothing off her, throwing it to the floor. She sat naked and ready for me.

My body squirmed under her, flames choking the surrounding air.

'Stay with me, Brynjar. I am what is real.' Her hand slid down the length of me. She snapped her fingers and my pants vanished. She gripped the base of my cock tighter. I moaned, arching my back.

'Tell me what you want.'

'Fuck, Emma: I want you. I love you.'

'I love you, too.' Her grin widened as she sheathed herself around me. Slamming into the hilt of me, she rocked her hips faster. She gripped my forearm, leaning back. My thrusts quickened, heat rising in the room. The fire spread, engulfing the bed.

'Stay with me,' she breathed. *'Almost...'* she gasped.

My pleasure rose. 'Emmy,' I whispered.

The vision faded and when I opened my eyes again, I was back in the dungeons, curled on the floor. Smoke burned in my nose, yet my skin was unharmed. I rolled to my knees and looked at my tormentor. Her face held no malice, only sadness.

Standing on shaky legs, I spoke in a steady tone. "I love you, Emma."

"Come Emma. We need to talk." Herrick grumbled. The pair of males behind her stormed off without another word, but she stood there, staring at me.

"I know you can't say it, but I love you." I winced as Herrick's curse opened up new cuts on my arms and dropped back to the ground. Fresh blood poured from my arms. I stared at the pink fluid and back at my mate. "I-I can exp..." I clasped my hand over the wound, standing.

Emma stood there frozen, showing no emotion. She looked through me, not seeing what was happening before her. I watched her, just begging for any kind of reaction.

Stepping closer to the bars that separated us, I pleaded with her. "Emma, please say something!"

Finally, she reached through the bars, careful not to touch them, and pulled my hand away from the cut, placing her own there. Her cool magic flowed through me, stitching the wound. '*I love you, my Kompis. No matter what.*' Her voice settled me as much as her magic had. '*I am sorry for the pain...*' Her eyes lowered to my hips. '*But not sorry for the pleasure.*'

My eyes followed hers to see the dampness she smiled at. '*That was... Different... I love you, Emma. Find a way to break from him, and soon, my love. Alfheim needs you.*'

'*What's happening at home?*' Her eyes widened.

'*Yggdrasil is on the brink of death and our people are grieving.*'

She sat there staring off into nothing for several minutes, as if she were working out a plan in her head. I tried to reach her through our mental bond, but only heard silence. Suddenly, she jumped up, wobbled on her feet and fell into the iron bars, searing her hands.

"Emma!" I shouted, jumping up to push her off the bars.

"I-I have to go. I need to know what he's done!"

"Emma, wait!" I gripped her wrist, bringing her as close to the bars as possible without touching them. She leaned in, kissing my lips softly. "Be careful, my Kompis," I added when we separated.

She nodded and walked off, leaving me in the dark.

CHAPTER 12

Aric

"I don't care what it takes. Find him and bring him here. Now!" I barked at my commanders. "I know what he is. The Mystic has answers I need. Just find him. If you have to send an army out in the town, do it! Just bring him to me." My voice held none of the lightheartedness it had mere months ago.

My focus on my men broke when a few of the villagers ushered Rajnish and Mayank to the center of the throne room where I stood.

My eyes widened at the sight of the men I'd sent with Brynjar. Black dust covered them from head to toe, their once beautiful wings torn and bleeding. They were practically dead on their feet.

"Bring the healers here, NOW!" I ordered the room. My stern gaze fell on the men who dragged them in here. "Why the Hel didn't you take them straight to the healers?"

'*Brynjar?*' I tried connecting with him again, but I couldn't sense him enough to contact him.

"We insisted," Mayank rasped out. "It's Brynjar, sir."

I stepped off my dais and approached my warriors. Flicking my wrist, two soft stools appeared and they sank into them. "What happened?" I knelt before my men.

"Sire, we tried to find Brynjar. He ordered us to leave but... we tried," Rajnish said, tear stains streaked his sooty face.

"We walked with him for half a day... then... I'm not sure what happened, sir." Mayank winced as he wiped fresh blood from his face. His mouth opened and closed several times before he looked away, unable to continue.

"He changed, sir," Rajnish supplied. "He stood still for a moment; I wasn't even sure he was breathing. Then when he turned to look at us, his eyes were a solid black. I've never seen anything like it, sir. He told us that our queen was in the grips of 'that monster' and he ordered us to warn you. But then he tore off his coat and took off into the electric storm. We waited... we tried to fly and follow him, but..."

"I understand. You did the right thing. Rest now. The healers will care for you." I nodded to the women that stood anxiously behind their patients. After a quick assessment they gestured to the men behind them who gripped Mayank and Rajnish by their hands and spirited them off to the infirmary.

Climbing back to my chair high on the dais took effort as I sagged under the weight of the news they brought.

"Damn it, Brynjar. I never should have let you go without me." I closed my eyes, stroking the scar on my palm.

'Where are you, brother?' I searched out again for a single thread of my sister's mate. A sudden sulfurous stench choked my nose, causing me to sit up, coughing.

Brushing off my sentry's concerned questions about my sudden reaction, I focused on Brynjar. He sat in the cold, dark cell, surrounded by the cries of pitiful creatures.

'Brynjar.' I whispered in his mind.

Brynjar's heart raced in response. *'Aric?'*

'Yes, you damn fool. What the fuck happened?'

'I'm in a cell in Svartalfheim. What do you think happened?' His voice thick with sarcasm.

'Cut the attitude. We don't have time for this.'

'Sorry, you're right. Emma just left... it's bad.'

My heart clinched at the heaviness in his voice. *'Tell me?'*

'She tortured me... Well, sort of. She is fighting his control, but she's still under his thumb. I don't know how to break it completely.'

My heart sank. After what I'd seen of my sister on the battlefield and now if she was torturing her mate, what wouldn't she do?

'Stay strong, brother. She is still in there. Remind her of how much she's loved.'

'I will. Aric... there's... I've... There's more to me than I've told you... than I even understand...'

'That can wait, Brynjar. Get home safely and we can deal with that as a family. That is all that matters.'

'Aric...'

'No. Get home. Bring your mate.'

'Thank you.'

I attempted to smile before I broke the connection, but only managed a weak grin. We both needed to hold onto a shred of hope. I stared off into the distance, rubbing my arms at the lingering chill after visiting Brynjar.

"Your Majesty," came a soldier's voice who approached the dais, clutching the arm of a tall, slender man. He wore a dark suit with a bright red shirt, hair slicked back to perfection. The wild grin he held told me everything I needed to know about the man. He appeared not much older than I was, but I knew better.

"Mystic." I gave the man a small nod.

The soldier kicked him in the back of the knees when he didn't bow back. "You bow to your king," he barked.

Flying down the steps, I looked the soldier in the eye. "That's enough. You're dismissed."

The officer bowed and left.

I bent low to whisper in the Mystic's ear. "My mother was kind to you. You defy me and you will wish again for that little hovel my mother trapped you in. Do you understand me, Mystic?" I growled. The man only nodded; eyes glued to the ground. "Good," I said. "Now stand."

I straightened as the Mystic rose to his feet and bowed. "My apologies, sire."

"Very well." My words were sharp. "You gave mother the prophecy that tore my sister and me apart?"

"Yes, sir." He tucked his chin to his chest.

"Explain the prophecy," I ordered.

"I... sire, prophecies are never clear."

"Cut the bullshit!" My voice echoed around the room.

"I believe, sir, that it means if the bond between you and your sister is broken, Yggdrasil will die." The man looked me dead in the eyes. "Sire... You and your sister are the Vörður of Yggdrasil."

I glared at him for a long moment. *Mystics and their damn riddles.* Breaking his gaze, I sighed, rubbing my temples. "Please, sit." I gestured to the now vacant stools behind me. "Explain."

The Mystic sat straight-backed, watching my every move as I sat next to him, eyes scanning the room.

"I won't speak of this in front of others." He crossed his arms.

Flicking a finger, I ushered my men out of the room.

After they left, the Mystic began. "Yggdrasil is more than the gateway to the realms, Sire. It's a warden tree. It... without Yggdrasil, Ragnarök will be upon us." The Mystic's voice broke as he slumped back in the chair.

I swallowed hard before I spoke again. "What does this have to do with Emma and I? And what is a Vörður?"

"The Great Tree needs a living soul to survive. It needs a pair of bonded souls. The last twins to be born in Alfheim sacrificed their souls for Yggdrasil."

"Why isn't this known to all?" I asked.

"Our ancestors were quite superstitious. They believed if others knew, they'd want to free the twins. Your father—"

"What does he have to do with this?" I snapped.

"I don't know what Herrick's plans are. His mind is shrouded in a cloud of darkness. I only know he wishes to destroy Yggdrasil."

"Why? Why would he want that?"

"Love's a bitch," The Mystic said flatly.

"Excuse me?"

"The gods tied your mother and father long ago. Together, they ruled Alfheim."

I sat upright. "Excuse me?"

"Yes, young one. They once lived happily together here in Alfheim."

"What the Hel happened?" I could never get mother to explain who he was or what happened.

"He... Well, it's ironic now, but he loved your mother so much, he wanted a child with her. He snuck into Asgard to beg the gods to grant him and your mother a baby. They denied him and the queen banished him for entering the forbidden home of the gods. His banishment pushed him towards darkness. She would go see him occasionally, but he kept spiraling into the darkness."

"So, he wants to destroy the world because our mother banished him?"

"Like I said... Love's a bitch. Their bond is still intact, even in death. When a bonded pair are separated, it can drive them mad. I believe he still loves her—even now—but he has spent decades in the dark and it has corrupted his soul. He no longer knows what love really is. He believes Alfheim abandoned him; that the gods owe him something."

"How do you know all this and why wait until now to tell me?" I questioned.

He scoffed. "I'm a seer, boy. And far older than anyone knows. I have worked hard at my anonymity. Do you really think my mother named me Mystic? I will not reveal my secrets to a child."

I closed my eyes and took a long, slow breath to stave off my anger. I couldn't worry about why Herrick was doing what he was doing, only that he would kill us all if he isn't stopped. So many unanswered questions raged on in my head, but I pushed them aside. Opening my eyes again, I looked at the Mystic. He was picking dirt from his nails.

Exhaling, I asked, "How can we save Yggdrasil?"

"You need Emma. It's not entirely the tree itself that is dying, but the twins that lay in the heart of Yggdrasil are dying. If you cannot save them, another set of twins will need to take their place. There is a bond that you and your sister have that no other creatures could ever have. You balance each other out. That, Your Majesty, is what it means to be a Vörður." The Mystic's eyes softened. Bile rose in my throat. "I am sorry, my king."

I slumped into my stool, clutching my chest, waved one of my guards back into the room, then spoke without looking at the Mystic. "I need you close, Mystic, in case I have further questions and you have a tendency to hide from troubles. My guard will escort you to a room. You can keep the luxury you have grown accustomed to, but if you cross me, I will follow through with my earlier threat."

The Mystic stood and turned to leave, but glanced over his shoulder. "You can still save her, Majesty. Heal your sister's heart and your mate will heal as well."

I sat wide-eyed unable to respond as he walked off.

CHAPTER 13

Emma

D amion's warm saltwater scent woke me, his arm draped over me as he slept. I had to keep up the ruse that we were together, even though his touch turned my stomach. My heart pounded against my ribs as I tried to slide out from under him, but he pulled me back to his chest until my wings pressed into him.

"Good morning, Emma," he whispered.

"Morning." My veins ran cold as his hardness pressed against me.

"Where are you heading off to this morning? Why not stay here with me?"

"I-I just wanted to shower."

"I could join you." He pressed harder into me.

"I'm still getting used to the wings. It's hard enough for me to shower by myself." I turned awkwardly in his embrace, my wings smacking him in the face as I moved. His smile made my stomach tighten. "I promise I'll be right back." I kissed his nose before sliding out from under him and bolting for the bathroom.

Scratching my skin where our bodies had met, every muscle tensed. Flipping on the water, I undressed and crawled into the shower, letting the water rush over me in a scorching heat.

My invisible cage closed in on me and my chest tightened. *Get a hold of yourself, Emma.* Gasping for breath, I formulated a plan.

With steel in my veins, I snapped my fingers getting dressed and snuck out my door before Damion noticed me and traveled deeper into the mountain. I descended the narrow steps until I reached the dungeons, ignoring all the screams and tears. I only came for one man.

"Bryn. Wake up, my Kompis." He was curled in the corner of his cell, his mass hard to hide in the tiny room. "Please Bryn, wake up."

His body twitched at my words, then he rolled over and opened his eyes slowly. "Emmy?" he asked, his voice rough. "What are you doing here?"

I dropped to my knees, reaching for him, ignoring the searing heat of the iron bars. "Come, my love."

He crawled to my outstretched hands, kissing them each in turn. "I love you, Emma."

"I love you, too, Bryn. I shouldn't be here... It isn't safe, but I needed to see your face. To tell you I'm sor—"

"Don't. Don't ever apologize to me."

He moved my hand to his face, placing it on his cheek. His touch warmed me. "We need to escape while I am still in control, but before we can, I have to learn more. Father is planning something. I-I just know there's more. I'm sorry, my love." I pulled my hand away from his face and looked at the floor. "I fear what he wants with me, and I have to know. Can you hold on? Just a little while longer?"

"For you, I can wait a lifetime." His eyes glistened in the firelight.

The squeak of the door had me jumping to my feet. "Shit! They found me."

"Emma, take this, hide it!" Brynjar reached behind him, pulling a piece of wood from his back.

My eyes widened, grasping the small twig. "Is this?"

"Your tree, Emma. Honestly, I'd forgotten I had it until it poked me in the thigh last night as I slept." He shrugged. "It's how I knew where you were. If you keep it with you, you will never lose yourself. Herrick doesn't know about your tree, so I doubt he'll be able to sense it."

Smiling, I lifted my skirt and held the tiny piece of wood against my thigh before producing a ribbon with a twirl of my finger and used it to secure the twig to my leg. I released the hem and looked at my mate.

My insides curdled as I spoke, but I stood tall. "I'm sorry for what I have to do. He won't believe me any other way." Hurting Brynjar hurt me just as much.

"I love you always, no matter what." He stood, bracing for the pain.

I blew him a kiss before focusing my energy on sucking the air from his cell and spoke loudly. "I told you. I'll end this right now if you tell me what Aric is planning."

Brynjar dropped to a knee, clutching his throat. My heart sank as I sucked the air from his cell.

"Well, aren't you eager this morning, daughter?" Herrick and Damion stepped up behind me.

I quickly let the air back into Brynjar's cell and turned to face Herrick. "You seem to bring out his snark. I thought if I questioned him without you, he might speak to me. As it turns out, the piece of filth," I flinched at my own words, "trusts no one. I doubt he ever has. He's keeping secrets even from me." My eyes fell to my mate. A look of guilt flashed over his face before turning cold again.

"Don't worry, daughter, we will break him, or he will die fighting. We came looking for you when Damion couldn't find you in the kitchens or training room. For now, we have better places to be." He glanced at Brynjar before walking back toward the exit.

Damion wrapped his arms around my waist. "You left me in that massive bed this morning. I missed you." He leaned in, forcing his lips on me.

A low growl echoed from the cell beside me.

I pulled away before Damion could fully penetrate my mouth and looked at my mate, then back to Damion. "Not while he's watching," I whispered.

"Awe, come on." He pulled me closer. "Could be fun."

Stepping out of his grasp, I said, "Not right now."

Damion straightened, but I saw the hurt in his eyes.

Steam puffed out of Brynjar's nostrils as he huffed out a hot breath in the cold dungeon. His eyes, black as night, drilled into Damion. My eyes dropped to his hands, or rather, his *paws*. Long, sharp claws replaced his fingers. He had partially shifted into some wild animal with thick black fur covering his palms and traveled up, stopping at his elbows. His face hardened, but still was the face of my mate.

In a flash, Brynjar stood, one paw pushing into the bars, the other slashing out toward the man beside me. "Don't touch her," he growled, holding onto the last bit of humanity he could.

Damion flinched, wrapping his arm around me tighter, but quickly regained his composure and laughed nervously. "See, Emma. Aren't you happy that we broke that bond?"

"Uh-huh," I whispered, not daring to speak more, for I might cry. My mate's hands remained paws as he glared at Damion. I needed to settle him before he destroyed my chance to find out Herrick's plans.

"Come. Let's go eat something."

"Sure. Give me a moment? Please." I didn't take my eyes off my mate for a long moment. When Damion didn't leave, I finally looked back at him. My skin crawled as I reached for his face. "I just need him to understand we are over, and I can't do that with you here. Please?" I spoke in the sweetest tone I could.

Damion kissed my crown lightly. "Hurry back so I can show you how much I missed you." He turned and headed off.

Moving to Bryn who still leaned into the bars, I waited until I heard the creak of the door shutting before I spoke.

"Bryn? Move off the bars, please." Concentrating on inhaling and exhaling while my mind was spinning with fear and too many questions, but I knew I had to stay calm for him.

His eyes snapped to my face. The black faded quickly back into his icy blue eyes. "Emma," he gasped. "What happened?"

I glanced down at his hands and watched as fur gave way to flesh.

"I... I didn't hurt you, did I?" He turned away.

"No... but..." I smirked, turning his face back toward mine. "If you could have reached him, I think you would have killed Damion. That would have solved one problem." He tried to look away again, but my hand stayed firm. "I love you always, no matter what. I'm not sure what just happened, but..." I smiled. Maybe the fairytales I grew up reading weren't as fictional as I once believed. "You say I am amazing?" I leaned closer to the bars, brushing my nose to his. "No matter what. You hear me?"

Brynjar smiled. "No matter what."

The aroma of bacon and eggs wafted through the hallway before I stepped into the dining room. Herrick and Damion, already deep in conversation, glanced up as I entered. I braced myself for what

I needed to do. Pushing the fear down, I opened the door further and sat beside Damion. He kissed me on the cheek, embracing me in a half hug.

He kept his arm around my side and whispered into my ear. "Does he understand now that you are mine?"

"I think he understands I'm where I need to be." I smiled.

"I told you, daughter, that he is a monster. You are far better off without him."

"Yes, Father." I cocked my head at the plate of bacon and eggs before me. "How is it you can have this kind of food? I wouldn't expect pigs or chickens to survive here."

"No. They don't." He took a bite from his plate. "I have farms on the surface, far from the mountain, that provide me sustenance. I'm not from this realm, so I can't survive on the same food the dark fae do."

I dug into my food. "You are not from here? Then where?"

"It's a long story. Suffice it to say, daughter, I used to rule in Alfheim."

Choking on my eggs, I gasped out, "You're what?"

"Yes. I am from your world. Long ago. Your mother banished me for some silly misunderstanding." He continued to eat without further explanation.

Swallowing hard at this news, I tried to focus my energy on Herrick and took another bite. I slipped through his defenses like water through a sieve. I stiffened at the ease with which I penetrated his mind, but I had little time to worry. Flashes of a life far from this dark hole rushed past me. Ancient gods towered above the sniveling man that would be my father. Pushing past his history, I searched for his present. A tiny beetle crawled up my leg. I tried to shake it off, but it excreted a thin line of liquid iron, burning my flesh. I let out a small squeak, pulling out of his head.

He took another bite without looking up. "Find what you were looking for, daughter?"

"I-I'm sorry. You..." I quickly checked to see if the partition in my mind was secure, hiding my true plans, and sighed inwardly when I found it intact.

"Don't fret. I let you look. I know I haven't told you much of my plans, but I wanted to gauge your reaction." He gazed up at me as I finished my plate. "You seem intrigued. Would you like to know more?"

I swallowed my last bite. "Yes, Father. Too many have lied to me. I never want to be left out again."

"I'm sorry, my dear. Never again. I promise."

"Thank you." Part of me wanted to believe him. He was the only parent I had... But then I remembered that he was the reason I had lost my mother, and I straightened in my chair.

"I've already succeeded in my plans and it's just a waiting game now. Yggdrasil must die before I can move. Once that happens, I will be able to take control of the Nine Realms. The others will scramble to figure out how to remake the tree before Ragnarök comes for us all and the secret will already be with me."

"I... I don't understand. What secret? Why must Yggdrasil be remade?"

"Yggdrasil is the gateway between worlds. You already know that, but it is also the protector of the realms. It requires a living host, one that will protect and control the flow between realms. The current hosts are Alfheim. They won't let me pass through. So, if I destroy them, I can remake the tree and have a host that answers to me, as well as staving off Ragnarök."

"I... I still don't understand."

He cocked his head. "Oh, but I think you do."

I thought, my hand resting on my thigh. I gulped when the wooden twig beneath my dress poked at me. *That's why he wanted me, and not Aric.*

"Understand now?"

"Does... Does that mean... I'll be trapped inside the new Yggdrasil?" I clamped a hand over my mouth.

"Well, yes, but you won't be alone." His gaze flicked over to Damion. "The heart of Yggdrasil requires a bonded pair."

Silently, I pleaded with Damion, my heart in my throat. "And you are okay with this?"

"Where you go, I go." He raised my hand to his lips. "Don't worry. We will still be able to have a life. Your father's powers of the mind run through you. We can have any life you can dream of."

Lead surrounded my heart and breath fled from my lungs, leaving me frozen. My hand shook in his grip. *'Bryn, please hear me. We have to get out of here, and soon!'*

I waited to hear his voice, but nothing came. Only a rush of blood flow from a racing heart that was not my own. Pushing the anxiety aside, I pulled Damion to me and traced the scars along his arms that he was cursed to not see. Kissing his cheek, I whispered in his ear. "Please, Damion, see what Herrick has done to you."

He stiffened at my words and pulled away, looking at Herrick. "If you will excuse us," Damion said. "I would like some time alone with her."

Herrick smiled. "I believe you have earned it."

Damion wrapped his fingers around my upper arm, pulling me from the chair. "Come along, Emma. We have some things to discuss."

He gave me a light kiss and taking me by the hand, he led the way back to my room.

CHAPTER 14

Aric

I paced nervously across the dais, hands clasped behind my back, as I focused on the floor under my bare feet.

'Brynjar! Answer me, damn it!'

Brynjar had become unreachable since speaking with the Mystic and I was desperate to talk to him. I needed him to know what was happening and to bring Emma home before it was too late.

Sleep had alluded me and I merely nibbled on the food High Chancellor Tavis brought me. My body refused to do either until my family was home.

The silent room erupted in shouts as its large doors opened and the party I'd been waiting for walked in. The three gods approached, still bickering with each other.

Surt reigned over Muspelheim, the realm of fire giants, and even in his smaller fae form, he exuded the power of his gigantic fire god strength. He gave off an air of self-importance—all gods did—but this man had helped my sister control her powers. And for that, I was in his debt.

Njörðr's realm sat peacefully upon the beaches of Vanaheim. I didn't enjoy the thought of asking for his help, as it always came at a cost, but I needed all the help I could get if we were to invade Herrick's realm.

My eyes turned last to the youngest of the leaders. Even compared to me, she was a child, but my sister's actions gave her her crown. Sigrid now reigned over her mother's realm. Skadi, Sigrid's mother, had been the Goddess of Ice who led Niflheim, until Emma had plunged an ice dagger through Skadi's chest during the battle. Convincing her to help would be the most challenging of them all. I gulped hard. She was here, at least, maybe it wouldn't be so difficult.

A rumble formed at the base of my throat at the argument Sigrid and Njörðr were still having. Surt, however, stood perfectly silent, looking at me. I let out a long breath, gathering my strength, gripping the hilt of my sword that now had a permanent spot on my hip.

"Enough," I whispered, voice low and menacing. The two leaders snapped their attention to me. "I swear if you two don't stop your petty bickering, it will kill us all."

Sigrid nodded her head at my command. Njörðr hesitated before he, too, nodded.

"You are in *my* realm. Therefore, you obey me. You vowed to follow my mother's command in this war, and now that loyalty falls to me. We are at war, and I, King Aric Rødt Tré, am the commander of this army. If either of you think you can do a better job, I suggest you kill me first." I spoke with a ferocity I didn't know I had.

Njörðr spoke first. "My apologies, Sire."

Sigrid glared at me with eyes that burned hotter than the fire god beside her, hand resting on her hilt.

I drew my sword, holding it to my side. "Please. Draw it." My arms shook and I had to rein in my fears before I overreacted, but her childish behavior was only fueling my fire.

"How dare you," she said through gritted teeth. "After what your sister did—"

"That was not my sister. Herrick controlled her." We stared at each other for a long moment before she relented.

The ice queen raised her hands to her side in surrender. "My apologies, Sire." She glowered at me. Her words dripped with sarcasm. "Won't happen again."

I backed away but kept a firm grip on my sword as I paced before the three rulers. Every nerve vibrated throughout my body.

"Sire," Surt broke the silence. "Why did you call us here?"

He spoke with a humbleness I would not have guessed he possessed, causing me to pause before the giant of a man.

"It's Emma. There's so much more to her than we knew. Brynjar went after her. I have been in contact with him, and he informed me that King Herrick is losing his control over her, but I haven't been able to reach him since. I worry something has happened. We need to go in and retrieve them."

"Why should we risk our armies for these two people?" Sigrid snapped.

Before I could speak again, I had to remember how to breathe. "You don't understand the full extent of the ramifications of leaving her with him." Exhaustion overcame me, and I collapsed to the steps of the dais behind me. I laid my sword across my lap as I continued. "Emma and I are the Vörður of Yggdrasil. Herrick is weakening our connection to the tree by separating us. Normally it feeds off the twins that lay inside it, but they are dying and it's looking to us to protect it. If we don't bring her back, the tree will die." The weight of the world crashed down upon my shoulders as I spoke, constricting the air in my lungs.

"I don't understand. If it dies, we will simply be locked in our own realms, right?" Sigrid asked.

Surt and Njörðr, however, stood wide-eyed and stared at me.

"Yggdrasil is the only thing that stands between our worlds and Ragnarök," I said flatly.

The girl queen finally registered the depth of need to save this one individual. She clasped a hand over her mouth. The four of them were silent for a long moment.

To my surprise, it was Njörðr who first offered assistance. "I will send my Flygeblad in right away."

"No." My voice was sharper than I intended. "Sorry. No one can fly in. The two men that went with Brynjar came back with their wings shredded. There's a vast electrical storm hanging over the mouth to Svartalfheim. We have to go in on foot."

"I can send my ice wolves to scout," Sigrid offered. "They can leave immediately."

I only nodded toward her. She turned away, bowing her head, issuing orders mentally.

Surt sat next to me, elbowing me in the ribs. "I knew you two were different." He looked at me, but I made no inclination of emotion. The fire god wrapped an arm over my shoulder. "We will find her. I will raze his realm to the ground in fire if I need to."

"I never thought you to be so sentimental, Surt." I laughed.

"Ah, well, I like Emma."

I smiled. I liked the giant god despite myself.

Sigrid rejoined the group. "They are heading out now. It won't take them long. We should gather our armies at the base of Yggdrasil and prepare to leave as soon as I get word back from my pack."

"Agreed," I said as I stood and sheathed my sword. Turning my attention to the others, I said. "Gather a small force of your best. Depending on what her wolves find I want to prepare to go in after them if we must. If they have wings, tell them to cover them and not to attempt to fly."

The three nodded their agreements and left to prepare for battle.

I only now noticed that the acting commander of my army, Brody, stood in the doorway to the throne room and I jerked my head, beckoning him forward.

Brody bowed as he approached. "My king, apologies for the intrusion. I have already sent orders out for our elite to join us at Yggdrasil. We will meet you there..." He cleared his throat and lowered his gaze. "In case you have other matters to attend to first?"

I bowed slightly. "Thank you, Commander."

Brody departed, leaving me alone. With a sigh, I straightened and headed for the infirmary.

She lay cold as ice on the bed before me, eyes closed as if she merely slept. I leaned over, kissing her forehead, my lips lingering there for a long moment.

I smoothed my hand over her hair. Falling to my knees, I whispered, "Please stay with me."

'Aric, my love. I'm not going anywhere.'

I smiled at her words in my head. *'I...'* How could I tell her I was leaving for battle when I just begged her to stay?

'You have to go. Bring her home, Aric. She is just as much my sister as she is yours.'

I let out a dry laugh. *'Have I told you how wonderful you are? She nearly killed you, and yet you hold no ill will.'*

'Emma's partner in Midgard came closer to killing me, and if I could have saved him, I would have. It's who I am, Aric. Save her.'

I closed my eyes, imagining Thyra's body pressing against mine, her warm embrace flooding me. Those lips I so longed to feel against mine lay motionless as she spoke again.

'Save her and maybe you will get your desire.'

'You wake up and I will demand the gods to tie you to me.' I pressed my lips to her cheek.

'Then go now and hurry home, my love.'

I stood, taking one last look at her before I rushed out the door.

CHAPTER 15

Brynjar

H er fear penetrated into the depths of my soul as I paced my tiny cell as much as I could. The slivers of her conversation with Herrick flowed through our bond, and my heart thrummed in my head, threatening to explode.

Martial arts had taught me how to handle fear, but feeling her terror and being unable to do anything about it was something new for me. I needed to get to my mate. I needed to keep her safe.

The rage boiled in my mind as images of a giant black beast flooded me. I watched as it tore through its enemies. My mate's voice echoed in my head, but I couldn't understand the words. Everything blurred in my vision. She needed me and I couldn't move, let alone speak back to her.

My mind stayed with Emma's as Damion dragged her back to her room. She shook at his touch, only fanning the flames within me.

I pulled myself from her mind and focused on the bars in front of me. They were made of iron. Just being this close to them should have weakened me, but I could sense a new magic within me growing stronger. I reached out to touch the bars and quickly pulled back. It still burned, but only slightly. Focusing on the unfamiliar magic within me, I touched the iron again. The tingle of their bite only tickled. My fingers wrapped around them and the buzz of magic poured into me through the bars.

Reaching back into my mate's mind, her words still eluded me, but I sent her as much strength as I could through our bond and sensed her smile a little.

I would tear through this entire mountain to get to her if I had to.

'Calm, my son. You need to focus if you're to keep her safe.' A voice echoed in my ears *'We don't have the time to explain everything. But as it is, I'll do what I can for you like this.'*

Visions of my childhood flashed through my mind. My mother and father sat on a beach wrapped in each other's arms. Sand covered my tiny body as I dug a hole going nowhere. My father's laugh had me peaking my head up above the mound. I scowled at him. He moved from behind my mother, stripped and shifted into a giant bear. I giggled and jumped out of the hole to run down the beach. My father chased after me for a while before I tripped and fell to the sand. His bear hovered over me and licked my face. I giggled again. He shifted back to his human form and knelt to pick me up before taking me back to where my mother sat smiling.

The happy scene faded and a new darker one appeared. I was crying as mother tore me away from my father's arms. She was yelling, and he was begging. I didn't understand. His anguished voice rang out in my ears even now.

A strange tingle crawled over my skin as his magic poured into me. It was unlike anything I'd experienced before. Fae magic was precise and elegant, but this was wild and uncontrolled.

I roared at its touch. The power of my new magic calmed at my voice and settled into place as if it had always been a part of me. Its warmth lessened my fears, and I was able to speak to my father.

'What's happening?' I couldn't fight the fear in my mind.

'You're fighting the change. It should've happened sooner, but my magic was blocked from you. I've tried for years to reach you, but our connection is weak. I don't know how much time we have. The Berserker magic is only now showing itself because of the level of danger your Kompis is in. This isn't just about her dying, but giving her life for all of us.'

'What... what change? I don't understand. I'm fae...with wings. I'm not a Berserker.'

'You are like me, son. You are the best of both your mother and me. You'll be able to fly high and roam great distances in your bear form. You can shift like I can. It should have happened naturally...'
He paused. *'This way will be more painful. I'm sorry, son. When it happens, hold on to her face in your mind and it will keep you sane. If you lose focus, the beast can control you. Stay strong and you will make it through.'*

'I'm afraid.'

'I know, son. Find me when you can, and I'll help you further. For now, you're on your own. I can't hold on any longer. Keep her safe, my son.'

His voice faded from my head as quickly as it had come into focus. I was alone again. I couldn't reach Emma. I couldn't reach Aric. Even my father was out of reach.

My body shook with fear and pain. Pain like never before. Every nerve vibrated under my skin. I needed to calm the fear, but the room spun.

Herrick's curse pulled at me as I reached for a shard of broken glass on the other side of the bars. The sharp edges found my tender forearms without a thought. The warm liquid dripped from the cuts I made. I didn't even feel the sting that I knew was there.

I should've—needed to feel pain, but only rage came as the bear within me growled. My father was right. I was like him, and the beast demanded to be released, but the fear I couldn't control him to protect Emma kept the monster caged.

Fur crawled up my arms, but I pushed it back down. I was locked in a battle with myself and didn't even flinch when my mate cried out in my mind.

Only when the echoing screams drew closer did I snap out of my trance.

King Herrick stood before me, smiling, as he watched me struggle. "I told her there was something wrong with you. I don't know what you are, but you aren't fae and not deserving of my child. She is in fact upstairs defiling your bond with Damion as we speak. She is yours no longer."

My arms stretched through the bars, needing to feel his skin between my fingers.

"She is mine," I growled through gritted teeth.

He laughed... he was fucking *laughing* at me. "I think not, boy. I believe it would give her pleasure to kill you herself."

The bear within me growled but calmed the instant Emma's voice echoed in my head. *'It's a lie, my Kompis. Hold on!'*

I reined my beast in, stepped away from the bars, and crossed my arms. Leaning against the wall I closed my eyes and spoke, "You cannot break us that easily." My voice was calm. I wanted to tear his throat out right then and there, but knew it was pointless to fight.

Herrick looked at me through cold eyes. "I have already broken her. She is Damion's now. I have seen it."

Now it was my turn to double over with laughter. "To think... the master of mind control has been controlled."

The bars vanished, and Herrick stepped up closer to me. My hands reached for him, but he quickly pinned them against my sides with his magic.

"You believe she has deceived me? I'm the only one that knows how to control another's mind. She couldn't possibly know how to lie to me." His words held menace, but his eyes were wide with fear.

I grinned. "You are by far the most arrogant man alive... for now."

He picked up a shard of glass from the littered floor and slashed it across my chest. I gasped at the pain but couldn't move.

"You dare threaten me, boy? I will watch you bleed out before me."

The image in my head of a giant bear huffing in what could only be a laugh had me grinning from ear to ear. "Look at me, you fool. Look at my blood. Look at my strength. I should be dead, yet here I stand."

Herrick's eyes fell to my chest and the pink blood dripping to the floor. His eyes widened as he quickly backed out of the cell, and the bars reappeared before he dropped his magic hold.

I sprinted forward, my hands gripped the bars as I yelled at his retreating figure. "You can't win! Not while we are bonded."

After he was gone, I went back to pacing my cell, searching mentally for my mate again. Once found, it was like she stood behind a veil. I could see her outline, I could feel her, but the connection was hazy.

'Emmy.' I tried to project, but my words hit a brick wall. Her fear had subsided, and sadness replaced it. It hurt to sense her but not able to help her, so I pulled out of her mind and studied the floor as I paced.

My breathing grew ragged as I walked in circles. If she didn't come to me soon, I would tear the walls down myself and take the entire mountain down with it. I tried to ignore the fear rising in my mate. Panicking wouldn't help her. I needed to calm myself and focus on her face, like my father had said.

We had to get out of here, and not just for our safety, but for Yggdrasil. Through our bond, I had seen Herrick's plans, and I knew the only way to save the ancient tree was with my father's clan, but we had to escape first.

Her father may have destroyed all hope for the future, but maybe mine could restore it. At the thought of my father, my beast huffed.

I lowered my guard slightly and watched as my fingers shifted into claws and fur then back to hands. Allowing myself this minor shift calmed me.

That was until I sensed her cries in my mind and all went red.

CHAPTER 16

Emma

D amion dragged me back to my room and flung me inside before slamming the door closed. I tripped over my feet and fell to the floor in a heap. He loomed over me. My heart pumped faster, like it was trying to get as many beats in before it stopped all together. I scurried backwards, flames licking the edges of his palms.

"Herrick is weak. He's let his arrogance overshadow what is right in front of him. Not me, Emma, I see right through you. I can smell the stench of fear within you."

Tears fell hard, but I refused to let them overtake me. Slowly, I stood, looking my accuser in the eyes, my jaw tight as I spoke. "What exactly are you saying, Damion?"

"I'm saying that Herrick will sacrifice us. And for what? His own gain? I know you aren't willing to let that happen. I sure as Hel won't allow it. We have a choice, Emma." His eyes softened as he stepped closer. "We die with him, or we take his place." He gently caressed my cheek.

My eyes widened. I was sure Damion had planned on killing me, not Herrick. Inhaling sharply, I reached out for my mate once again. *'Brynjar? Please, we have to get out now. Answer me!'*

The wave of anger that flowed through me had not come from my own mind. My mate's raspy breath whispered in my ear as if he stood wordlessly at my side.

Damion's crisp voice brought me back to the room. "What do you say, my love?"

"W-what?"

"Will you help me destroy him? Herrick?"

I flinched as Damion leaned in, brushing his lips to mine. Pain and hurt flashed in his eyes before he squeezed his molten hand around my arm, searing my skin.

"What does that mutt have that I don't?" he barked. He pulled me closer, forcing his tongue inside my mouth. I bit down hard, tasting the coppery tang of blood in my mouth. Damion shoved me to the ground.

Spitting blood to the floor I begged him, "Damion, please see the truth of what Herrick has done to you! Look, please, look at yourself and see!"

He wiped the blood from his mouth and stepped in front of the mirror. He stood there for a long moment, cocking his head to the side.

"Please see it, Damion," I begged not daring to stand up. "He has a hold of you. The only way to break free is for you to see what he's done to you."

He rolled his eyes but looked from me to his reflection. He cocked his head and stood there for a long moment. When he finally looked away, wide eyed, I knew he saw the scars.

"You see it now? Don't you?" I asked, tears burning my eyes.

He clinched his jaw, refusing to look up at me.

"Damion," I moved to stand but fell back down when his hardened eyes glared at me.

His chest heaved as he roared, slamming his fist into the wall. His eyes never looked back at me.

I reached a shaky hand out for the hem of his pants. I needed to run, to break out my mate and be free, but the pain radiating off Damion at what Herrick had done to him broke my heart. "Damion, please help us—me. You can come too, but we have to leave now!"

His burning gaze fell on me as I stood and moved closer to him, but he jerked away before I could touch him.

When he spoke again, his voice was cold and distant. "You're no better than him. I thought you actually cared for me. I thought we but no... it was yet another mind trick from you wasn't it."

"I—I'm so sorry Damion. I didn't mean to hurt you it's just I'm already mated—"

"Don't..." His entire body tensed as he looked back at the mirror.

With his back to me I moved, taking careful steps toward the door.

His face turned, freezing me in place. "Emma, I loved you and that might have saved me." His body ignited in flames. "You... go now before— Just go!"

I slammed the door behind me. Damion's screams from the room we'd shared, coming from somewhere deep in his gut, sent chills through me, and heat radiated off the door. I could only imagine the destruction from the torrent of flames I assumed he'd unleashed as they tore through the room.

Placing a hand to the door, I whispered, "I am sorry, Damion," before I ran for the dungeons and my mate.

I was breathing hard when I reached his cell. What I saw made me gasp.

"Brynjar?" My voice shook.

Giant paws had replaced my mate's hands. Dark fur crawled up his arms, covering his chest, his face taut, but still his golden skin. His eyes focused on me struggling to fight against his shift.

"Emma," he breathed, his words sharp and pained. "Couldn't answer. Leaving?"

I closed my eyes, straining my mind and slowly, the iron bars lifted but I couldn't raise them higher than a few feet from the floor before they stopped.

"Can't push further," I said in a strained voice. "Damion knows and I'm sure Herrick will know soon enough."

Brynjar lowered his body to the floor, laying himself as flat as he could go with his wings. He sucked in a breath and used one paw to grip the underside of the cell door and pulled himself free. The cold iron did nothing to his fur covered hand.

I released the bars as soon as he cleared them. Sighing in relief, I looked at my mate as he stood. I outstretched my hand to caress his face.

He pulled away and spoke, his words coming easier than before. "You were right about one thing. I have been hiding something from you. I knew I wasn't a pure fae but I didn't know I was this..." He looked to his claws.

I pulled his face back to mine, leaning in, and kissing him deeply. "No matter what," I whispered. His breathing evened out and paws reverted back to his hands as he shifted back to my Brynjar. "Run now. Explain later." I turned and led us toward the exit.

"Emma." Drew's familiar voice halted my steps. I had almost forgotten the pitiful humans that I once called family. "Emma help us!" He begged.

I turned and walked toward the cell he and his mother cowered in. My mate followed close behind me. They looked up at me in desperation. These two pushed me to the brink of throwing myself off a cliff. I should let them rot. Anger filled me at the sight of them. Brynjar's cool hand wrapped around mine, calming me. The moans and cries of the other's I'd blocked out now flooded my ears. I sighed giving in and lifted the bars of every cell door. I slammed the bars back down when everyone was out.

Staring at my stepfamily, I spoke as calmly as I could. "I will not help you more than this. It is more than you deserve. I can't tell you what to do, but I'd hide here until its safe. Herrick will fight us escaping. If we succeed that means he's dead and it should be safe for you. If not... he will probably kill you anyway."

My heart raced as I turned and walked away from the dungeons. My steps were light as I hugged the walls of Herrick's fortress. I headed straight for the weapons room and slipped inside as quietly as possible. Darkness surrounded us as Brynjar closed the door behind him but I flicked my wrist, producing a small fireball in my hand. We stood in a room wall to wall with blades of all kinds.

"I figured we might need these." Pulling a pair of long daggers from the wall, I strapped them to my hips.

I turned back to my mate and smiled. The tension from the dungeon faded and he was just my mate again. "How?" I asked him. "How are you so calm right now? You looked as if you'd tear off my head a few minutes ago."

His purr from across the room sent a flutter in my stomach. "You." He said flatly as he strode over to me in a single stride, wrapped his arms around my waist and pulled me closer. "You are the calm in my storm. Now that I have you in my arms again all is right with the world." He leaned in kissing me fiercely.

Pulling away, I said, "We are in the heart of the enemy's lair and you want to do this now?" I laughed as he pulled me tighter. His hard body pressed into me.

"Nothing else matters to me. After everything," He paused looking far away and I feared he was thinking of all the things I did with Damion. "I just want to feel you against me. To know this is real." He held me tight.

I brushed my lips to his, "It's real. So real if Herrick catches us, we're dead." I pushed out of his arms.

"Then we better hurry out of this place." He said with a grin. I could gaze at his smile for the rest of my life.

I nodded. "There's only one way out and I'm sure Herrick will have it heavily guarded," I said unsheathing one of my blades and moved to the door. He grabbed two long swords holding them at his side.

"Like we did at the tree?" he asked.

We fought side by side to defend our home. Literally tied together by the leather strap of our mating bond.

"Together," I said.

"No matter what." He responded.

The silence was eerily creepy as we slipped into the hall and up to the training room before we saw another soul. The dark fae turned on us as we approached.

The beings lined the hall, blocking the path to the exit. Herrick's tall, dark form stood behind their protective wall.

Brynjar raised his blades and stood beside me. A small horde of the creatures charged us leaving the rest to protect their king. Brynjar extended his wings high into the sky. His feet left the ground and he spun around so he was behind the threat. I grinned at my mate as we ran towards the enemy, sandwiching them in.

We thrust and jabbed our way toward each other, cutting down the monsters one by one in a dark and violent ballet of blood. I reached for my mate and stood beside him as we strode towards Herrick, who scowled behind his forces. A feeling of unease gripped me. This was too easy. Herrick hadn't made any moves against us, only sending his fae to die for him.

'Bryn, wait...' I tried to pull him back and fortify my mental shield but Herrick's voice shattered my control.

'Have you learned nothing, daughter?'

I crumpled on the spot as searing pain ripped through my body. My vision blurred as I lay there. Flashes of light filtered through my mind.

Brynjar dropped his sword and roared as black fur rippled over his back. His pants tore as muscles doubled, then tripled in size. Massive paws replaced his hands and feet. His face contorted into a long brown snout. His growl echoed off the stone walls.

I watched Herrick's minions scatter, leaving him to face the massive black bear that challenged him. The ground shook when Bryn's front paws hit the rocks as the bear that was my mate stalked toward Herrick.

The dark fae king stood rooted on the spot. "You... You can't exist," he stammered.

My mate circled Herrick. The king's eyes darted around, looking for a way out. He tried to follow his dark fae, but the bear cut off his escape. He stood frozen in place, terrified. Even in my haze, I could see him shaking.

"You're only legend." Herrick raised his hands drawing at his magic as a small ball of fire formed in his palms.

"Bryn," I whispered.

Herrick pushed the flames towards my mate, who effortlessly batted it away with his massive paw and continued to close in on him. He moved backwards, tripping over one of his fallen fae.

"P-please..." he begged, reaching his hands out blindly searching. His fingers clasped around the hilt of a sword and he swung out wildly, making contact with the outside of Brynjar's arm.

The bear roared, taking a step back and shaking his entire body. A small trickle of blood flowed through his fur, matting it in place.

Herrick stood to shaky legs and raised the sword. Brynjar's massive body lunged. His jaws gripped Herrick by the wrist, snapping it from his body. Herrick's screams echoed in the hall as he collapsed to the ground holding the stump where his hand used to be.

The bear stood and with one swift swipe of his paw, tore through Herrick's chest like paper. His body fell to the ground with a soft thump and the bear clamped down on his throat for good measure.

The pain subsided from my head the moment Herrick collapsed.

The bear snorted and huffed at the body before turning to me. He approached me slowly. Nudging my head with his snout, he slumped to the floor, whining.

I focused my vision on the black mass before me, smiling as I reached my hand out to scratch the fur between his eyes.

"No matter what, my Kompis."

He groaned as his body slowly returned to his fae form and rolled onto his back. Bryn clutched his chest. "Ah, fuck, that hurts."

I shifted around to his side. "So, that's some secret you've been keeping."

"I... I've never done that. I didn't know I could. Seeing you laying there in pain must have snapped something inside me." He rested a hand on my shoulder. "Are... are you all right?"

I nodded.

"I guess I have a lot of explaining to do," Bryn continued. "But let's get out of here first."

I laughed and pressed my lips to his, but the copper tang pulled me off his mouth quickly. I stood, spitting the taste out.

"You're naked and covered in blood and you're asking if I'm okay?" I reached for his hand, helping him to his feet. "I think we should get the Hel out of here before Damion comes looking for us."

We ran until we reached the center of the large caldera. I scanned the walls for a way up and saw none.

Brynjar's laugh behind me broke my focus. "What?" I asked.

He stroked my spine, brushing his fingers against the white feathers of my wings in a silent reminder.

"Shit." I rolled my eyes. "Still not used to those yet."

He stepped in front of me, leaning in to kiss me again. I turned my head so his lips fell on my cheek instead. "I do love you, but you're disgusting right now."

"Fair enough. How much flying have you done?"

"Not much." I gulped.

"There is a massive electrical storm above our heads. My... abilities keep my wings relatively safe. I'm not sure what would happen to yours, so let's get to the top and land. From there we can walk." His fingers grazed my jawline.

"How long will that take?" I buried my head in his chest.

"You want home in a hurry?" His chest rumbled with laughter. "For you, I think I can muster the strength to fly us both straight to the gateway. Tuck your wings in as tight as you can and turn around." I did as requested and without a second thought, he tightened his grip and launched skyward.

I closed my eyes and held on to my mate. Deafening wind rushed past my ears. The icy chill gripped me. I shivered and Brynjar squeezed me tighter. I twitched in his arms as lightning rippled around us and buried my face in his chest, praying we would make it through the storm. When my feet finally hit the ground, I let out a sigh of relief.

My heart sank as I gazed upon the once mesmerizing gateway. The massive vine weaved doors that sprang to life at my touch the first time I saw it now wilted. I spun on my heel to look at my mate.

"He's already won." My voice shattered.

"Not yet. We have you now, so we still have hope." He kissed the top of my head. "Let's go home." He led me forward.

The cold nothingness of the gateway froze my veins. I shielded my eyes from the bright light of my home.

"Emma! Brynjar!" My brother's voice came from somewhere in front of me.

I focused my eyes, and the small army came into view. "We were about to come rescue you two. Looks like we are too late." He laughed. His gaze fell to Bryn beside me. "What in Hel's name happened to you?"

"It's a long story. One in which I will tell you but," Bryn looked at me, still clutching my hand, "after I clean up and welcome my Kompis home."

Aric nodded. "Very well. We have a lot to discuss, so make it quick." Brynjar shot him a menacing look. "Well, take your time. Rest up tonight and we will talk in the morning."

Brynjar bowed slightly and strode off as the army parted, letting us pass, arm in arm with me.

CHAPTER 17

Damion

Fire filled me at the sight of my marred skin, and a lifetime of torment flooded back to me. The man I thought of as father had stolen everything from me. And now his daughter had destroyed my heart. How could I have been so blinded by my own love for her to see she didn't love me too?

The inferno that engulfed me raged on, spilling out of me. Flames licked up my arms as I shoved the mirror to the floor, shattering it. Turning to the bed I shared with Emma, I placed a hand on the sheets, erasing the night together I thought we had, burning the bed to ashes. It had all been a lie. She loved *him*.

I paced the room until the fire demolished everything. My hand reached for the door handle, melting it and setting the wood on fire, and walked through the flames. Dark fae rushed past me, attempting to extinguish the fire that was consuming their home.

Sounds of battle raged on somewhere within the mountain, but I ignored it. That was Herrick's problem. Even if he was fighting Emma... I told myself I no longer cared. As I walked to my room, burning the ground with every step, my anger slowly dissipated, extinguishing the flames. My skin was still warm, but I was no longer scorching all I touched.

Water called to my heated body and my feet moved straight to the bath, my brain a fog of pain and fear. I flicked the showerhead on and stepped into the tub. The water cooled my heated skin.

I sank to the floor of the tub and let the water wash over me in a haze. Overwhelming grief took hold of me as I wrapped my arms around my knees and sobbed. My body shook with the force of my tears. Emotions poured out of me. Hatred for Herrick. Emma's betrayal. The death of my family. Everything hit me at once.

I plugged the tub and let myself sink down as the water filled the space. I was utterly on my own. I could drown and no one would notice or care. The water covered my face, and I closed my eyes, letting it take me under.

The green tail from my dreams flashed in my memory again and I felt more at peace than I had a moment ago. As I submerged in the warm water, I looked down at my legs. Iridescent green flakes formed like freckles over my legs.

I cocked my head in curiosity as my fingers grazed their scaly texture. In a blink, I was back in my memory. The burn from the water I expected never came. My body relaxed against the fluid motion of it.

Breathing came so naturally that I couldn't tell if I was really here or still in my memory. My tail flapped as I swam around moving faster under the water than I ever had on land. Lights up ahead caught my eyes as I swam closer to the city that had formed before me. Tall, spiral towers jutted up from the ocean floor enclosing the city. I moved into the quiet center. A large glass domed greenhouse sat in the heart, glowing. I pushed the doors open with ease and swam inside. I couldn't explain it, but I knew this place. My hands reached out for the strange plants that grew all around me, dripping with strange fruit.

"You have come back, I see," a woman's singsong voice spoke. I spun around to see the woman from my dream. Her bright green tail flicked from side to side as her long dark hair flowed down the front of her. She had called me her son but the image of the mother I remembered blurred.

I stared at her for a moment, unsure of what to say.

"I don't understand. How?" I asked. "Why am I here?" I tried to clear my mind.

"You are in great pain, my child. The spell Herrick held over you is breaking and you are seeing your past for the first time in years." She answered.

"Child? Son? Who are you?" I asked the woman. The truth of who she was filled me, but I needed to hear her say it. My heart ached to hear it.

She reached her hand out brushing her fingers over my cheek. "I am your mother, of course." Her arms raised, waiting for my embrace.

I didn't move. "How? I'm fae. I have legs and breathe air not water. How can I possibly be here?"

Her smile faltered. "Of course you don't remember, do you? You were a small child when he took you from us." She dropped her hands.

"I... I remember..." What did I remember from that day? Everything was hazy. I rubbed at my eyes, trying to clear my head and focus on the first time I met Herrick.

I looked back at my childhood and tried to pull something from it. Swimming flashed in my memory. Swimming not with feet, but with a tail.

All at once, the memories of the day I thought my family had died came into my mind. The day my family had been killed happened in this very city before me, where I had grown up.

Mercenaries had been sent in to destroy the city. I fled and hid in this very chamber. They hadn't discovered me until all the screams had died out.

I looked at the woman that called herself my mother. Her tail matched mine.

"How did you escape? What happened to my tail?" I had too many questions.

"We are water nymphs. We can take either human or nymph form. So, once he had you out of the water, your tail changed into legs. When the attack started, I was already in the city. I went looking for you. I thought you would have fled to the caves, but when you weren't there, I came back here. Herrick's men had already destroyed the city and there was no trace of you." She placed her palm on my chest.

A sharp pain seared through my torso. I closed my eyes at the pain and swam away from her.

"I leave you with this gift." She looked at where her hand touched my chest. I followed her gaze and saw the massive red welt forming. "She will help you avenge your family."

The stabbing pain intensified, pulling me back to the bath in Svartalfheim.

The moment I opened my eyes again, the pain vanished. My tail, too, had disappeared and my legs were restored. I smiled as I stepped out of the tub and walked to look at my reflection in the mirror over the sink.

My reflection hadn't changed, except for one new addition. I leaned in, looking at the dark swirls tattooed on my flesh.

A dark beauty of the sea swam across my chest, stretching from shoulder to shoulder, and her black tail snaked around my ribs, just under my left arm. She held a black trident in her right hand.

My fingers grazed over her. I watched as she twirled around, spiking my skin with her trident. I pulled back with a yelp, looking at the blood that dripped from my hand. When I looked back at the mirror again and she was back in place, swimming across my body. My hand reached out to touch her again, but before I could get close, she brandished the trident and hissed at me.

'Find me when you are ready, my son.' I heard my mother's voice in my head.

I knew the woman's words to be true. She was my mother. My mind knew this, but my heart refused to accept it. Still, I needed to get home, even though I didn't know where home was.

Shuddering at the thought of all the things Herrick had done to me, I stepped out of the bathroom heading towards my closet to get dressed. I was not an ordinary fae after all. Herrick blocked my history from me. Why now? Why was I seeing my mother after all these years? How had I grown scales under the water? Was I getting stronger or Herrick weaker? I absentmindedly pulled on a pair of loose pants and walked back to my room. I studied my arms as I walked. The green scales on my forearms remained even though the fins were gone.

An icy wave rushed over me, and I knew Herrick was dead and the spell that had connected us together broke. His past actions were clear to me now. He never truly cared for me, and now he was gone... The man that had raised me was gone. I should have been filled with sadness, instead I felt nothing for the man.

I grinned before walking out of my room to survey the damage Emma had left in her wake.

Herrick had caged me. I could walk the earth and swim the seas. He had merely wanted the Nine Realms, I wanted more. I would have the lands of the gods but the waters would bow to me as well.

CHAPTER 18

Brynjar

We hurried through the crowd of faces staring at us. I tried to block out the murmurs and whispers but words like 'Queen,' 'blood,' and 'battle,' pulled me away from my mate. After thinking she was lost to me, I wanted to share her with no one. My reunited mate and I practically flew to my home, high in the treetops.

I took the stairs to my treehouse two at a time, pulling her up with me. The second she closed the door behind her I spun her around and held on tight to my mate, burying my face in her neck.

Taking in a deep inhale of her scent, I spoke. "I was so afraid for you, Emmy."

Her sobs shook through my body.

I pulled away just enough to look her in the face. "You are home, my Kompis. You are safe." I kissed her tears away.

Her smile grew but didn't quite reach her eyes. She pulled out of my embrace, taking my hand, and pulled me to the bedroom.

The curves of Emma's hips swayed from side to side as she walked and my chest tightened at the primal hunger that burned in my gut.

I closed the door behind us. Her fingers dug into my hair, scraping my scalp as I pulled her into my arms brushing my lips to hers

She pressed a finger to my lips. "I love you, I do, but," she pulled out of my grasp, "you're covered in blood."

I growled in protest but dragged her with me toward the bathroom. I snapped to remove the tattered remains of our clothes and started the shower.

The rush of warmth from the water spread over me as I guided the two of us into my massive shower. Our wings took up most of the space, so I pressed our bodies together, pulling her under the showerhead. She reached beside us for a bar of soap. Her bubbly hands spread across my chest and up my neck as she scrubbed me clean from head to toe, lingering a bit in the middle just long enough that her absence left me wanting more. My mind struggled to believe this was real. We were home and she was in my arms again. She wrapped her hands around my back, pulling me into her. I kissed her neck just to prove to myself she really was here.

My hands rested awkwardly on her back, just under her wings as my fingertips stroked her feathers. Her body trembled against mine as her smile faded and she cried. I held her tighter letting her pour out everything she was feeling. We escaped with our lives, yet Herrick had left scars I couldn't see. I'd kill him over and over again if I could. She was hurting and all I could do was watch. My beautiful mate sobbed until the water ran cold.

"Emmy," I exhaled. She looked at me with puffy eyes and I brushed the wet locks from her face. "We should go to bed." I wanted this woman with every ounce of my soul, but there would be time for that later. Tonight, I simply wanted to hold her. To know she was real.

We stepped out of the shower, and I wrapped a towel around her, doing my best to be careful with her wings, before grabbing my own towel. With my hand in hers, I led her back into our bedroom.

She leaned against me as we walked. I breathed in her scent. The dull shine to her skin lingered, and I prayed to the gods to take her sadness.

Her wing entangled around my legs as she dragged them alongside of us and before I could react, we both went crashing to the floor, me landing on top of her.

"Shit," Emma groaned. "I thought you said slamming your wings into things didn't hurt that bad?"

I laughed at the memory of her shoving me into the door.

"I lied." I grinned at her. "Are you alright?"

The feel of her beneath me ignited something deep within, but I tried to push my need aside.

"Yeah," she whispered. "I've got to learn how to control these things. She brushed her fingers over my jaw sending a shiver down my spine.

Her grin had me shifting to my elbows, straddling her hips and I pressed into her, devouring her lips.

I pulled up slightly. "I... I... We need to sleep." I started to sit up, but her hand reached for me.

"No..." She caressed my cheek.

"Are... are you okay? Your wings?" I asked.

She wiggled under me, screwing up her face. With a snap of my fingers, I placed a pillow under her head. "Better?" I asked.

Emma smiled. "Much." She paused. "Thank you for saving me."

"You saved me."

"No... If you hadn't come, I'd still be there. You broke his hold..."

"I told you. I love you. I couldn't sit around and do nothing without you." I stroked her cheek then pulled away quickly.

"Don't..." she whispered, closing her eyes. "Don't stop... Don't ever stop touching me."

She pulled open her towel and I watched her face for a long moment. She opened her eyes and looked back at me. "Please."

My breath caught in my throat as I looked down at her. I wanted to taste every inch of this woman. Her lips met mine as I leaned in, kissing her softly. Her heartbeat pulsed under my kiss on her neck as I moved to explore her body.

My tongue flicked over the hard bud of her nipples as I traveled lower, her back arching beneath me.

"I haven't even started, my love," I exhaled against her stomach.

My lips caressed the curve of her hips, following the line down to her core. She parted her legs for me and I inhaled in the scent of her, memorizing every detail. I smiled at the moan that escaped her lips as the tip of my tongue gently teased her slit.

She raised her hips as I slid my fingers over her wetness. I thrust my fingers inside her as I licked the nub there. Crooking my fingers inside her, I beckoned her to succumb.

"Bryn," she breathed. I moved faster as she rocked against me. "Bryn," she gasped. My hand began to cramp but her moans urged me on. It wasn't long until she pulled the pillow over her face and screamed into it. She pushed my face away and wiggled backwards staring at me with those fierce eyes.

"Well that didn't take long."

She threw the pillow at me. "Shut up. I missed you."

"I missed you too." My hands traveled up her legs.

"Now, I want you to fuck me. She growled.

I sat up, pulling the pillow with me and placing it under her ass.

"Are you sure?" I asked as I knelt in front of her. Her legs wrapped around me pulling me closer.

"Yes."

I leaned over her, pushing into her slowly. Her hands stroked the edges of my wings and bringing every nerve to life. Our bodies melded into one as I moved inside her. My climax was already rising when she grinned, flipping me over. She sat on top of me, hips rocking against mine.

I reached for her soft face. Her eyes widened suddenly, and she smacked my hand away, jumping off me.

"Emmy?" I stood grazing her wings. She shook under my touch. "Emmy, my Kompis, talk to me." My heart shattered to see her so broken. I wanted to snap my fingers and make it all better.

She turned, hands covering her nakedness, tears trailing down her cheeks. I reached for her, but she pulled away.

"I-I am sorry," she sobbed and lowered her head, heaving for breath. "Forgive me. For what I did... with Damion."

"Emmy." I pulled her into me, wrapping my wings around her. "You did nothing. There is nothing to forgive." I kissed the top of her head as she cried into my chest.

"No... You don't understand." Her words came out muffled. "What I made him think..."

I tightened my embrace. "We are connected, Emma, by the gods. I know everything."

Emma trembled. "And still, you want me?"

I pulled her face out from hiding, looking into those brilliant eyes. "You hear me right now, my Kompis. I will always love you. Remember? No matter what. You know what I am and still you want me, don't you?" She nodded. "Then why in the Nine Realms would you ever think I wouldn't want you?" I kissed her tenderly.

"I-I'm sorry."

"Come on. Let's go to sleep." I guided her to the bed, sliding between the sheets.

She laid her head on my chest, hands wandering. "What about you?"

Her fingers clasped around my still erect shaft.

"I... will survive," I gasped.

She smiled, sliding on top of me.

"That won't do." Leaning down, she kissed my neck. She moved her hands, reaching around, guiding my length into her slickness, and buried me between her thighs.

Her warmth engulfed me. I dug my fingers into her hips while she rocked against me, pulling a moan from my lips. With the ferocity in which she moved, I wouldn't have enough time to touch every inch of her skin. To memorize the silkiness of her body against mine as sweat dripped down her chest. I reached up, desperate to caress her, and cupped her breasts in my hands. She clutched tighter around me as I pinched her nipples.

"Bryn," she gasped as her hips rocked faster and faster, making my body tingle all over.

"I do love the way you make my name sound." I pulled her hand to my lips, kissing each finger in turn before sucking them into my mouth. She threw her head back, moaning. Her body shook as she came against me.

She fell onto me, breath ragged. I sat up and wrapped my wings around her as my massive hands gripped her hips, guiding her up and down. My own release hinged on the cusp and only just hanging on, with the spasms of her coming around me.

I took her breasts into my mouth, biting the tender flesh.

"Bryn, my Kompis, how I have missed you." Her fiery breath on my ear drove me deeper. I drew her closer as I pulled her down harder on my cock.

Words lost all meaning. Time was irrelevant. Only My Kompis and I existed. I pulled her chest to my face, breathing hard, as she rode me. My climax rose, but her moans held it at bay.

"Bryn," she breathed. "Fuck, don't stop."

Ignoring the heat rising within me, I bit down hard and slid my hand between our bodies, rubbing the nub at the apex of her thighs.

She threw back her head, grinding her hips against me harder. The moans and gasps that escaped her lips brought me over the edge as I exploded into her. Every muscle relaxed as I came. We were free. She was really here in my bed again and I'd never take my eyes off my mate as long as I lived.

I rested my head against her breasts, trying to regain my breath.

"Bryn," she said first. "No matter what."

I laughed, falling back onto the bed. "No matter what." I pulled her off me and she lay facing me as I dragged my finger down the bridge of her nose. "Always." I softly pressed my lips to hers.

I traced the features of her face even after her breathing fell into the steady rhythm of sleep.

CHAPTER 19

Emma

T he aroma of lilacs and petrichor washed over me, rousing me from sleep. I brushed my fingers through my mate's wings as I reached for him.

I'm really home.

Blood rushed to my face as he turned those cool eyes on me. The soft tips of his fingers traced the lines of my lips.

"Good morning, my Kompis," Brynjar said.

Tears fell from my eyes. "It wasn't a dream. It all happened, didn't it?"

Brynjar nodded. "But you are home now. You are safe."

"Am I? Are any of us safe?" I wiped the tears away. "Herrick might be dead, but Damion isn't. Bryn... I thought I could save him, but..."

"I will keep you safe. No matter what." His brawny arm pulled me against him. "I won't lose you again."

The tears flowed freely into his chest until I couldn't cry anymore. His massive hands gently stroked my back, easing my breathing.

"Shh, Emmy, I got you."

His very presence calmed my heart. Taking one last long breath, I looked up at him. "We better get to Aric and get this over with."

Kissing my forehead, he asked, "What if I want to be selfish and keep you here all day?"

I chuckled lightly. "Then we will have to replace your door when Aric's soldiers break it down."

"Damn. You're probably right." He smiled at me before he stood.

Reluctantly, I dragged myself out of the bed and turned to my mate. He stood there in glorious beauty. The softness of his skin sent heat to my core as I stroked his naked chest. My fingers traveled lower, lingering on the curve of his hips. He pulled me closer, devouring me in a deep kiss.

"If we don't go now, I *will* keep you here all day." He whispered into my ear.

With a sigh, I snapped my fingers, and we were both clothed. "Fine... Later?" I grinned.

"Promise."

The warm morning air sent a rush of joy through my body while the smooth steps cooled my bare feet as I glided toward the earth.

Brynjar clasped my hand and strode forward leading me through the crowd as I watched my feet. I heard the whispers, sensed the stares. My chest tightened. The thumping of my beating heart raced out of control. The battlefield flashed through my mind. Blood coated my shaking hands. I clutched my neck as invisible hands gripped my throat.

I tore my hand from his grasp and bolted for a small alley between buildings. Gravity pulled me down to the ground, sobbing. I stuck my head between my knees and rocked from side to side.

Flames licked around me, boiling my blood. I gasped for breath, but the fire sucked the air out from around me.

"Emmy!"

I raised my head at the sounds of Brynjar's voice. His footsteps grew louder as he drew closer. Tears streamed down my face as smoke burned my lungs.

He knelt before me, placing his hand on my chest. "Match my breathing," he directed.

I tried to pull my eyes away from his stare, but his hand kept my head in place. His cool eyes never left mine.

"Don't look away. Emmy, please don't feel you need to hide anything from me."

'I can't do this.' I thought to myself.

'Yes, you can. Fight it, Emma. Warmth spread over me at his voice inside my head. *'I love you and I won't give up on you. Not ever. Now breathe, damn it.'*

Melting into his touch, the fist at my throat relented, bringing glorious air to my lungs. My vision cleared, transporting me back to the moment.

"I-I don't know what happened," I said. "I was back on the battlefield. It was my fault. It was—"

"No. It was Herrick's, and he's paid for what he did to you. We are safe from him. Look." He turned his palms up, exposing the pink underside of his forearms. The unblemished skin was smooth again. "The scars are gone, remember. Look at your own arms." Slowly, I turned my arms over. Somewhere in the depths of my mind I knew what I'd see, but in the grips of panic I feared my skin would be marred. But panic was wrong. The cuts were healed, leaving no trace they had ever been there. Even the words Herrick had carved into my flesh were gone. My breath came easier with every moment that passed. I had been so wrapped up in my own sorrow that I hadn't noticed I was finally free of his curse.

"Better?"

I nodded.

"Do you want to walk or spirit? Or I guess we could fly too?" He grazed my wings behind my back with a smile.

The rhythmic beat of my heart threatened to increase at the thought of flight. Shaking my head, I said, "I need to learn how to control it first. Will you spirit us? I don't trust myself."

He pulled me to my feet before wrapping his strong arms around me. Darkness and cold surrounded me, the quiet nothingness hugging me like an old friend. We reemerged at the edge of the castle, standing before the sentries guarding the bridge.

The pair of massive soldiers quickly hit their knees in a deep bow at the sight of us.

"My Queen," they spoke together.

The pride in Brynjar's eyes glowed as I turned to look at him. He bowed low to me as well, smiling as he stood. His arm hooked around my elbow as we strode past.

'What was that about?' I asked, fighting to stay calm.

'With the death of your mother, you and your brother are the sole heirs to the throne. You, my Kompis, are also my Queen.' He brought my fingers to his lips, kissing them softly.

Aric

I paced around the dais, heart racing with every step, gripping the hilt of my sword. The creak of the door drew my eyes away from my own weapon. I flew straight to my sister, embracing her tightly.

"Thor almighty!" I swore under my breath. "I was so worried about you, Emma! From now on you stay here." Pulling away, I looked at Brynjar. "You too, brother." We clasped arms.

"What's wrong, Aric?" Emma asked, gripping my arm.

Swallowing hard, I said, "There is a fire. It is... bad." My eyes filled with tears. "I nearly sent warriors to your door."

Emma clasped her hands over her mouth. "A fire? Where?"

"Yggdrasil." I hardly believed it was my own voice that spoke.

Emma's eyes widened as she turned to Brynjar. With a nod, the three of us spirited away.

The heat hit me before I reemerged in front of the Great Tree and I had to shield my eyes from the light that emanated from where the tree should've been. Flames climbed through the branches over the bark, tiny slivers of brown peeking through the red and orange tongues that licked at the bark. I froze and watched it burn.

A cool breeze rushed past me. Emma stood to my side, drawing up water from the ground, forming it into a massive cyclone.

She strained her face as she tried to push it toward the inferno. Brynjar and I placed our hands on her shoulders, lending her our strength. Between the three of us, the water-clone doused the flames. Emma's body slacked, collapsing into her mate's arms.

"Emma!" I shouted at my sister.

"I'm fine," she said in a shaky voice. "How bad is it?"

Fae surrounded us, but no one moved. I doubted any of them drew breath. Scorched vanilla flooded my senses as I approached the massive tree. Black marks crawled up its base revealing four words.

"What is it?" Emma asked from behind me. She brushed past, reaching her hand out for the tree. Her fingers traced over the unburned letters in the bark.

You should have stayed.

"What does it mean, Emma?" I asked her.

"I-I think we need to talk, brother." She looked around. "But not here."

I nodded and the three of us spirited back to the throne room.

I quickly turned toward Emma and Brynjar. "Now, tell me what happened to you and how the Hel that," I pointed out to where Yggdrasil stood, "happened? What does it mean? The words?"

Emma took Brynjar's hand before she spoke.

"I think I might have unleashed something even worse than Herrick." She looked at her mate. "I... well, let's just say that King Herrick's rein has ended."

"The blood yesterday? Was Herrick's?" I asked and Brynjar nodded at my question. "But it was all over your face?"

"I... I'm sorry. There are certain things my mother hid from me about my past. I always knew there was something different about me, but I never dug deeper. I should have...." He took Emma's hand in his. "Especially after I met Emma."

"So, the rumors are true?" Brynjar's eyes widened at my accusation. I shrugged my shoulders. "Fae talk."

"My father is human. Well... part human, I guess." He looked down for a moment before looking back up at me. "You've got to understand I didn't remember any of this until I was locked in that dungeon. Even my childhood memories had been altered to erase all trace of my father." He looked at me, eyes pleading to understand. I nodded for him to continue. "He is a warrior of an old clan of Berserkers. Essentially, they are shifters. Legends say they'd wear animal skin into battle and would transform. Over the generations they gained control of their shift. I never thought that was part of who I was until I saw Emma in danger." He looked at her. "When we were trying to escape, Herrick invaded her mind. I thought he would kill her. I lost control, and fully shifted... I... well... I tore out his throat."

Silence filled the room for a long moment. I slumped onto the throne before I spoke again. "Okay... so if he's dead, who burned Yggdrasil?" I asked slowly.

"I believe that would be Damion," Emma said. "He was Herrick's... apprentice, I suppose. He's been under Herrick's controlling spell for years, being brainwashed and tortured. Herrick tried to break my bond with Brynjar by forcing Damion and I together. His plan was to destroy Yggdrasil and make a new one with Damion and I as the heart. When I refused Damion, he lost it. I hurt him... badly. I- I don't know what he is capable of."

I rose, walking over to my sister, brushing her tears away and pulling her into a hug. "I am sorry, Emma. I never want you to hurt like this again." I stepped back. "Is there anything else you need to tell me?"

She wouldn't look me in the eye.

"Emma, I know there is more." I saw the tears welling up in her eyes. "I will not push you but remember, I am always here for you to talk to."

"I know... thanks." She reached for her mate's hands. "I'm exhausted from putting out that fire. I need food and sleep."

"Very well, sister." I looked at Brynjar. "Keep her safe."

He nodded. "With my life." They strode out into the hall, leaving me alone once again.

CHAPTER 20

Damion

E mma and the mutt left bodies in their wake as they made their escape. Blood and guts littered the floor. The stench of death hung in the air as I stepped over the corpses walking toward the center of the space in a haze. I nearly gagged on the stench.

I stepped up to what Emma and Brynjar left of the man who raised me. The dark fae that survived had all retreated far from the battle leaving me alone with what remained of Herrick. They had torn the only father I could remember to shreds. He would cause me pain no longer, yet my scars remained, dug too deep into me for magic to remove. My fingers traced the words he etched into my skin. Each phrase I read weakened me, but the dark siren on my chest gave me strength.

I looked down at my bare chest as she swam down to my stomach to get a better look at the massacre. Her delight was my own. This creature connected me to my world. I could feel the water slipping through my hair as if I were really there. I raised my hand to her tentatively, bracing for pain. She lowered her trident and pressed her palm to mine. I grazed my fingertip over her hand and electricity sparked between us.

My mind was back in the water, swimming around the town I was born in. I flipped my tail and shot upward. That was what freedom tasted like, and I had to get home. I blinked and once again stood among the disemboweled flesh.

"M-Master?" a voice from behind me asked.

I turned my eyes to the shaking fae. The pounding of my own heart deafened me. A rage that wasn't mine filled me. *Pathetic creatures.* Herrick had tormented them into submission.

"What now?" he asked.

I grinned and vanished on the spot, spiriting to our gateway. Herrick had succeeded in his plans. It really was dying. The once vibrant color was faded and the ashen vines were falling off in places. My heart ached at seeing the destruction he caused.

Lightning struck all around me bringing me out of my thoughts and hardening my heart once again. I raised my hands to the sky and called the storm to me. Magic poured into me until I couldn't contain it anymore and I released it towards the dying gateway connecting the Nine Realms. I screamed but no sounds came from my mouth as flames shot from my hands and I placed them upon the gateway between worlds. Fire consumed what remained of the vines. I used my finger to write a single phrase before I stepped back and watched it burn.

The heat nearly knocked me to the ground, but I stood and watched the chaos as if through someone else's eyes. I could almost hear the screams from the light fae, as I knew they would scramble to put the fire out. A forced smile spread across my face. Even as the fire was extinguished, I knew I had them shaking.

I turned my back to the tree and slowly walked back to my realm. *My realm.* No longer Herrick's. Nor the dark fae's. But mine for the taking. Lightning crashed all around me but never touched me.

Dark fae walked up to me as I reached the base of the mountain, their faces filled with horror.

"What have you done?" one asked.

I looked at him, and a bolt of lightning struck him down.

"Any other questions?" I grinned. The rest bowed low before me. A high-pitched cackle echoed in my head as I strode off back home.

I clenched my fists as I paced my bedroom. My throat constricted and my heart raced. I rubbed at my chest, wishing the world to slow.

"I couldn't have. I didn't. It wasn't me." I spoke to no one.

I watched on helplessly as my own hands ignited Yggdrasil, unable to stop myself.

The siren swam frantically across my chest. She dragged me closer to the edge of madness with her emotions raging on, her anger evident by the scowl on her face. I pulled a shirt over my head to cover her and the moment I couldn't see her, her voice in my head faded.

The need to destroy all who stood between me and my goals still lingered in my mind, yet I wished I could have stopped myself from burning Yggdrasil. My hands shook as I looked down at them. They were my hands, though they felt foreign. I tucked them under my arms, shaking my head.

"No, no, no." I begged.

I couldn't separate myself from the siren no matter how badly I wished her to leave me be. Even with her out of sight, I knew she was there. I fought the hatred burning deep within me. Hatred for Herrick for what he'd done to me and my family. Hatred for all of

Alfheim for allowing him the freedom to do the things he did. And even hatred for Emma for leaving but I still loved Emma as well. It was no use.

The siren's anger won as I walked over to my dresser and pulled a knife from the drawer. Emma's image fluttered to my mind as I moved my shaking hand to my skin and carved into my flesh. I'd have her back one way or another. Only when the green tinged blood dripped to the floor did I stop. I cocked my head at the emerald liquid pooling at me feet. Herrick's influence was so deeply ingrained in me that the change in my blood color surprised me.

"Fuck!" I shouted, dropping the blade.

I gripped my hair, yanking it tight. Two desires floated about my brain, pulling me in different directions. I dropped to my knees as my breath fled from me, leaving me gasping.

'Water. I need water.' I heard the siren's voice in my head. My feet moved at her words and I stood, walking automatically toward the bathroom.

"No," I growled. My hands braced on the doorway, holding me in place.

If water is what she needed, then denying her that might mean freedom. Sharp stabs to my chest brought me to my knees. Green spots soaked through my shirt.

"No!" I barked out. "I won't give you water." I told her.

She continued to jab me with her trident, but I refused to move. I collapsed and hugged my knees to my chest.

"Stop," I begged.

She didn't relent until the pain consumed me.

I woke, shivering, on the floor, my blood-soaked shirt clinging to me. The pain had subsided slightly so with a grunt, I rolled over to my side and stood. I walked into the bathroom and tore my shirt off. Dark green welts dotted across my chest, but the siren slept. She looked as exhausted as I felt.

Taking a rag from the shower, I ran it under warm water from the sink and gently cleansed the wounds she left, careful not to touch her. *How can I kill something that is a part of me?* I was still a captive. But this siren was a gift... a gift from my mother.

I scoffed at the idea of this *gift*. My mother wanted her revenge. It didn't matter if it cost her her son. I closed my eyes and rubbed my temples. I was only a tool. For Herrick, and now my own flesh and blood.

Looking back to my reflection, I made the choice to fight the siren, even if it killed me. I threw the rag into the sink and grabbed a fresh shirt from the closet before heading to bed.

CHAPTER 21

Brynjar

I woke to a hard smack across my face. My tall beauty of a mate looked small beside me, curled into a twitching ball, sweat pouring from her skin. Pulling her face to my chest, I wrapped my arms around her, stroking her back between her wings.

"Shhhh, Emma, it's just a dream," I said.

"No... no. Thyra!"

"Emma! Wake up!" I shook her arm gently. "Emmy!"

She winced as she rolled over onto her back, wings pressing into her spine. "Bryn?" she breathed.

Her face scrunched in pain. "You were dreaming."

"Bryn? Tell me it was all just a dream? Please?"

I kissed her forehead. "I'm sorry, my Kompis, it really happened."

"Mother? Skadi?" Tears rolled down her face as she asked. "Thyra?"

"My love, your mother and Skadi are dead, but there is still hope for Thyra."

She sat up, practically jumping from the bed. "What?" Wiping the tears from her face, Emma smiled. "She's alive?"

A smiled crept across my face. "Yes, she is. But—"

She scrambled out of the massive bed. "What? Where? Why didn't you tell me?"

"Slow down, Emma." She halted her steps toward the bathroom and looked back to me. "She is alive, yes, but she is hurt badly. The healers haven't been able to close the wounds. They had to put her in a deep sleep. They don't know how to stop it. I'm sorry, Emma." I hung my head low.

"Where is she? I have to see her. Maybe... maybe I can help her." She walked into the bathroom and reemerged a few moments later, fully dressed. "Let's go... now."

I chuckled slightly at her demand. "Yes, ma'am." I stood, snapped my fingers, and walked out with my mate.

We entered the cold, silent infirmary, walking straight to where Thyra lay. The icy chill of the day we brought her here crept through my veins. Aric sat in the chair beside her bed, sleeping with his head beside the unconscious fae. Emma moved to stand beside her friend, tears falling down her face.

I walked to the other side of her bed, gently rousing my King.

"Aric," I whispered.

He sat up, face wrinkled and red, at the sound of his name. His eyes fell to his sister, who only stared at Thyra.

"Em, she doesn't blame you," Aric said, his voice barely above a whisper.

She snapped her head to her brother. "How? How do you know?"

Aric shrugged.

"She is his Kompis," I answered for him. "He can hear her thoughts, even like this."

Emma fell back into the chair behind her, head in her hands, sobbing into her palms as she spoke. "You must hate me, Aric. I nearly killed your mate."

He walked around the bed to his sister, placing his hands on her back. "I could never. Besides, she thinks you can fix it. If you are willing to try?"

Emma peered through her fingers at Thyra. "How?"

"All fae have some ability to heal, and some are better at it than others. Thyra feels that with your empath and mental abilities, you can draw on the powers of others to heal her, but..." Aric looked back at me.

"But what, Aric?" Emma demanded. "Look at me and tell me the truth. Can I save her?"

"It's dangerous, Em. If you draw too much, it could... it could kill you, or the others. You can't risk it."

"Don't." The sharp edge to her voice had Aric backing up. I covered my face with my hand to hide the grin. "After everything I have seen and done, don't tell me what I can't do, Aric." Her eyes pleaded with me for support.

My tear-filled eyes didn't leave my mate's face as I spoke, "Give her what she needs. We will help her."

Aric shuffled off to the door behind us without another word.

I walked around the bed to where my mate sat. Kneeling before her, I took her hands, raising them to my lips. "I have seen some amazing things in my life, but none compares to you, Emmy. My dreams have never been wrong and I... Well, let's just say I know you can do this, my beautiful Kompis." I took her face in my hands, kissing her deeply.

"What... what do you mean? What have your dreams shown you?" she asked when I pulled away.

"Dreams can be misinterpreted... I don't normally share them but—"

The murmurs from behind us halted my words. The two of us stood to see the fae now entering the room. Aric led the group of five healers to the bedside.

"She needs their knowledge and skill. And our strength. And... and my love for Thyra." He swallowed hard. Emma stepped up to her brother and wrapped her arms around him.

"I love you, Aric. I will fix this. I promise." She kissed his cheek. "What now?"

"From what I understand, you already know what to do." Aric said. "You did it at Yggdrasil yesterday. You drew on mine and Brynjar's power and strength to help you put out the flames. You know how to heal, but to fix something so deep you need to draw on all of our powers. There's enough of us here that you only need to take a little from each of us. All we need to do is touch you and you will feel us there. I believe in you, sister." He rested his forehead to hers and whispered, "Thank you for trying."

She smiled at him before turning back to the bed. The other fae stepped behind her. Aric stood on her right and I on her left. I gripped her hand, placing a small kiss on her cheek. "Take whatever you need from me, my love." The others all placed a hand on her as she laid her free hand over the punctures in Thyra's middle.

"I'm sorry for what I have done to you, my friend. I pray to Odin I can take this back." She closed her eyes.

A tendril of electricity wrapped around me, pulling me toward her. I planted my feet in an effort to stand upright. The tug on my power only grew, my knees weakened with every moment that passed. I watched as Thyra's skin stitched back together. Tiny threads of tissue reached out toward each other. They pulled and tugged until the holes closed up. I leaned on the side of the bed closing my eyes.

"Thyra." I heard Aric whisper but couldn't even look up. I focused on my mate, giving her all the strength I could.

The tug suddenly released, sending me crashing to the floor.

"Bryn!" Emma gasped, kneeling beside me.

"I'm alright," I replied, my voice weak. "What about Thyra?"

Emma smiled and took my hand, helping me up. "See for yourself."

Thyra lay there, blinking. Red flesh replaced the holes that had been there a moment ago. Her violet eyes fell upon Aric, and she smiled.

Aric pushed through the healers and knelt beside her bed. Brushing her hair from her face, he kissed her tenderly, tears streaming down his face. "Thyra, I... I love you."

She smiled back at him. "About damn time you admit that. I love you too, Aric." Her eyes moved to Emma before she reached her hand out. "Thank you, my friend."

Emma leaned hard against me, shying away from Thyra. "I... I caused your pain. It was the least I could do. I am..." She turned in my arms, burying her face in my chest. I stroked her hair.

"Emma, turn around," I whispered in her ear.

Thyra sat up on the edge of her bed, reaching out for my mate. She wrapped her arms around Emma the moment she turned around. Her tiny frame tucked under Emma's arms.

"It wasn't your fault. You saved me and I am forever grateful. But our work has only just begun."

Emma broke away from her embrace, leaning back into me. "What... what do you mean?"

"You were able to bring me back from the brink of death. I believe you can do the same for Yggdrasil. When you were there, did you learn what he did to the tree?"

"I... I think I do. The tree has kept him banished and he wanted to destroy it so he could create a new tree with Damion and myself as the heart. Damion is his... *was* his minion." Emma looked away from Thyra's gaze.

"Emma and I are the Vörður of Yggdrasil." I stared at my brother as he continued. "We are its protectors. If it should fall, it would be on us to find a way to recreate it. Currently, the heart of Yggdrasil is another set of fae twins. The way I understand it, they are the 'gatekeepers.' They are the ones that allow us to pass through the realms." Everyone looked at Aric, who shrugged. "The Mystic told me. He is now resting comfortably in a suite with two armed guards at the door."

"That makes sense now. Herrick wanted to split us apart to weaken the bond we have with the tree. Once I started to doubt myself... All the fighting we did, Aric. The pain and cutting he forced us to do." Emma's eyes found mine. "Every thought I had about this world he implanted to break my bonds to you and Aric. He knew he would never get to the tree if we were strong. Then he... I don't really know... I saw these bug things in his mind... They looked like an ash beetle but it was a bright silver color. I think that's what is happening to Yggdrasil. They are eating it and leaving their toxin's behind. Its... iron." She sagged into my arms.

I lowered Emma into a chair before I spoke. "I think I might know how to deal with that part." I looked to Aric, then to the healers still standing there. Aric dismissed them, and they bowed before leaving the room.

"Go ahead, Brynjar," Aric said. "Thyra already knows. Sorry, I confided in her when I had no one else."

I gulped down the lump in my throat. "Well..." I swallowed hard and looked at my mate. "I didn't really have time to explain what happened when we were in Svartalfheim, but I think because of my heritage my father's clan might be the answer. When I was locked in that iron cage Herrick put me in, I discovered something... interesting. The iron did not have the same effect on me as that iron bolt I pulled out of Emma's shoulder. Whatever my mother did to me blocked the power from my father clan. Those abilities are only just now emerging. Herrick's iron cage should have weakened me by being that close to it, but it didn't. My mother didn't tell me much about my father, but I think we need to find him."

I turned my back to them rubbing at my temples.

"What is it Bryn?" Emma's cool voice called me back.

"Damn it... I hate sharing my dreams, as they aren't always clear, but I dreamt of him while I was in Svartalfheim... or at least I think it was a dream? Iron gives them strength." I looked at Thyra. "If Emma can do what she did just now with you, Thyra, and draw the bugs from the tree, I think my father's clan can deal with the iron." I reached a hand out for Emma. "I have vague memories of him. My mother's block is fading. I think his clan is somewhere in northern Norway. That's about all I can remember of him. I'm not sure how welcoming they'll be."

"If it will save our worlds, we need to find him, Bryn." Emma took my hand. "It would be safer if it were just the two of us going."

"I think we need to officially crown the two of you before you go off on another adventure, your Majesties." Everyone jumped as Surt's gravelly voice came from behind us.

We all turned to greet the fire god as he entered the room.

"It's good to see you home again, Miss Emma." He bowed low. Emma dropped my hand and ran to the god, wrapping him in a hug, her head just barely reaching his sternum.

Shock filled me at how happy I was to see him again. I had been jealous before and now... now I got the impression through our bond that Surt was the father Emma had always wished for.

She stepped back, bowing to him. "Thank you for teaching me to harness my emotions. You helped me more than you know."

"You're welcome." He stepped to Aric. "You have taken over in your mother's place. Everyone is calling you the King and Queen of Alfheim, but without the ceremony to bind you to your oath, the title is empty. The binding will place a shield over you protecting you from mortal danger, so you shouldn't go off to Midgard until that is official."

Emma looked at her brother cocking her head.

"He's correct, Em. Alfheim has not needed a crowning ceremony in a very long time." Aric told her then looked at Surt. "Surt, will you help us?"

The fire god, giant even in his fae form, lowered his head. "It would be my honor. I have already set things in motion. We can move forward tonight, if it pleases your Majesties?"

Aric looked at his sister and nodded.

"Very well. We will see you tonight." Surt smiled at me as he kissed Emma's cheek before departing.

CHAPTER 22

Aric

The reflection in the giant mirror couldn't be me. The emerald pants and vest clinging to my body like a viper.

King.

I shook the title from my head. I'd been filling that role for weeks now. What difference would a crown make?

Thyra's thin arms wrapped around my middle, forcing her fiery head between my arm and ribs. I lazily draped my arm over her back.

"You look delicious, my King," Thyra said.

I reached around and pulled her in front of me. Her dusty pink dress hugged her chest and waist, flowing freely to the ground.

"And you look devastating." I raised her chin, brushing my lips against hers.

The gentle rap at the door tore us apart.

My sister's voice wafted in. "Aric. It's time."

"We better go." I gripped Thyra's hand before walking out of the room.

Emma wore the same emerald color as me but in an elegant, V-neck, floor-length dress. Her mate, Brynjar, stood behind her, clad in black. I offered my sister and Thyra both an arm and the four of us strolled out of the castle and toward the Great Tree, Yggdrasil.

Every citizen of Alfheim—and many of our allies—filled the open field. I gulped as we walked toward the Tree, all eyes turned to us.

Surt, Njörðr, and Sigrid stood at the head of the crowd.

'Now it is your turn to not let me fall, sister.'

Emma laughed. *'Never, brother. Together, we can do this.'*

We stepped up together to the base of Yggdrasil, our partners stepping aside.

Surt's massive form stepped between the tree and us, motioning for the crowd to sit. "Today is a historic day for the Nine Realms and for Alfheim." He spoke loud for all to hear. "As the ruler of Muspelheim I proceeded over your mother's coronation, and I'm proud to be here again today. Kneel, Aric Rødt Tre."

I inhaled sharply. "Wait."

Surt cocked his head. "Excuse me?"

My face flushed but I ignored the god. I wiped my sweating palms on my pants as I looked back at Thyra and reached out to her, taking her by the hand and pulling her up to me.

"I waited until I thought I lost you to admit you are my Kompis. I can't wait a moment longer." I broke my gaze to look at Surt. "I just want to be me when I tie my life to hers. Would you?"

The giant fire god chuckled. "Never let it be said I am not a romantic at heart. Princess, do you mind?"

Emma wrapped her arms around me, kissing my cheek before stepping to the side.

Surt's booming voice echoed above the crowd. "The future King wishes to be tied to his Kompis before I crown him. Do we indulge him?" The cheering of the crowd was deafening. "The people have agreed." His gaze fell to Brynjar.

"Master Alm, since Thyra has no living males in her line, will you protect her honor? Will you also swear allegiance to her mate?"

Brynjar stepped beside me, put a fist to his chest, and bowed. "I will protect them both with my life." He turned to me, clasping me in a half hug and whispered in my ear, "If you hurt her, you will regret it." He winked, stepping back to his mate.

"Aric and Thyra," Surt began. "The gods have entwined you together, though it took a little longer than normal. Will you follow the path they laid out for you?"

I grasped both of Thyra's hands, looking her in the eyes. "I will," we spoke together.

"Tying yourself to another being—especially a future king—is not to be taken lightly. Will you promise yourselves to no one but each other?"

"I will."

"Will you include each other in this equal partnership?"

"I will."

Emma flicked her wrist, producing a thin leather strap. She handed one end to her mate and stepped up to Thyra and me.

"Will you bind yourselves together, never to be parted?" Surt asked.

"I will."

Brynjar tied one end of the band around my right wrist while Emma did the same to Thyra's left.

Sigrid stepped up to us, holding a small wooden cup.

"Drink the sap of Yggdrasil and if the gods truly bless this union, they will mark you and bind you." Sigrid handed the cup to me.

I took the cup and placed it to my lips. The sweet honey dripped down my throat, warming me. Thyra took the cup from me, drinking it before handing it back to Surt.

My heart thrummed so loud I thought the world could hear it. I tightened my grip on our tied hands as we watched the last rays of light stretch out toward us. I whispered a tiny prayer the gods would find us worthy and only when I felt the leather binds tighten around us did I let out a breath. The searing heat of the mating mark burned into my hand.

"The gods have tied you together," Surt announced, and the crowd erupted into cheers.

I kissed my mate deeply, not caring about the eyes that watched.

Fae lights flicked on as the last rays of light sunk behind the earth.

Surt cleared his throat a long moment later, breaking us apart. "Might I continue with the coronation now?"

"Thank you for indulging me," I said. "Yes, we may proceed."

Emma stepped to my left and clasped my hand in hers.

"Aric, Emma, long did your mother rein. She was a just and fair queen. Emma, I know you haven't known your origins long, but Queen Astrid had a brilliant team at her side, and so shall you. If ever you are in need, we shall be there." He raised his arms to us. "Kneel," the fire god commanded.

I tugged at the bonds that held me to Thyra as I knelt beside my sister.

He looked at our two mates. "As their bonded mates, will you kneel with them?"

They knelt beside us.

"Aric Rødt Tre the Tenacious, may you always fight for what you believe in." With a flick of his wrist, he laid a dark, wooden crown upon my head.

"Thyra Embla the Gentle, may you always show the strength and courage that is deep within you." He laid a small, flowery wooden crown upon her head.

Surt turned to my sister. "Emma Rødt Tre the Valiant, may your heart always be strong enough to do what must be done for your people." The crown he laid upon her head was an ash wood with vines carved around it.

"Brynjar Alm the Indomitable, may you always be the fortress in which we stand." The crown he laid upon his brow was a simple, but strong, thick wooden ring.

"Arise, King Aric, King Brynjar, Queen Emma, Queen Thyra." We stood before the fire god as he led the chant. "Long live King Aric. Long live Queen Emma. Long live Queen Thyra. Long live King Brynjar."

I embraced my sister, pulling my new mate in with me. Emma laughed, wrapping her hands around her new sister and me. Even Brynjar's brawny arms slapped me on the back.

Turning awkwardly, the four of us eyed the crowd. Every fae and creature knelt before their new kings and queens. I gripped my shaking arm around Emma.

'We survived.'

'And that was the easy part. Aric, what are we going to do if Bryn's father won't help us?'

Her voice shook inside my mind. I leaned over, kissing her temple.

'We cannot afford to think like that, Emma. We need their help, so do what you must to make it happen. I love you, Sister.'

She leaned into me, hugging me tighter. *'I love you too, Brother.'*

I released her and stepped closer to the crowd. "Rise, my people. We have thwarted one enemy, but that doesn't mean the war is over. Rest tonight, for tomorrow is a new day and we must prepare for what is to come."

I looked at Thyra as the crowd departed. "I wish to take you home with me, my Kompis."

"As you wish, my king." Thyra inclined her head with a laugh.

"Aric." Brynjar's voice halted me. "Emma and I will be leaving right away. It'll be a long journey from the nearest gate to my father's clan. The sooner we leave, the better."

I turned to my sister, tears in her eyes. "I'm so happy for you two." She hugged us both. "Take care of her." Emma kissed us each on the cheek before stepping back.

Brynjar clapped me on the shoulder. "Congratulations, my friend!"

"When this is all over, we will celebrate properly." I told them.

My sister smiled and nodded her head before she snapped her fingers, her dress replaced with dark jeans, hiking boots, and a long sleeve flannel shirt. Her wings vanished before my eyes. She shrugged with a smile, "I figured out this glamour thing."

Emma picked up the pack that magically appeared at her feet and threw it over her shoulder. Her mate, now dressed in similar clothes, took her hand.

"Bring her back safe, Brynjar," My voice shook as I spoke.

"I will, Your Majesty." He nodded before walking up to Yggdrasil, touching the spot that would take them to Midgard and vanished before my eyes.

"What was that about home?" Thyra's warm voice washed over me.

I wiped the tears from my eyes before pulling my mate into me. "I wish to take you home and show you how thankful I am for you." I leaned in, kissing her softly.

CHAPTER 23

Brynjar

The crisp morning air of Midgard bit my face as we stepped through the gateway. I shielded my eyes from the bright light that awaited us. The small forest came into focus around me as I shook off the chill.

I sat on the short stone wall beside the massive gate. Its metal frame rusted to the point of nearly falling down and the vines that interwove it was all that held it together. Emma stood in front of the ruins of a wall beside me, her hand grazing the stones.

"Where are we?" She asked.

"We are in a forest in Denmark," I answered.

"Denmark? But we need to be in Norway. How are we going to get there?"

"I said it will be a long journey." I stood, placing my hand on her back. "We will have to walk or find human transport. Let's just make sure we keep our glamour up so we don't scare the humans with our wings. Flying's an option, but I'd only recommend that at night. I'd honestly recommend we might want to rest our wings for when we really need it."

"What do you mean 'really need it'?"

"I'm sorry to have dragged you into this, Emma." I brushed my fingers over her cheek.

"Bryn, you are my Kompis. I refuse to be separated from you again. Where you go, I go. Now, where's your father?"

"My father's clan is on an island far off the northern border of Norway. I doubt even I could fly the whole way, but if we take a boat or a plane all the way to the island, they'll kill us if they thought we were human before we could even get to shore so flying in will assure them that we are anything but human. I know you haven't had a lot of time to practice flying, but I'll be right there with you. They aren't fans of the fae, but they despise humans."

I leaned in, kissing her for a moment. My fingers dug into the hair at the nape of her neck as I rested my forehead on hers.

"If anything happens to you, I swear I will kill them all." A low growl rumbled deep within me.

"Your inner bear is showing." She chuckled into my chest. "Come on, if we have a long journey we might as well start now." She wrapped her arm around mine, interlacing our fingers. "Which way?"

I closed my eyes, soaking in the light and sounds from the world.

"The longer we can avoid humanity, the better, so..." I inhaled a deep breath. "All I really know is we need to head north There is a town not too far so to avoid that we'll have to go southeast for a ways, then back up north." I squeezed her hand as I started forward.

A strange chirping sound coming from Emma's bag halted my steps.

"What the Hel is that sound?" I asked her.

She cocked her head, listening. "Shit," she laughed, digging into her bag and pulled out a small black square. "It's my phone. I forgot it was in here!"

I leaned over her, looking at the contraption. "What's a phone?"

I glared at her as she laughed in her hand for a long moment before she spoke again. "I'm sorry, Bryn. You're in my realm now. I guess I'll have to teach you about my world." She pressed her finger into the device that held her image. "It's a human thing. You and I can talk to each other using our minds, no matter where we are, but with this I can talk to anyone in the world." She kept pressing the device, bringing up new images. "How is it still working?" Emma seemed to ask herself.

"Human technology doesn't work in our realm," I told her. "But Aric once told me that the energy and magic in our realm can keep its batteries... what's the word? Charged?" I clenched my jaw as she giggled.

"Uhm. Good to know." She shrugged. "Uh, okay." She looked back to the phone for a moment before she stood and handed it to me. "Look, we are here, and we need to get here, right?"

The green and blue images flew across the device as she dragged her fingers over it.

I couldn't hide my wonderment. "What is this?"

"It's a map. We are here in Denmark, but we need to get to northern Norway, right? Do you know where your father's clan is exactly?"

"My mother only said he lived on an island of bears. Since my vision of him, I've had flashes of memories come back to me but nothing clear."

Emma took the phone from my hands and moved her fingers from image to image. She squinted her face up as she worked until she turned back to me.

"Here, could this be it? Bear Island? It's far north of Norway and looks pretty secluded."

She showed me more images I couldn't understand. My heart raced. "I-I don't know."

She chuckled at me.

"Don't laugh!" I fought back the urge to scream at her.

"I'm sorry, Bryn. I'm used to you being so comfortable in your surroundings. Okay, sit." She guided me back to the wall. "Alfheim has a vast library filled with information about everything, right?" I nodded. Emma continued, "This phone can hold all that information and so much more. Technology is one of humanity's greatest achievements. I just googled bear and island... Sorry... I searched for those things kind of like I did in the library back home when I looked for Yggdrasil, and this is what I found. I think it's where we need to go." The more she talked the less I understood. Her words blurred together as the world around me spun. She sat beside me and slid her arm around my waist, pulling me into a hug. "Just breathe, my Kompis. I'll take care of everything." We sat in silence for a few minutes and once everything stilled she continued. "Unfortunately, If we traveled by foot, it'll take us weeks."

My face flushed at the panic that rose in my chest again. I'd faced down monsters. Hel, I *was* a monster compared to other fae, yet I trembled at the idea of crossing through the human realm. Even with my gorgeous mate at my side. I must have let some of my fear slip across our bond because she tensed at my side.

Her arm wrapped tight around me as she relaxed. "I'm sorry, Bryn. I didn't think this would be this big of a deal for you. You went through Hel to get me out of Herrick's grasp. If you can do that, you can do anything."

A bit of her calming magic flowed over me, and I relaxed as well. "No, I'm sorry. I just haven't been around humans much and I'm a little afraid of them."

She chuckled. "The big bad bear is afraid of teeny tiny humans?"

I glared at her.

"Sorry." Her face tightened. "You gotta admit. It is a bit funny."

I watched her fight a laugh until I couldn't take it, and I broke into laughter with her.

"You're right. It is a bit funny. I feared I'd lost you, but I got you back. I can make it through here so long as you are with me." I interlaced her fingers with mine and pulled her to me. Her lips tasted so sweet pressed against mine.

She pushed back. "Let me figure out a route. I can buy tickets if we need them." She went back to her magic work with the device in her hand. "I wish we could just spirit there. It would make this so much easier." She mumbled.

"We can only spirit to places we've been before. Remember?" I reminded her.

"Yeah I know." She said not looking up from her phone. "T here..." she spoke to me. "I think I have it. We need to get to Copenhagen and board a ferry to Norway. How do you feel about boats?"

Bile rose in my throat. Water scared me far more than humans did. "I-I don't think I can do this... Let's just go home. We can figure out another way to save Yggdrasil."

Her slender fingers slid into my hair, pulling me to her. Her kiss was fierce. She pulled away, grinning ear to ear. "Since I met you, you've always been the strong one. We do need your father's help so let me help you through this." She kissed my nose. "Besides, I already have the tickets." She stood, pulling me to my feet. "We better get walking. Our boat leaves tonight."

I wrapped my arms around her, holding her tight. "Have I told you lately how much I love you?"

"Nope..." She stole a quick kiss.

"Well, Queen Emma Rødt Tre Alm, I adore you." I kissed her deeply before pulling away. "Now, show me your world."

"Alm, eh? I like it." She pressed her fingers back into her phone before she spoke again. "This way, my love."

CHapTer 24

Emma

Brynjar's arm wrapped around my waist as we strode onto the stones cutting through the middle of the forest. I pulled my phone back out, looking at the map. I glanced from my phone to the circular foot path we stood on. There were eight different branches moving out from its center.

I looked up and pointed to the road heading slightly south-east. "This way." I told him.

The forest wasn't maintained and it took us nearly an hour just to get clear of the trees. At this rate, we would miss our ferry.

I gulped hard before I spoke. "Bryn, I know you don't like humans, but we have to find a quicker way. I think we need to hitchhike."

He pulled me to a stop. "Need to what?"

I sighed. "I'm sorry Bryn. I grew up here so these things come naturally to me." She placed a hand on Bryn's arm. "I will help you. Hitchhiking means to ask strangers for a ride in their cars. I normally wouldn't recommend it, but we aren't humans, so I think we'll be safe. If we don't do it, we won't make it there in time."

He let out a long breath. "Okay."

"Thank you, Bryn." I leaned in to kiss him, but a sharp pain sent me to my knees. I spit out the sour taste of my own blood as I bit my tongue. My arm burned as something etched words into my flesh.

Brynjar knelt beside me, eyes wide as he pulled my arm away from my chest. "That bastard learned a thing or two from Herrick. I should have killed him too." He wrapped me in his embrace.

I looked down at the welts on my arm. '*You are mine.*' His words replaced Herrick's scars. I pushed the fear and pain away as I stood.

"I am yours." I looked at my mate. He smiled as he stood while kissing me. My arm still burned, but I brushed it aside to feel Brynjar's quickened heartbeat. "I love you and only you. We stopped Herrick, and we will stop Damion."

He held me tighter. "I love you too, my Kompis."

"Why does my blood taste so sour?" I asked into his chest.

His laugh gently jerked my body. "You never wondered why fae bleed white? It's because we have a higher concentration of magnesium in our blood. And that is why it tastes so sour." His hands ran down my spine. "You know, you pick the strangest times to wonder about things."

I grinned. "I know. It distracts me." Pulling out of his grasp, I placed my hand over the wounds and staved the bleeding. The pain lingered but at least I wouldn't attract attention as we walked. "Let's keep going."

Once we reached a main road, I started walking backward and snapped my fingers producing a sign reading "Copenhagen" and waited. It wasn't long before a tour bus stopped and opened the door.

"Need a lift?" the driver asked.

"Yes, sir," I answered.

"Climb on up."

I magically pulled a fifty-dollar bill from my pocket and handed it to the driver as I dragged Brynjar behind me up the steps. "Thanks." I told the driver and handed him the cash.

He looked at the bill before pocketing it. "Americans?"

"Yeah. I'm Emma. This is my husband, Ben." I told him. Brynjar looked as if he might pass out. I forced him into an empty seat behind the driver. Even with the glamour, my wings were still there and I had to adjust the way I sat so I wasn't squishing them or looked awkward to the humans. "We're backpacking up to Norway for our honeymoon."

"Well, you're in luck." He motioned over his shoulder. "These ladies are heading that way, too."

I looked behind me. The bus was full of gray and white-haired women, all eyeing us like we were shiny new toys.

"Where y'all from?" the lady next to us asked me.

"Tennessee," I answered with a smile. "We just got married and wanted to do something different. I'm Emma. This is Ben."

"That's sweet, dear. I'm June." Her hair was so black it was nearly blue, but her smile was genuine. "This is my tour group. We're just a bunch of old biitties with too much time on our hands so we travel the world together. I'm from Ohio and these ladies are from all over the place. You heading anywhere in particular or just where your feet take you?"

"Well, we're heading towards northern Norway."

The old lady leaned her thick frame forward, looking at Brynjar, then back to me. Brynjar's face was stone and his body just as rigid.

"He don't talk much, do he?" she asked.

"No, he isn't that comfortable around hu—people." I corrected myself quickly. "We thought if we hitchhiked, it might break him out of his shell. You are the first to pick us up, so he's a bit nervous." I clasped his hand, letting my magic flow into him until he relaxed.

"I'm... I'm sorry," Brynjar finally spoke. "I'm trying to learn to not be so shy. My apologies, ma'am." Brynjar bowed his head to the lady.

"My my, it's been a long time since I've seen such manners from a young man. It's a refreshing change." June said to him.

"I was raised to respect my elders and women. My mother taught me that without mothers, we would die out." His voice was starting to sound more like himself.

June smiled. "Well, she did very well, son."

"Thank you." He sighed.

"You wouldn't happen to have an extra pillow, would you?" I asked June. "We slept on the ground last night and I'm feeling a little sleepy."

"'Course, dear." She stood, nearly hitting the ceiling of the bus as she walked toward the back.

I turned to look at Brynjar. "You doing okay? Shouldn't be long before we get to the first ferry and then we will board another larger one and we can stay locked up in our room the whole time." I winked at him.

"That sounds nice." His growl rippled through me as he kissed me.

The throat clearing beside me broke us apart. "Here's a couple of pillows for you. If you really need them." June grinned at us.

I blushed as I took the pillows. "Thanks."

Brynjar took one, leaning against the window and I laid the other across his chest as I snuggled in close to him. I didn't really want to sleep, but I wanted to talk even less.

Thankfully, we disembarked from the bus an hour later. The ladies pressed on further into town. We gave them our thanks before walking toward the pier and the ferry that would take us up to Norway.

CHAPTER 25

Damion

It had been days since I had begun to starve the siren of water. She spent her strength trying to force me to feed her need but the longer I didn't give in the weaker she became. My chest and sides marred with fresh wounds I knew would leave scars and my body ached for sleep, but I couldn't give in just yet. I feared she would take over if I relaxed enough to sleep.

My massive room closed in on me as I paced the floor. Just another day, and I was sure the creature would die. I had poured so much magic into myself to stay awake. Herrick's dark fae made sure I ate, but I refused to let them into the room. With the siren silenced I couldn't allow the dark fae serve me like they had Herrick. I was not Herrick, and I wanted to see his people freed, not serving me.

The longer I stayed awake, the more lost memories flashed in my head. My mind began to crack and all at once, I was pulled back into my childhood.

My mother and father were the leaders of our clan in the oceans of Midgard. Herrick had gathered a powerful and fierce force of our enemies that attacked all at once. Our waters ran red.

My home burned as they dragged me away. The white flames raged on through the water, reducing everything I loved to ashes.

In that moment, I hardened my seven-year-old face and vowed to destroy everyone that caused me this pain.

The men who stole me threw me onto the beach and before I could crawl back to the water, more arms grabbed me. My tiny body fought, but these men were four times my size. Out of the water, I was useless with my tail. Something hard cracked over the back of my head and the next thing I knew I woke up in Svartalfheim with Herrick watching over me.

It was the first time I saw my legs. And the first lie he told me. He said he saved me from those mercenaries. That he fought them off to protect me. He told me my family was dead. But I knew better now.

My mother's face kept invading my mind, but I denied her entry. I rubbed at my temples as I thought of her, trying to block her out of my head. I knew she wanted to connect to me. I knew she wanted me to find water. But I couldn't. I knew if the siren was strong again, she would force me to continue Herricks war with the light fae. I was at war with myself. On one hand, Emma had betrayed me and left with that mutt.

On the other hand, I loved her—I swayed on my feet at the thought of Emma—even if I knew it was wrong... I still loved her. I needed to free myself of this siren on my chest and then of this Hel I had called home.

Unable to stand upright any longer, I sank into a chair, holding my head in my hands, trying to stop the world from spinning. Closing my eyes, I leaned back in the chair, laying my head on the side.

Just a moment's rest is all I need and I will be... My thoughts dragged into the nothing.

I woke up in the bathtub, my tail splashing water to the floor, and flopped out, shouting, "No!"

My muscles tensed, and my body shook as my tail split and my legs formed.

No, no, no, this isn't happening!

I clutched at my stomach as I sat up, resting my back against the cool stone wall. The siren swan across my chest and around my back. "No, no, no!" I screamed.

Only when hot liquid dripped onto my naked thigh did I feel the searing pain radiating throughout my arm.

Slowly, I looked down. The scars on my arms opened up and the words 'You are mine' were carved deep into my flesh. Out of the corner of my eye, I saw the knife, my other hand wrapped around its hilt.

Determined to end this one way or another, I placed the tip of the blade to my chest. A small trickle of blood ran down my skin. I pushed harder, but she pushed back.

Stepping out of the bath and glaring at my reflection enraged me. The siren looked healthy again as she smirked at me. I stabbed at her, piercing my own flesh instead as she swam away. I growled with each stab but still I tried again and again. She dodged my blade each time. She waggled her finger at me and cackled.

I dropped the knife into the sink and hung my head in defeat, pulled the rag from the sink and wiped the blood from my chest. With a snap, I dressed and headed out of my room.

As I walked, dark fae stopped and bowed to me, but I ignored them all. Stopping the siren from carrying out Herricks plans consumed my thoughts. And only one place could keep the world safe from me.

My feet found the doors to the dungeons automatically and my chest constricted at the memories I held on to the moment I stepped inside. Emma had been a force to reckon with. Even under her Herrick's control.

Ease settled over me as I walked into the darkness. Emma had freed Herrick's prisoners, so the cells were empty. The place was so quiet I could hear the mice scurrying about.

The siren panicked, holding me in place. She fought me and stabbed at me, but I resolved my will, forcing my feet forward, I found a cell with thick manacles hanging in the center of the room.

I took a deep breath before stepping inside. No one knew I was here. I would die along with the siren. I sighed, knowing the world and Emma would be safe from me. I could have made it easier on myself and jumped off a cliff or something, but I couldn't risk the siren being able to heal a broken body. She needed to die, and this was the only way. It would be slow and painful, but everyone would be safe from me.

Manacles hung from the ceiling in the center of the room. These were not mere handcuffs but were designed for magic users. Their iron gloves would keep me or the siren from using my magic. I stepped under them snapping my fingers and the gloves enclosed both of my hands and stretched to my wrists.

The siren screamed in my head, desperate for a way out. Knowing there was no escape for either of us, I smiled.

CHaPTeR 26

Aric

We strolled back to the massive castle I now called home. Our bound hands kept us close, but I longed to be closer as I curled my fingers around hers and leaned into her. The smile that sat on my mate's face hadn't faded since the gods tied us together.

Part of me wanted to rush home and devour the tiny beauty at my side, but another part wanted to simply walk with her. Only yesterday I thought I would lose her forever, so I'd savor every moment with her at my side. We merely smiled back at all the bows and the "Your Majesty's" that followed us through the town. Thyra was the only one I saw.

My eyes watched her even as we glided past the guards and through the castle. We strolled up to the room my mother had given me when Emma and I first arrived at the castle.

I pulled her against me before she could reach for the door. She spun around on my chest with a laugh, but my face was solemn.

"What's the matter, my love?" she asked.

"I am sorry it took you nearly dying for me to admit that you are my Kompis." I wiped at the tears forming in my eyes.

She had to stand on her tiptoes to press her lips to mine.

"It all worked out in the end. Now, are you going to take me inside and bed me?"

I grinned and deepened her kiss. With a flick of my wrist, the door opened. Her feet moved back through the door without breaking our contact.

She sat on the edge of the bed, pulling my body with her.

I laughed, showing her our bound hands. "This should be interesting."

Her smile melted me. She snapped her fingers and the pair of us were fully exposed to one another. I was no stranger to the nakedness of a woman, but this woman—my woman—froze my heart. Her free hand trailed down my chest, resting on my hip.

She slid her body further up the bed, tugging at our bond. Climbing on to the bed, I straddled her hips and drank her in. My gaze lingered on her abdomen as fire built within me. The three pink scars across just below her chest pulled me back to the battlefield.

Her palm rested on my cheek before she spoke. "Aric, my Kompis, I'm all right," she whispered.

"Did it..." I brushed my fingers along the scars, ignoring the beauty past them. "Did it hurt?" I shook my head. "Of course it did. I'm sorry I'm such an idiot."

She sat up. "All I remember is you. Keeping you safe was all that mattered, so I jumped in front of you. Then I saw your face. The pain there hurt me more than the trident did. Then there was nothing for the longest time—until I heard your voice." She pulled her gaze away. "The scars will fade," she said in a quiet voice.

Fear flashed in her eyes. "You are perfect just the way you are." I touched the still red and jagged skin. "These scars show how resilient... and stubborn you are." I leaned down and kissed her stomach softly. "I wouldn't change a thing."

Her free hand grasped my hair and pulled me up toward her face until my lips connected with the tender skin just below her ear. I traced her jawline, kissing her mouth before traveling lower to the soft skin on her neck that tasted sweet on my tongue.

I lowered my body to cup her full breast in my hand as I slid my tongue over the peak. My body hardened at her touch. Pulling her to the edge of the bed, I knelt on the floor between her legs as she lifted and rested them on my shoulders. Even her thighs made me quake. My lips longed to kiss every inch of her.

She gasped as I kissed everywhere but where she wanted. Her hips, her thighs, the little creases where the inside of her legs met her body. Everywhere but her core. Thyra sighed as I lowered my mouth to her and exhaled.

"My gods, Aric," she breathed. Her legs shook, though I'd barely touched her. She inhaled sharply as my tongue found its mark and licked up her as I slid my fingers inside her.

Fuck, she feels so good. My body longed to be inside her, but right now was all about her. I worked my fingers and tongue until she was gripping my hair... hard. She pulled at me until I could hardly breathe. I quickened my pace as she arched her back and shattered in an exuberant scream. I traced her core with my tongue, taking one last taste before I stood.

She wrapped her legs around me, pulling me closer. My heart raced. I couldn't take her beauty anymore and sheathed myself within her in a quick motion.

Her warmth nearly sent me over the edge as she tightened around me. Pulling out, I pushed her back up onto the bed and crawled on top of her. She raised her hips to me and pulled a pillow under her. She moaned as I sank back into her.

My wings unfurled and stretched wide as we made love. Her fingers grazed the edges of my feathers, sending goosebumps down my body. She wrapped her legs around my hips as I slid into her. Her body tensed around me, clamping me in place. She inhaled sharply, holding it in for a moment.

"Oh, my gods," she breathed out. I exploded into her the moment she relaxed her hold on me and slid in and out of her filling her until I was empty.

Collapsing, I buried my head into her chest. Her fingers ran through my hair as we lay there, trying to catch our breath.

"I love you, my Kompis, no matter how long it took you to reciprocate," she whispered.

"I love you, too, my mate." I kissed between her breasts.

She giggled at the touch. "Don't you start that again," she scolded me, which only made me want to kiss her more.

Straddling her again, I pinned her to the bed. She wiggled under my weight, but she laughed and succumbed to desire.

We spent the rest of the night exploring each other.

Too soon would the sun rise, and I'd be called to my duty as King.

The knock on our door roused me. We had spent all night in each other's arms and I couldn't stand the thought of not feeling her skin on mine. With a sigh, I moved to drag myself out of bed, but the ties that bound me to my sleeping mate stopped me.

"Enter." I spoke softly as to not wake Thyra.

The High Chancellor walked in and bowed the moment he closed the door behind him and spoke low. "I'm sorry to wake you, Sire, but you need to make a decision."

I groaned. I'd been putting off this duty. We had lost so many when Herrick had ambushed us and replacing our leaders had become harder than I'd anticipated. It had only been a few months but appointing a new High Commander was my utmost priority and it wasn't like I could just pick one. They had to be approved by the council, and they refused to agree on anything.

"The council will meet with you shortly." Tavis bowed.

I nodded. "Thanks. We'll be there soon." My mate lay curled up against my hip sound asleep. Watching her peaceful slumber eased the ache in my chest. I could watch her for hours, but I had duties to attend to and I couldn't go anywhere without her at the moment. Stroking the side of her face, I smiled to see her twitch.

She slowly opened her eyes. "What is it, Aric?"

"I have to go to a council meeting to replace my High Commander."

She sat up, wrapping her arm around me and I nearly lost it at her warmth.

Pulling out of my mate's grasp, I said, "We should get dressed and head that way. I'm sorry I have to drag you with me." I raised our joined hands.

"My Kompis, I would go with you even without the ties." She kissed me softly before sliding off the bed. With a snap, we dressed and headed for the war room.

The entire counsel was deep in conversation when we entered the room. Its deep mahogany wood walls stretched up high in the sky. Its open ceiling revealing the midday sun warmed me, but the cool grass floor calmed me. We kept nothing secret from the gods so even our confidential meetings were open spaces.

None of the council noticed as we walked to the front of the room. My chest tightened as I clamped down my jaw. Part of me wished I could stay hidden, but I was their king now and they would respect that.

Taking a deep breath, I summoned the strength before I bellowed out, "Silence!" and slammed my fist on the table.

Every face jerked to me.

"Enough of your bickering and disrespect. I am your king, and you will treat me as such or meet my blade!" I snapped. Several of the council knelt low, kissing the grass under their feet. Others sat glaring at me. Pulling Thyra behind me, I walked up to the nearest defiant fae, drawing my sword on him and shook as I pressed it to his throat. "I warned you once, Lord Racnid. If you do not obey, I will remove your head right here for all to see."

The fae under my blade lowered to the ground, bowing low, his wings flattened out behind him. Everyone else who had disrespected me followed suit.

"I am the rightful King of Alfheim and the next one to challenge that authority will not see sunrise. Do I make myself clear?"

The murmured voices all agreed, but their faces stayed low.

"You may rise and sit." I waited for them to sit before I continued. "As you all know, the position of High Commander would naturally go to me if my mother were still alive. As it were, she is not and that leaves it to me to make the choice but the High Commander needs to be approved by a majority of the council as well. I highly recommend you listen to my suggestion." I eyed the room, daring anyone to challenge me.

"Who is your choice?" Lord Racnid spoke with malice in his voice.

Swallowing hard, I spoke loudly. "Mayank Suresh." The room exploded in protest. I shut my eyes at the noise. I knew this would be a fight. Mayank was a good leader, but his current rank wasn't technically high enough for this position, but I was used to getting my way, and this was no different. So, I shouted over the noise. "Quiet and listen!"

Silence fell over the room.

My eyes scanned the council's faces before I spoke. "When no one else wanted to go, Mayank volunteered to follow Brynjar to Svartalfheim to save Queen Emma. He, along with Rajnish, risked their lives to save my sister and her mate. If anyone is worthy to be *my* High Commander, it is one of them. Mayank has the ability to control emotions at a level to rival my mother's. He can calm an army with a single thought. He will be my High Commander and Rajnish will be his lieutenant. That is my decision and I suggest you agree." I sat, pulling my mate down with me.

I stared at them one by one waiting for their approval.

Her voice echoed in my mind. '*Well done, my King.*'

'*It wasn't too harsh?*' I thought back to her, not really caring if I came across as harsh to this spoiled crowd.

'*Just the right amount.* She squeezed my fingers.

One by one, the council stood with their fists to their chest and agreed with the new appointments before departing. The room slowly cleared, leaving only my mate, High Chancellor, and myself.

High Chancellor Tavis spoke first. "Your mother would be proud. The council is difficult to rein in, and you skillfully got them to see things your way. It is never easy being King, Sire, but you do it well. Now, I suggest you two go eat something. You look as though you haven't slept." He winked at us as he strolled out of the room.

I leaned into Thyra and spoke. "I think he is right. We should eat and get some more rest. I'll inform Mayank and Rajnish of their new assignments later." She kissed my cheek and pulled me to the kitchens.

CHAPTER 27

Emma

Brynjar and I walked toward the pier. Wrapping my arm through the crook of his, I tried to keep him calm. He wasn't thrilled being around humans and his body tensed the moment he saw the small boat. Seeing him not be the strong and composed one was worrying me. Nothing ever got to him, but I could see now why he rarely came to Midgard.

"Just breathe. I'll be with you always. No matter what." I reminded him, and he sighed, relaxing into me.

We joined the queue to get onto the ferry as I interlaced my fingers with his and gave a little squeeze.

"We're only here for the night, but we will have our own cabin. All to ourselves." I looked over at him to see a tiny half-grin forming on his face. "We can do whatever you'd like." I tried to contain the girly giggle at the thoughts running through my head but failed.

Midgard wasn't as scary as he had believed it to be, and I wanted him to relax and try to enjoy himself.

The line grew shorter as we waited for our turn. Brynjar's body loosened slightly as he leaned against me. I let my hand slip under his shirt and teased my fingers at the waistband of his jeans.

He chuckled. "If you don't stop that, we won't make it to the boat."

I pulled my hand away slightly but lingered on his lower back. Finally, it was our turn to board, and I handed our tickets to the attendant.

"What brings you all the way to our lovely country?" he asked us.

"It's our honeymoon," I chimed in.

The man's fake smile spread touching his eyes. "Well then, don't let me keep you. Here's your key. Your cabin will be about halfway down the first corridor. It's a pleasure to have you with us. Enjoy the ride." He winked at Brynjar, who laughed. I tugged him up the slipway and onto the ferry.

We headed down the narrow hallway. I had to walk in front of Brynjar, but I never dropped his hand. I didn't even mind that his palm was sweaty in mine. After all we'd been through, I just wanted to be near him. Finding our cabin, we stopped and I unlocked the door.

Squeezing in, we didn't need to "look around." There were two pull-down cots barely wide enough to hold one normal sized human, and that was about it. We could touch all four sides of the room without moving.

"Well, at least it's just for the night. The next boat is bigger. I promise." I looked at my mate, who only stared wide eyed. "Bryn?" He didn't move. He didn't even blink.

I dropped my bag and pulled his off before I dragged him back into the hallway. Hauling him down the hall and back out onto the deck before he gasped out a breath.

"Bryn?" I asked again.

One of the crewmen approached. "Is he okay? He looks green."

"Claustrophobic, I think. He took one look at our *room* and froze." I looked up at the girl that spoke to us. She was petite with dark brown pixie cut hair. Her hazel eyes looked at my mate with concern.

"I'll go get him some water. There's a bench up front." She pointed to the bow of the ship. Brynjar moved on his own and slumped down into the seat.

"I'm sorry, my love. I have proven useless to you." He gave me a sad smile.

"Never, my Kompis. I nearly lost my mind when I learned I was the daughter of the Queen of Alfheim. Earth is very different from your world. You are used to nature and an openness that is rare here. Midgard is full of metal and electronics. You have every right to be uncomfortable."

"Here's some water." The stewardess' voice broke into my thoughts. "Do you need anything else?" she asked.

"I think we'll be fine. Thank you." I took the bottle of water from her and opened it. Brynjar took it from me and studied it.

"It's not the same as drinking straight from the purest stream, but it's the best we got here on earth." I opened the other bottle and drank, nearly spitting it out. After the pure food and water from Alfheim, this tasted like dirty pond water. Forcing it down my throat, I said, "Not the same at all."

Instead of drinking it, I poured a little of it down Brynjar's shirt. He arched his back as the cool liquid flowed down his spine.

"Now what?" he finally asked. "I can't go back to that *room*, but I desperately need to stretch out." He wiggled his shoulders from side to side.

Glancing around, I noticed the captain walking off toward the bridge and the crew preparing to launch. I turned to the slowly setting sun before I responded. "It'll be dark soon." I smiled at my mate. "Maybe we can shield ourselves and drop the glamour for a bit?"

"That would be nice. Can you build a shield? I feel really stupid for saying this, but I just don't think I have the energy for it." He lowered his head.

I leaned down and kissed his cheek. "For you, I could move mountains. Remember?"

He looked up and smiled at me. "No matter what."

He wrapped an arm around my back, and I rested my head on his chest. We sat like that until the moon had risen and the deck had cleared.

I stood and faced my mate. Leaning down, I kissed his cheek and whispered in his ear, "Ready?"

He pulled me onto his lap, kissing me deeply. Dragging my face away from his, I told him, "I can either do this or make a shield. I don't think I could do both."

The growl rumble deep within him, vibrating along my chest. "I need you, Emmy." He pulled me closer, kissing my neck. Heat boiled in my core. I needed him too, but not here. Pushing myself off him, I found the magic within me.

Closing my eyes, I reached for the wall within my mind. I let it grow until it was no longer within my own head but surrounding us. When I opened my eyes and looked at Brynjar he breathed easier.

"We're shielded." I told him.

He stood and together we shook off our glamour and stretched our wings wide. Their edges brushed my shield.

Brynjar loosely tucked his wings behind his back and stepped up to me. His strong arms wrapped around me, grasping my ass and pulled me closer. My wings folded around him as he pressed his lips to mine. Heat rushed to my core. Everything faded from my mind but his body. There was no concern for Yggdrasil or finding his father's clan. Only he and I existed.

Pulling away from his kiss and resting my head on his chest, I gazed up at the night sky. The stars were bright out tonight and the moon was nearly full.

Glass shattering and the yelp of the steward that gave us water brought me back to reality. I looked at the girl that stood, frozen in fear.

"Shit." I said. Brynjar and I quickly glamoured ourselves again. "You're such a bad influence!"

He shrugged. "Couldn't help myself."

"I told you I couldn't do both and you distracted me." We walked cautiously toward the now sobbing girl. Looking from her to Brynjar, I asked, "What do we do?"

No one had ever told me what would happen if someone saw what we really were, but it couldn't be anything good.

He knelt in front of her and gently cupped her chin in his hand. He spoke to her in a low and even, almost hypnotic tone. "What's your name?"

"A-Addy."

"It's a pleasure to meet you, Addy. I know you're afraid, but you don't have to be. We are as human as you are. There is nothing unusual about us. You just happened to catch us in a compromising position."

He offered her his hand and helped her stand. "In a moment you will blush and walk quickly away, only thinking you found the newlyweds out on the deck."

"Yes, the newlyweds were enjoying the privacy," she said robotically.

"Good," Brynjar said before pulling me back into him. "I'm so sorry, miss. You have a good evening as well." His voice returned to its normal tone.

"I... Yes... you too." Addy's face flushed, and she turned and hurried off in the opposite direction.

Burying my face in my mate's chest, I laughed. We laughed together. Tears streamed down my face from before we stopped.

"Damn you, Bryn." I halfheartedly punched him in the arm. "I told you I couldn't hold up the shield and have you so close."

His lips found my jaw. "I'm sorry. I find I just can't help myself."

I pushed away. "Stop it. We can't get into trouble like that again! What did you even do to that girl?"

"It's simple in theory, tougher to actually do. I changed her memories. Not all fae can do it, and it takes a lot out of you." He swayed on his feet as he said it.

Wrapping my arms around him, I asked, "You think you can handle that tiny room for a few hours of sleep now?"

He sank into me. "I think I'll have to."

We walked sideways down the hallway until we reached our cabin. I deposited him on the bottom bunk, laying a blanket over him. Our lips brushed together as we whispered, "goodnight" before I pulled myself up to the top bunk and sunk into sleep.

CHAPTER 28

Aric

P ounding fists on my door woke me. Groaning, I sat up and rubbed my eyes at the same time as Thyra.

Mayank's panicked voice came from the other side of the door. "King Aric!"

I looked at my mate, who only snapped her fingers to clothe us and pulled me by our bound hands out of the bed. We walked groggily to the door and I opened it, allowing Mayank to enter.

"Good morning, Mayank." I suppressed a yawn. "I've been meaning to get in touch with you, but can this wait? We just woke up."

"No, sir, this can't. It is Lord Racnid. He is causing quite a fuss in the village."

I blinked the sleep out of my eyes. "He's what? What the Hel is he doing?"

As one Thyra and I walked to my wall of weapons and I strapped my long sword to my hip and Thyra grabbed a bo staff while Mayank elaborated.

"He is stirring the villagers into a fight and rallying support for a vote of no confidence against you. He's using Emma and the fact that you have only known of your heritage for a short time to try and divide the people."

"How the Hel can one spoiled fae cause such a fuss in such a short time? It can't be half a day since I sent him to his knees."

"It seems other spoiled fae are joining him for support."

I grumbled a few choice words before stepping out into the hall. "Where is he?"

Mayank took the lead. "Follow me."

Once we got closer to the main hall, fae scurried past us in a panic. One even bumped into me and moved on without acknowledging who they hit. The tension only thickened as we walked out into the morning light.

My feet halted at the end of the bridge leading into town. The sentries typically posted there were nowhere in sight and people were running in all directions.

I stared off toward the village. Smoke rose from the center of town, and fae ran from the fire. "What in Helheim has he started?"

I spun my mate into my arms and spirited to the source of the smoke. What once was the butcher shop was now engulfed in flames. Thyra sprung into action without a second thought, working with other fae to summon water and extinguish the fire. She lifted our bound hands as she worked and I watched on, helpless.

My gaze shifted to a sobbing woman wrapped in her mate's arms. The butcher was a stout man, taller than I, but broader. He watched, stoned faced, as his livelihood was reduced to smoldering ashes.

When the flames were gone Thyra and I walked up to the butcher and his wife. He turned to me and gave a slight bow of the head before looking back to what was left of his shop.

"What happened?" I asked as his wife continued to sob in his arms.

"I refused to join him against you, so he torched my shop. My mate was still sleeping upstairs. It was all I could do to get her out of there." He glanced down at her then pulled his bulky arm away, revealing a massive burn stretching from his fingers to his elbow. "No one else helped us... Maybe they were too afraid of him or just too stunned by his actions. I'm not sure."

Thyra placed her free hand gently over his arm and let her magic flow, healing his wounds. The searing red flesh was replaced by dark skin. He flexed his hand and stretched his arm out before looking up at Thyra. "Thanks."

"I will send for the vine weavers to repair your home and shop right away," I told the grieving couple. The butcher only managed a nod, still looking at the ruins of his home.

I turned my attention to one of the onlookers. "Did anyone see where Racnid went?"

"He ran off toward the north and he had a small group with him," one of the males informed me.

"Is Sigrid and her army still camped in the north?" Mayank asked.

Ice ran through my veins. Sigrid had vowed to avenge her mother and wanted my head as much as Racnid did. If the two of them joined forces, I'd be in trouble.

"I need to speak to Surt. Have him meet me in my throne room," I told Mayank. "And you as well as Rajnish. Find the two of them and come quickly."

He nodded and spirited off to find them. Not stopping to ask her, I pulled Thyra against me and spirited us directly into our throne room.

Where once there stood a single throne, now stood four. The room was silent as a grave. My guards stood on the outer walls, watching me. I stood upon the dais and paced, dragging my mate behind me. She pulled at the bonds that tied us together, stopping me from moving.

"Take a breath, my love. You are no use to us in a panic." Her soft voice melted my anxiety.

"You are always right." I wrapped my unbound arm around her, pressing my lips to hers. "What will we do if he joins with Sigrid?"

"You will do whatever you must in order to keep us safe. Racnid is your responsibility. Sigrid is the queen of her own realm. You cannot stand against her without the aid of others. Talk to Surt and go from there. One step at a time, my love." She gently pressed her lips to my cheek before pulling me back to our thrones. "Sit and try to relax before they get here."

She was right so I took in a deep breath and did as she asked. I would take it one step at a time. Assess the situation and go forward from there.

We sat in silence for several minutes before the doors to the throne room opened and Surt, Mayank, and Rajnish entered. The two warriors knelt before me, and Surt bowed slightly.

"Your Majesty," they all said at once.

"Stand, we have much to discuss." I stood as well and stepped off the dais. "Lord Racnid has defected and is trying to raise an army to join in his coup. I fear he is attempting to involve Sigrid. I need your help to stop this."

Surt spoke first. "Have you gone to her camp? What about Njörðr?"

"I wanted your advice before I proceeded."

"Wise choice." He cocked a grin. "Would you like me to speak to Sigrid and maybe even Njörðr? If she is in league with Racnid, it will only be a matter of time before that snake Njörðr joins them."

"Thank you."

Surt placed a fist to his chest and bowed. He turned and left to seek out the others. I rubbed my brow and sat back down on my throne.

Mayank broke the silence. "Sir?"

"Yes?"

"I sent scouts out looking for Racnid and any other of his cronies. So far, it appears the Guard is secured. We are all behind you, Your Majesty."

I raised my head to my High Commander. "Thank you, Mayank."

A small pop sounded and Surt stood gripping Njörðr by the back of his neck as they approached.

"I could not get to Sigrid. She has raised a shield around her camp, but I caught this one," he shoved Njörðr forward, causing him to stumble before righting himself, "trying to flee. He has always been a coward, but I never assumed he'd back out of a fight like this."

The god straightened and looked at me. "She is powerful and just as crazy. She wants your throne as much as this Lord Racnid does. There is no winning against them."

My hand gripped the pommel of my sword as I stared at him. "So, what were you going to do? Run and hide? Do you know what the punishment for treason is?"

"Treason?" Njörðr squealed out. "Retreating is not treason."

"You back out of our agreement and bury your head in the sand, I will call it a treasonous act. I'm not thrilled with the idea of execution, but for you I'd make an exception."

Njörðr shook at my words. He dropped to one knee and bowed his head low. "I beg your humble forgiveness, my king."

"Rise. If you attempt to flee again, I will see that my blade removes your head. Do you understand me?"

"Yes, Your Majesty." He stood slowly.

Turning my attention to Surt, "Sigrid has joined Racnid's cause, then? How in the Nine Realms did she raise a shield in my realm?"

"She had help." Surt rubbed his temples. "Racnid was standing at the edge of the field when I arrived. He just grinned at me when I tried to remove the shield. He is arrogant and I wish to witness his death."

I scoffed. "I will save you a seat, my friend."

CHAPTER 29

Emma

W e disembarked the small ferry in the morning and stretched our legs on the dock. The attendant at the office told us our next ferry wouldn't be ready to board for a few more hours and directed us to some shops further down the pier.

I took hold of Brynjar's hand, and we strolled in the direction of the shops. We passed large glass windows filled with their displays just lighting up as their owners opened their doors. They smiled at us as we walked, wishing us a good morning. The cobblestone beneath our feet felt more like home than anything else we'd seen in Midgard so far. Brynjar clutched his stomach when it let out an audible growl.

"I think we should find some food," I said.

The aroma of coffee guided my feet. We continued to walk until we came upon a modern-looking building with a café sign above the door. Dragging Brynjar inside, I breathed in the scent.

"Good morning. How may I help you?" the barista asked as we stepped up to the counter.

He was of average height, with dark eyes and hair. The black apron around his neck had the name of the cafe written across it, though I couldn't pronounce the word.

"Hi. We're not from around here. It's our honeymoon." I pulled my mate to the counter. "He's not a coffee kinda guy, but I definitely need some caffeine. We are also starving. What do you recommend?"

The barista's grin widened. "Welcome to our little hamlet. I will make something for you. Please, have a seat."

I nodded my thanks and pulled Brynjar to a table. We slumped into the booth. I was as exhausted as he looked.

"You going to be okay?" I asked him.

"Yeah, it's just all so new."

"Well, at least we're here early and no one's here."

The sounds of steam and metal clinking on metal filled the little café. Our barista was at our table a moment later, holding a tray.

"Here we are. A cappuccino for the lady." He laid the cup in front of me. He had neatly made a heart shape on the top of it.

"An orange juice for the gentleman. And two kanel-bolles—apologies, you would probably call it a cinnamon roll." He lowered the now empty tray and bowed slightly. "Please enjoy, on the house to celebrate your nuptials."

"Awe! Thank you!" I smiled widely.

"Entirely my pleasure, ma'am. Enjoy our country." He bowed again before getting back to the bar.

The water on the ferry might not have tasted good, but the coffee was divine. Even the food was amazing. As I finished my last bite, I looked up to see the barista dashing from one end of the bar to the other so fast I had to focus to see him. Once he stopped moving, I saw it. His ears were as pointed as mine. I gasped.

"What?" Brynjar looked around, startled.

"Look at the barista," I whispered before I stood and walked to him.

He bowed as I approached. "I'm surprised it took you that long to see me, Your Majesty."

"You're... but..." I shook my head. "I must be more exhausted than I thought."

"Not all of us fae hate Midgard, my lady. Some of us rather enjoy the life of a human."

"But..."

He chuckled. "I do believe your ferry will be boarding soon. I love Midgard but I also have family in Alfheim. Please do what you can to save Yggdrasil." He handed me a brown bag and a box. "More pastries and coffee for your trip."

I gaped at him. "But how did you know?"

"You're a seer." Brynjar's words made me jump. "I'm right, aren't I?"

The barista bowed. "I am, my king. As are you? We shall meet again, but for now you better get going."

I bowed and turned to leave.

"She doesn't know, does she?" I heard the barista asked Brynjar as I walked to the door.

When my mate joined me outside I asked, "What did he mean by that?"

He wrapped his arms around me and kissed me deeply. "I'll tell you when the time is right. Let's get to our boat before we get arrested for indecent exposure." He grinned mischievously.

I frowned at him. "Fine. Let's go." I pulled out of his grasp and walked back to the pier.

This boat was massive compared to our last one. It stood several stories high and was about four times longer than the first one. They gave us a map to find our room.

The large glass door on the far wall of our suite opened up to a balcony overlooking the pier. The bed stood in the middle of the spacious room. We even had a private full bath.

We deposited our things on the small table in the corner of the room. I stepped up to the glass door and opened the blinds and stared out toward the icy waters. I glanced over my shoulder to see a fierce look in Bryn's eyes.

He wrapped his arms around me before I could blink. I elbowed him in the ribs, opened the door and stepped out onto the balcony.

"You're still hiding things from me," I said.

"I'm sorry. You know how I am about my dreams. And they are constantly changing. I don't want to get your hopes up but... Well let's just say if nothing changes our story ends well. Can you live with that for now?" He stepped up behind me running his hands through my hair.

I sighed. "I guess."

He smiled and pulled me back into the room and snapped his fingers. The door and blinds closed behind me.

I laughed as he attacked my neck with rough kisses. Our glamour dropped, and he enveloped me with his wings.

"I want to worship you, my Kompis," He breathed into my ear. He pressed his mouth to mine, parting my lips roughly.

Pulling away, I asked, "Can I take a breath first?"

"I'll breathe for you." His kiss deepened. His passion thrummed down to my toes as he pressed his stiffness into my hip, making me forget my irritation.

I snapped my fingers and removed our clothes before he could rip them off. His growl rumbled through me as I wrapped my leg around him. His naked flesh felt hot against mine.

He stepped back, pulling me to the bed and gently sat on the edge, unfurling his wings behind him. I straddled his lap, placing my knees on either side of him as he pressed his lips between my breasts kissing tenderly.

"I love you, my Kompis." I raked my hands through his hair. His wings—along with other parts—sprang to life at my touch.

"I love you too, my mate," he breathed out.

My hand reached between us, down to the length of him. He moaned as I stroked him. I guided him to my slickness and lowered my body over him.

I gasped at the sensation. My wings stretched wide as he filled me. I rocked against his hips in slow, deliberate motions. He buried his face in my chest and wrapped his arms around my back, stroking my wings. Tiny pinpricks of electricity burst out around his fingers. My new wings felt every slight touch.

I threw my head back, exposing my chest to my mate. He took the opportunity to kiss, lick, and tease my nipples. My hands wrapped around the nape of his neck as I rocked harder against him. Heat radiated through my core.

"Fuck," I moaned. "Oh my gods, Bryn." I dug my nails into his skin.

"Oh, really?" He laughed, gripping my ass, and stood. The sudden movement sent an electric pulse through my body. He turned and laid me gently on my back, avoiding smashing my wings.

Pulling out, he knelt in front of me. "I want you on my tongue," he said before spreading my legs. I jolted as he licked at the wetness between my thighs. He plunged two fingers into me, wiggling them inside. His mouth worshipped me until he sent me over the edge. I pulled a pillow over my face and screamed. The orgasm came in wave after wave, rippling over my body.

Before it subsided, he plunged his cock back into me. His hands traced up the length of me until they found the peaks of my breasts. He twirled my nipples between his finger and thumb.

"My gods, you feel so good." I heard his muffled voice through the pillow. I was gasping into it as he slammed into me over and over again.

"Fuck, fuck, fuck..." was all I could say. His breath came in sharp inhales and exhales as he growled. His hands gripped my hips as he pounded harder and harder.

"Oh my gods, Emmy." With one last thrust, he burst into me. I wrapped my legs around him and pulled him down. He pulled the pillow from my face, kissing my lips. "I. Love. You," he said with every kiss.

"Uh huh..." I gasped. He rolled off me, laying on his side.

His fingers brushed against my skin, sending shivers over my body. I laughed and rolled onto my side to face him.

"I don't think I will ever grow tired of that." He smiled.

"Oh, just wait until the boat is moving... that could be really fun too!" My smile grew.

"I believe we won't be leaving this cabin the whole time." He pulled me closer, kissing me softly.

CHAPTER 30

Brynjar

E ven though the room was larger, it still caged me in and exhausting ourselves in each other's arms did little to distract me from the size of the space. It took some convincing to get Emma to leave the comforts of our retreat for a walk, and I hated tucking away my wings, but if I didn't get out soon, I'd go insane.

Emma held the map in her hand when I stepped out of the small bathroom and the grin across her face had me reconsidering my decision to leave.

"What?" I asked her skeptically.

"I've always wanted to dress a man. Now, I think I will." She tucked the map into her back pocket and dragged me from the room.

I had to breathe deep as we raced down the hall. Alfheim was so open that I couldn't breathe normally in the tight Midgardian corridors. Thankfully, the hall led to a set of large stairs. We walked up one deck, and it opened up into a large shopping area.

"Now what?" I asked my mate.

She pulled me closer and her lips brushed against mine as she spoke. "Your human clothes are outdated, my love. I've seen what Aric has worn and you and he both look as if you're stuck in the 80's. I have to fix this atrocity."

She laughed and dragged me behind her as she walked through the sea of eager shoppers, and I had to gulp down the anxiety that was building within me. Humans weren't all that bad—if one ignored their blatant arrogance and general entitled attitude. Or at least, I tried to convince myself of that.

"Come on, slowpoke," Emma yelled at me. I hadn't even noticed that I had stopped moving or that she'd dropped my hand.

The tiny hairs on the back of my neck stood on end as I stayed rooted in place, looking around. Something was off, like someone was watching us, but I couldn't pinpoint it. Maybe it was just my anxiety building. The unease didn't leave me even when Emma returned to slip her hand in mine.

She finally slowed down when we reached her intended destination. The storefront looked much like Lena's shop back home did. Only made from cold metal rather than rich wood. The fabrics that hung from the windows were in much brighter hues than I was used to, but I let my mate pull me inside.

The girl at the front of the shop greeted us. "Good afternoon. Is there anything I can help you find?" She was small, even by human standards. Her blond hair was dipped in purple die and piled high on top of her head.

"First, we need to get rid of these acid-wash jeans," Emma said, tugging at my waistband. "I wish to burn them all."

"Oh, that's easy. Men's jeans are up front on the left." She looked me up and down. "Then I assume you need some shirts? They will be just behind those. Dressing rooms are on the back wall in the center. Let me know if you need any help with anything." Her hands worked as she talked, pointing in the directions she spoke of.

"Thanks," Emma said as we walked past her.

"Good luck," I heard the girl whisper behind me.

We walked up to a wall full of jeans with styles of all kinds. Some were so dark they were nearly black. A few I thought would cut off circulation if I put them on. I pointed to them and asked Emma, "Are those in the right section? They look like they'd fit you better."

She laughed out loud at the question. "Those are skinny jeans. Some girls like them on guys, but I'd hate to cut off blood flow." She grabbed me by the belt loops, pulling me into a kiss.

I gripped her wrist and pulled away. "Emma, you better stop that or else I'll be doomed to this wardrobe forever." I stole a quick kiss before returning to the wall of jeans. Pulling a few down, I asked, "How about these?"

"I like your choices. Let's find some shirts to go with them. It's going to be cold where we're going, yes?"

"Yes, but remember, I don't get as cold as you will."

"Still, if you walk around in the snow half-naked, people will stare."

Shaking the image of her bared to the world from my head, I followed her. The section of shirts was three times as large, and I was lost in a sea of colors.

"Here, I'll make it easy for you," she said as she flipped through the clothes, pulling a few from the rack. "Let's go try these on."

I followed her into the dressing room.

She hung the clothes on the hook and turned to face me with a grin then snapped. The dark, straight legged jeans and a forest green long-sleeved textured shirt appeared on me. Her fingers fumbled with the buttons around my neck. "Leave these three undone. Looks sexier." Her lips traced the exposed skin sending blood rushing straight to my dick.

With another snap, I now wore the faded and torn jeans and a button-up shirt.

She grinned and rolled up the sleeves. "I do so love a man in a Roper shirt." Her fingers hooked in my belt loops and yanked me into her embrace. "You are so hot, my love."

"We better get out of here before you snap your fingers again." My lips lingered along her jaw before I snapped and returned to my 80's attire.

She demanded that I get some new shoes as well, so we left the store with five new pairs of jeans, about ten shirts, a pair of high-top shoes and leather boots.

Once back out into the main hall, I asked her, "Where is all this money coming from? I know our currency doesn't really convert."

"How else? Magic."

"Yes, but from where?" My voice was sterner than I had meant it to be.

"Relax. It's my father's. Or it was his."

I gaped at her.

"No, not Herrick's, my human father's. He was wealthy and with Drew and that witch most likely dead, it is legally mine. Right?" She gave me her best irresistible smile and I dropped the subject.

"Now, how about some food? And can we send the bags back to the room?" she asked me. I snapped my fingers and replaced my 80's clothes with the outfit she so enjoyed and sent the rest to the room.

That nagging feeling of someone watching followed me to the food court. I kept looking around while we waited for our food, but couldn't find the source. Emma's hand on my forearm broke me out of my trance.

"What's wrong? You've been distracted since we left the store."

"I... I don't know. Maybe I'm just being a soldier. Something feels off." I kept looking around as I spoke, not even noticing when the girl from the restaurant brought us our food.

We ate in silence and headed back to our room. The eerie feeling intensified the closer we got to the stairs. I stopped, pulling my mate to a halt beside me.

"Emma," I breathed.

"I know, I can feel them, too." Her hand twirled at her side. She handed me the newly formed steel sword she created from the metal around us before she produced a pair of daggers for herself.

We turned to face what I'd felt all day. Three towering figures stood before us, and their pointed ears gave them away: they were dark fae. Their hair as all dark but in different styles. One was cropped short, one was long and pulled back, the other's hung low around his ears. All of them glared at us.

The one with the long hair spoke first. "Our master wishes you to come with us. And we won't take no for an answer."

"Who is your master?" I asked.

"Ask your mate. She got *real* intimate with him in Svartalfheim," the crop-haired guy said.

The memory of Emma and Damion flashed in my mind, and I had to remind myself it was fiction.

"What if we refuse? Are you going to try to kill us?" I asked.

"We won't try. We *will* kill you and take her with us. We'd rather not in front of her, though." Long hair nodded to my mate.

"You will be the ones to die," Emma spoke up beside me.

"I think not, Majesty."

I raised the sword and lunged towards the one that spoke. The tip of my blade scaped across his skin as he moved to avoid the blow.

"Nice try," he mocked.

Emma's magic built up beside me. She pushed it forward, sending flames toward him, but it split around the three of them.

"You think he'd send us to you without protection? Your magic won't work on us." He grinned. "Please, just come with us. I'd hate to hurt you."

This time, she threw a dagger at him. It sailed through the air faster than natural, aided by her magic. It met its mark and sank deep in the long haired dark fae's chest. He clutched at the blade as he fell to the floor.

The other two moved into fighting positions, gripping swords of their own.

Emma knelt and yanked the dagger from the dead fae's body. The moment it was free, his body shook and broke apart, leaving only dust. I looked on in amazement, unsure of what just happened.

My mate's voice brought me back to reality. "Do you wish to continue?"

The two gripped their swords tighter and charged me together. I blocked one, but the other's blade found my ribs slicing deep, bringing me to my knees. I heard Emma scream. Then the two dark fae disappeared. I lay on the cold metal as Emma's face faded in and out of view.

I woke up back in our room after the sun had set.

"Wh-what happened?" I croaked out.

Emma's hand clasped around mine, but it was an unfamiliar face I saw first.

"You were stabbed, my king." The face of the man who spoke slowly came into focus. His light hair was neatly parted and laid flat against his scalp. Blue eyes and crooked nose came into view next.

The man's grin spread as I tried to sit up. "Glad you're back with us, Majesty."

It wasn't until I was fully upright that I saw his very fae ears.

"You're..." I tried to say.

"Yes, Sire. I'm fae. I'm also a doctor in both this realm and ours. You are very lucky I was here. Well, I say luck. She," he jerked his thumb to Emma at my side, "says her brother sent me. Our queen doesn't trust that I just happened to be here and believes King Aric had you followed, but either way, you are both lucky. Thankfully, I was the only witness. Her Majesty's scream sent them fleeing."

"I told you. Please call me Emma."

He nodded. "Very well, Emma."

"What happened to the one she killed?" I asked. "He just vanished."

"That was me as well. Sorry I couldn't warn you. It's a little disturbing to watch if you don't know what's happening. That's my magic. I'm very adapt at... disposing of bodies. It's complicated but essentially my magic allows me to return anything back to its original form. Those creatures were created from ash. That's why your mother sent me to Midgard so many years ago. I'm the one she called when things got out of hand."

"How long was I out for?" I touched my side, where the sting of the blade had been, but only found a small sliver of disturbed skin.

"It's been a little over a day. I was starting to worry about you." Emma squeezed my hand. "We are nearly there, and I was afraid we'd miss our stop." She grinned.

"Oh, so not worried I'd die, but worried we'd be stuck here?" I pulled her into a kiss.

The doctor spoke up. "I'm glad you are doing better. I will leave you be."

"Doc, wait," I called. He turned around. "Thank you for saving our lives."

"It was my pleasure, Majesty. Emma has my phone number if you need anything else. Rest for now. Tomorrow, you will disembark and will need your strength for the final stretch of your journey." He bowed before exiting the room.

I turned to Emma waiting at my side to find her eyes filled with tears.

Her entire body was visibly shaking. "Never do that to me again, you hear me?"

I pulled her onto the bed with me. "Never again." I kissed her deeply, sliding her under me.

Her smile widened as I caressed her body.

"I love you, my Kompis." I kissed her jaw.

"I love you too," she sighed.

CHAPTER 31

Aric

There was no point in delaying the inevitable. My new enemies could be holed up in their little shield for months. I had to end this now before others were injured. I didn't even wait for Surt or Njörðr's approval and immediately spirited toward the traitors, dragging my mate with me. I hated bringing her closer to the danger I faced, but it would be against the gods to try to remove the ties ourselves. They'd only be removed when they deemed us worthy and that could take days or even weeks.

We paced—I paced, the ties that bound us forced Thyra to follow—in front of the invisible wall, waiting for someone to show their face. The shield was completely invisible, not even a shimmer to it. I only found it when I ran smack into it. When we saw no one, I paced more. Racnid's actions was an attack on my leadership skills.

"Hold still, my love," Thyra spoke beside me.

I halted my steps to look at my mate. "What is it?" I asked as calmly as I could.

"I can... I can feel a weakness. In their shield." With her eyes closed, she dragged me closer to the wall between us and our enemy. "Right here." She brought our tied hands up and laid them on a spot. "Feel it. Not with your hands, but with your magic."

I shut my eyes and reached out with my magic. It was like the laces of clothing that kept my shirts on around my wings. It was there, but only as thin ropes stretching across the shield to keep it closed.

"Can we undo it?" I asked her without opening my eyes and her magic poured into the opening as a response. I did the same, dumping every emotion I had into it until it strained before the breaking crack echoed across the valley. Then, with an ear-splitting shatter, the wall came down.

So too did the ties that bound Thyra and me together. She looked at me with glistening eyes.

She flung her arms around me. "I guess the gods approve, my love."

"I'm glad we did not anger the gods by interrupting the crowning to bind you two." Surt's gruff voice rang out from behind us. Thyra untangled herself from me but stayed close by my side. He looked back to where the shield had been before he continued, "And you did a fine job taking down Racnid's shielding. Now what are your commands?"

"Find the traitorous Sigrid and Racnid—and watch them hang," I said. "I'd prefer the entire realm to bear witness to their deaths, but that all depends on them."

"I'd say I'm surprised that they're hiding, but maybe Sigrid is luring you into a trap?" Njörðr suggested.

"I've thought of that. Why don't you two," I looked at Surt and Njörðr, "head around the side of the camp and sneak up behind them." I gripped the hilt of my sword, turned, and marched toward the heart of their camp.

Sigrid's' people scattered the moment they saw me coming. They opened a path leading right to their queen. Not one of her men chose to fight. A smug smile spread across my face. Sigrid hated me, but her people didn't want me dead.

Racnid and Sigrid stood in the center of the makeshift ice realm, weapons in hand. A few of my fae stood behind them, trembling. I too was shaking, but not out of fear, but rage. It was time to show them why I was the rightful King.

"I told you, Sigrid, that if you ever defy me again in my own house, you will feel my cold steel across your neck. Do you still wish to stand with your partner in treason?" I asked coldly.

She tightened her grip on her sword. "Your sister killed my mother. It is only fitting that I take from her as well." She raised her sword and charged. I sidestepped, and she skidded past me. Sigrid turned on her heel and screamed through gritted teeth.

I stepped back, trying to deescalate the situation. I might be a skilled fighter, but that didn't mean I enjoyed it. If I could save her from her own anger, I would.

"I don't want to fight you, Sigrid." I unsheathed my sword but left it at my side. "But I will kill you if you force my hand."

She ran again. Not like the great huntress she was, more like a cornered animal. Wild and uncontrolled.

"Sigrid, stop!" Surt cried out from behind me, but still, she didn't slow.

The look in her eyes told me all I needed to know. She'd never stop. Even if I let her live, she would be my enemy forever. I had to end this now.

Sigrid's movements turned sloppy and she left herself open. In one swift motion, I thrust my blade through her chest.

She gasped as she fell to the ground.

I looked down at her. "I warned you. I tried to save you. Your death is on you."

"Forgive me, Mother," she gasped out.

I pulled my blade from her body and stood then looked to Racnid and his party. "You all now have a choice to make. Stand with me or against me."

One by one, they all knelt, except Racnid. He stared at me as if he debated on charging as well.

Finally, he spoke but made no move to account. "I cannot, in good conscience, follow you. I don't believe you will be a good leader. You're Herrick's son and you'll bring about the death of our world."

Thyra stepped forward first. Her hands lifted, twisting his arms behind his back and forcing him to drop the sword. Vines wrapped around his wrists as she stepped behind him. Within moments, Thyra had Racnid secured and kneeling in front of me.

"The traitor, my king," she said with a slight bow.

"Thank you, my love." I turned to Surt. "You deal with many traitors in your day?"

"Very few but I know how to deal with him. Bring him to the front of the castle." He nodded to Thyra before he looked at Njörðr. "Can we trust you to stay here and deal with Sigrid's people?"

"Y-yes." Njörðr stepped closer to Sigrid's body. Her people were already attending to her. The Ice Queen's high commander stepped around her and bowed low before me.

"I regret that we couldn't stop her act of vengeance. We hold nothing against you for her death. We came to aid your mother and now you in this fight against Herrick's forces. While we are here, we are at your command, your Majesty. And once we depart from your realm, we are still your friends." He placed his fist to his chest and continued. "We give our oath. You're our ally now and forever, my king."

I tapped him lightly on the shoulder. "Rise. And thank you. I'm sure there is much to discuss amongst your people. I'll leave you to it. If you have need of anything before you leave, please let someone in my court know."

He stood. "Thank you, Sire." And he turned to deal with his people.

We walked slowly through town so all could see the traitor. We passed the butcher and his mate. She was still clutching tight to him, but he looked on in silent satisfaction.

Everyone we passed joined our slow parade back to the castle. As we approached, I saw that my sentries were back in place looking a little worse for wear, but still fit for duty. I nodded in their direction as Surt led us around the river.

He stopped. "Here's good," he said and snapped his fingers, building a small platform five feet off the ground.

The giant god of war grabbed the front of Racnid's shirt and tossed him up on the platform. "You'll stay up there until it is done."

I whispered so only Surt could hear me. "Now what?" *When this was all over I'd have to brush up on civics.* There was so much I didn't know or understand yet I was forced to lead. I unclenched my jaw trying to relax.

"A few more minutes and I believe everyone will have joined us." Surt said.

I hadn't noticed until he said it, but a large crowd had gathered around us. Surt leaned in close to Thyra and spoke something

I couldn't hear. Her eyes widened, but as he stepped away, she nodded.

"After you, my king." He motioned to where the traitor stood.

"What did you say to her?"

"I told her what she needed to do. If you're to show your might, you will need to address your people and warn them of what will happen if they betray you," Surt told me.

'What is going on?' I asked Thyra so no one else could hear.

Her words came so quickly I had to struggle to keep up. *'It will be difficult, my Kompis. But I will be with you the whole time.'* She gripped my hand.

I gulped as I flapped my wings to stand beside Racnid on the platform. Thyra spirited behind me.

My hands shook, so I wrapped them behind my back, gripping my arms tight. Thyra forced Racnid to his knees and I stepped up beside him.

"Today I come to you all not as a friend but as your leader. My mother entrusted your safety to my sister and I. While I don't enjoy this part of leadership, it must be done. You all must remember that I'm no longer a friend. I'm your King, and you should treat me as such. I may not be like most. I welcome other's opinions, but I have the final say and my word is not to be defied. When you step out of line, this will be the consequence. One has already lost their life for attempting to rise against me. And this one," I pointed to the fae silently crying at my feet, "won't die, but he will wish he were dead." I bent down and tore his shirt from his chest. "He will no longer be considered fae." I gripped my sword, ripped it from its scabbard, and sliced through the base of his wings.

He fell face first, screaming and writhing in pain. Thyra knelt beside him, placed her hands over the bleeding sores, and healed them quickly. He gasped in relief as Thyra helped him back into a kneeling position.

Tears glistened in my mate's eyes, but she said nothing as she straightened and danced around him. As she moved, she pulled his magic from his body. His appearance changed as she performed the ritual. His ears rounded and his eyes lost their glow. When she finished, he looked human. His jaw clenched but made no other sign of emotion as I bent to cut his bindings free.

I stood and addressed my people again. "He's free to go about his life here in Alfheim, but won't be allowed to leave, ever. He no longer has the ability to hurt anyone, so I expect you all to treat him well. If any harm comes to this man, the one who does it will suffer the same fate. Do you all understand?" I asked in a booming voice.

Every fae before me knelt low. I turned to Racnid. "You're free to go, but I promise you if you try to rise against me again or harm any of our people, you will wish I killed you instead."

He refused to meet anyone's eyes as he stood and tried to spirit. He slumped to his knees in tears. Thyra gently grasped his shoulder and spirited the two of them down to the ground. Racnid slunk away from the crowd, who parted to give him space.

I floated to the ground beside my mate. "I'm sorry you had to do that. If I would've known..."

"I'm sorry you had to kill Sigrid. It is part of our duty now to protect our people. We both did what we must."

I wrapped her in my arms, kissing the top of her head. We stood like that until the crowd had departed, leaving only Surt looking on.

"You did well, Majesties. It's never easy stripping a fae of everything that makes them fae. I think you should get her home to rest." He nodded to Thyra and spirited away.

"He's right. I could sleep for days," she said.
I hugged her tight and spirited us into our bedroom.

CHAPTER 32

Emma

Disembarking from the ferry the next day was a relief. Being caged in gave me more anxiety than an open fight would have. The doctor waved us over before we left the pier.

"I just wanted to let you know I'll be sticking around the area. I know I can't come with you, but it is still my duty to make sure you'll be safe. If you need me, you know how to find me."

I nodded my agreements with him before he departed.

"Come on, we need to find our pilot." I threw my backpack over my shoulder and headed for the other side of the peer. "We have one more part of the journey before we are there."

The small inlet was full of boats docking and disembarking, and my fae ears picked up every sound. I pulled out my phone, looking for the small airfield.

"Should be just up ahead." I clasped my mate's hand and pulled him closer. He stared at nothing. "Hey, we're almost there."

"That's the problem," he said without looking at me.

"What do you mean?"

"The closer we get, the more nervous I am. I have these vague memories of him when I was little. I don't really know why we stopped visiting him." He finally looked at me. "What if it's my fault we never came back?"

"I don't have the best experience with fathers so... But I doubt it was anyone's fault. We have to try at least. Right?" I gave his hand a little squeeze. "Besides, how could anyone hate you? I believe in you and so should you." I kissed his cheek. "Now, let's find the pilot and get going."

The airfield—if you could call a dirt strip and single hanger an airfield—stood solitary in an open field, a single prop plane sat on the only section of blacktop.

I looked at Brynjar. "You ready for this?"

"Not sure. How about you? We'll have to jump from that thing and fly. You ready to test out those wings?"

I grinned and tugged him forward.

A tall, thin man with a scruffy beard and long, curly hair pulled back in a ponytail strode out from the hanger as we approached. His jeans were stained with grease, but the opposite was true of his clean, green sweater. He wiped his hands on a red rag as we approached.

"You the newlyweds?" he asked us.

"Yeah. I'm Emma and this is my husband, Ben." I smiled.

"Morning. I'm Jonas. You sure you two want to go to Bear Island? There's really nothing there."

"We're sure." I told him.

He shrugged and walked off toward the plane to open the door and tossed his bag on the pilot's seat. Jonas flipped the seat down when we joined him.

"Not much room but hop in. I gotta top off the tank and we'll be ready."

We peered into the plane as our pilot went to prepare.

"It's smaller than that first cabin," Brynjar whispered.

"Yeah, but there are windows and we won't be here long. What are we going to tell him just before we jump out?"

"Hel if I know. This is your show." He laughed.

"Gee, thanks!" I jabbed him in the ribs before climbing in.

We only had to wait a few minutes before we were in the air. I'd only been on a large plane once and taking off in a smaller aircraft was shakier than that experience.

The pilot's voice chirped in our headsets. "So, what makes two newlyweds from America come all the way to Bear Island?"

I thought for a minute before an idea came to me. "Well, we're sorta adventurers—daredevils, if you will. We do all kinds of crazy things like base jumping and stuff." I ignored Brynjar's questioning eyes.

"Okay, but what's on Bear Island? Why can't you do that stuff closer to home?"

This guy wasn't going to let it go.

"We like to travel to new places and see lands few humans have," I said flatly, staring out the window.

Jonas shrugged. "If that's what keeps life interesting, I guess."

With that, he stopped asking questions.

Brynjar's voice in my head broke the silence about an hour later. *'We're getting closer. We should go soon.'*

I nodded and shifted in my seat. We both strapped our backpacks to our chests. With one last look at my mate, I climbed up to the seat next to our pilot.

"You know how I said we do all kinds of crazy things?" I asked into my headset.

Jonas looked at me, wide-eyed.

"This is one of those things. I'm sorry, but we don't want you to keep going." I focused on my magic and sent everything I could to Jonas, hoping the spell would work. "In fact, the moment we're out, I need you to head back home and forget you ever took the plane out today. You will live your life without ever remembering you met us. Do you understand?"

"Yes, ma'am," Our pilot said mechanically. I turned and looked at Brynjar.

He nodded. "Ready when you are."

I opened the door and a sudden rush of cold air pushed me back into my seat. I exhaled, every nerve buzzed, and my vision blurred. If I jumped and couldn't handle my wings, I'd drown—in freezing cold water.

The image of a dying Yggdrasil popped in my head, so I pushed forward and dove headfirst out of the tiny aircraft. The air rushed past my ears, deafening me.

'Drop your glamour,' I heard Brynjar's voice say.

I focused my mind, letting my true self out. The wind tugged at my wings, sending pain rippling down my spine. With a wince, I squeezed my wings tighter to my back, afraid to move.

'Open them, damn it, Emma! You're falling too fast!'

'I can't! It hurts!'

'Do it! Make it quick! It'll burn, but you'll live!' His voice sounded distant.

I shut my eyes and braced for the pain. My wings spread wide, catching the wind. Stabbing pain bore into the spot where they met my back, but I held on. My descent slowed, and I was gliding.

'Good! Now follow me.' My mate's form appeared in front of me, heading toward the only landmass in the water below. I stared at his back in flight. Every muscle rippled down his back.

'Damn, I'm liking the view!' I shouted to his mind.

'Focus, Emma.' I heard the grin in his voice.

I flapped my wings and followed my mate to his father's home. Every muscle in my back ached as the island grew closer. We circled it once before we spotted a group of people standing on the shore and even from this height, I could see they were all armed and were wearing stern expressions.

'The second we land, take a knee. I don't know how they will react to us. I love you my Kompis.' His internal voice was shaking.

'I will. I love you too!'

Brynjar twisted and angled his body so he descended toward the group. I forced my sore wings to follow. He landed gracefully on the beach and knelt before the strangers while I landed in a heap, tasting sand.

"We beg an audience with Espen the Mighty," Brynjar spoke without lifting his head.

I raised my gaze to see one of the warriors step up to him, spear pointed at his neck. My body tensed.

"And who asks this of us?" The man's voice was rough. Dark fur draped down his back and around his body like a second skin.

Brynjar lifted his eyes and slowly stood, not breaking contact with the man.

"I am Brynjar Armel Alm. King of Alfheim and this is my queen, Emma Marie Rødt Tre Alm." His voice rang out with strength he hadn't had a moment ago.

The man that stood before him lowered his weapon. A grin slowly grew on his face. "My son! You have returned to me!" Espen clasped my mate around the shoulders and Bryn relaxed. The man turned to where I sat. "And why is your mate cowering in the sand? Rise my child and welcome!"

I stood and brushed the sand from my body.

Brynjar's father let out a deep laugh. "New to the wings? Or are you just terrible at flying?"

I tried to smile. "They're new... It's complicated. And I'm exhausted." It took all my strength not to collapse back into the sand.

My mate's arm quickly wrapped around my waist, helping me stand. I leaned into him gratefully.

"Might we take this conversation somewhere else?" Bryn asked his father.

"Yes, yes." He turned to his people. "My friends, this is my family. My long-lost love bore me a son and here he is, returned to me. Please fetch them some food and water. We will retire to my cabin to let them rest from their long journey." The people behind him nodded and headed back into the woods. He turned his attention back to the pair of us. "Please, come. Rest while they gather supplies. We'll talk once you have eaten." He stepped up to us, pulling us both into his embrace. He kissed each of us on the cheek before he turned and started walking along a narrow path in the trees.

CHapTer 33

Damion

D ays blurred together as the darkness surrounded me. I sagged at my weight. Fresh blood dripped to the stone floor as the chains bit into my flesh. I drifted in and out of consciousness. The once vibrant siren on my chest no longer swam or stabbed at me. Instead, she lay in a heap, gasping for breath.

The end drew closer. I had robbed my body of nutrients. How long had it been since Emma left me? Since I chained myself up here? Fuzzy images of my life as a siren and as a fae swirled around my mind, but I couldn't hold on to a single thought.

A squeak roused me from my haze. I tried to lift my head, but the weight of it crippled me. The light footsteps slowed as they approached. With all the strength I had, I lifted my eyes enough to see the fae that stood before me. His tiny body shook and dark skin blended into the rocks around him, but his bright eyes shined in the black room.

His voice broke. "Master?"

"Don't..." I whispered. Sand coated my throat. "Don't call me Master."

"What else should I call you?"

"Damion. I'm no one's master." My voice grew stronger as I spoke.

"But we need a master."

"I choose you to rein in my stead."

"Sir?"

"You heard me. You are the new leader of Svartalfheim."

"But you don't even know my name, Sir."

"I know you came down here when no one else would." I coughed hard, spitting up blood. The life drained out of me with every breath.

The dark fae reached for the door, keys in hand.

"No!" I barked out. "Not while she lives."

I wheezed as I tried to catch my breath. Every ounce of me begged for death. My stomach shriveled in on me, and my muscles ached. My knees gave out, pulling the chains tight on my wrists. I winced as the iron dug deeper.

My body shook as I wept dry tears. A bright light shone from the corner of my eye and I blinked at the vision before me. The figure stood in the corner of my cell and smiled.

"I'm ready," I whispered to the figure.

"Sire?" the dark fae asked.

My head dropped as everything vanished.

I swam back in my home waters. My small body wove through the crowd at the center of town while Mother and Father hovered in front of their people.

Father's strong shoulders straightened as his booming voice spread through the crowd. "The rumors of Herrick having a spy in our midst are simply that. They are only rumors."

Murmurs erupted. The people screamed and cried. Everyone questioned him. I didn't understand. Why were they questioning his word?

"Silence!" He shouted above the noise. The people hushed. "Have I not promised to keep you safe? Why do you question me now? Please, trust me. I will protect you no matter what happens. I give you my word."

His stone face watched the people until they departed. He gripped my mother's hand and swam toward home. My gut churned. I hustled off toward my shortcut, praying to the gods I bet them home.

I snuck into my room, leaving the door ajar. They arrived shortly after me. Silence filled the space for a long moment before Father spoke. My heart sank at the new quality of his voice as I listened to their conversation through the cracked door.

"I don't know how much longer I can lie to my people." Father spoke in hushed tones to mother. "We need to find the spy."

I peeked out my door and watched them. Father's back was to me. I watched as mother gripped his arm, her eyes locked on his while her other hand reached for something behind her.

"I know how much you love *your* people." Something un-motherly seeped from her words. "You have always put them above all else." Her gaze turned from the loving mother I thought I knew to something else entirely. Her eyes hardened, and a scowl spread across her face.

I caught the glint of light moments before she pulled the dagger out from behind her back. I clasped my hands over my mouth a moment too late as she plunged it into Father's chest. "You have always loved your people more than me. I am your spy, and it is too late to save your people."

My mind froze for an instant as the sounds of my dying father pulled at my heart. I retreated further into my room before she noticed me. What had I just seen? It had to be a lie.

"Damion?" Her voice echoed down the hall. My heart raced. I dove though the open window and swam away.

The screams of the people emanated all around me as my eyes scanned the village. Mercenaries pulled the people from their homes. The water turned red with the blood of those that resisted.

My mind raced for an escape. *The caves*. I searched for a clear path toward my favorite retreat.

I swam for it. Mother's calls rang out behind me. She would find me there. Where? Where else? The garden. The vines scared me. She wouldn't look for me there. I gulped down hard and swam in the opposite direction.

The fighting hadn't reached the center of the town where the dome sat. I pushed open the door and closed my eyes as I swam inside.

My heart beat faster and faster. They'd see my shadow. I knew they would. I forced my eyes open. Vines, vines, vines everywhere. Tears streamed down my cheeks. I swam closer to the creepy, crawling plants.

I shuddered as I pushed past the plants and swam under the tables and curled into a ball. I covered my ears and waited for the noise to settle. But the quiet never came, instead the door shattered and the fae filtered in.

My breathing grew ragged. I tried to cover my mouth, but the moment I moved, I heard one of them shout. "Over there!"

I shot up and tried to swim away, but they grabbed me by the tail and pulled me back. I screamed, they laughed.

I woke in my bedroom in Svartalfheim. My vision blurred. I tried to move, but my limbs were heavy, unmovable. I blinked. Death should've taken my body from me. I should be floating in the nothingness. Shouldn't I?

A shiver ran down my spine. I shouldn't be cold. Igulped down sulfurous air. Breathing? Was I actually breathing? I tried to focus my eyes, but the world spun.

"Settle, Sire. You are still healing," a voice spoke.

"No... I can't be..." my voice rasped out.

"You are alive... for now."

"The siren?" I tried to move my hand to my chest, but something pinned me down.

"She is dead," The voice answered me. "But you are severely weakened. I... I don't know how else to help you."

"You should have let me die." Tears fell down the side of my face and into my ears. I shut my eyes and begged the gods to end this misery.

CHAPTER 34

Brynjar

W e followed my father's men further and further into the barren island. The sharp rocks cut into my hands as we climbed the side of the cliff. I pulled my pack from my chest, grabbed the jacket Emma had bought me and put it on uncomfortably over my wings, but I was warmer. My eyes fell on my mate, who was grinning.

"Cold?" She laughed.

"Where I come from, it's always warm. I'm not used to the cold," I shivered.

"Sorry. Where I come from, this is an ordinary winter day." I stared at her as she raced up the side of the rocks with ease. She had grown stronger since she left us on the battlefield. My chest tightened, remembering waking up to find her gone.

When we reached the top of the mountain, my hand wrapped around hers, pulling her into me and held on tight. My lips found hers. I savored the taste of her until a cough in front of us broke us apart. I lifted my head to see my father staring at the two of us.

"I can tell you are newly mated, but can it wait," he gestured to a cave ahead, "until we get inside?"

I flushed. Emma and I walked hand in hand, following them inside.

'What was that about?' My mate's voice echoed in my head.

'I don't want to miss a moment with you. I remember what it felt like to lose you. I can't ever feel that way again. '

She wrapped her arm around my waist in a sideways hug. *'No matter what, my Kompis.'*

I couldn't describe how it warmed me to hear those words from her without it causing either of us pain. My chest swelled at everything we had been through in such a short time. I held her closer to me as we entered the cave.

Narrow walls closed in on me as we walked. Voices echoed around me. The chill bit at my bones until my jaw was trembling. The darkness finally released me when we reached an open space carved out of the stone. Wooden torches lined the walls as my father and his men led us around the outer walls. Smaller domed huts sat around the outer cave walls and a large fire pit in the center. A few smaller archways were carved into the main cave walls. My father stopped at the largest one and the others walked inside. We stopped when we reached him.

"What is this place?" I asked him.

"This is my home. We have much to talk about, my son."

I nodded as we walked inside.

A space similar to the one we just left only on a much larger scale. The massive, cavernous space stretched out further than I could see. Sunlight spilled in from holes high above us, illuminating the room. This was not like the caves of Svartalfheim. Where Herrick's home was dark and cold, this was inviting. The sandy walls absorbed the heat from the many fires spread out around the space. Smaller dome structures encircled one larger one.

I stopped walking and looked back the way we came. "If this is your home, what was that?" I asked my father.

"That is where our warriors sleep to protect the rest of the village. We have an intricate tunnel system with many caves such as this." He spread his arms wide indicating this space.

He clapped me on the back as he led the way to the central building. All eyes turned on us as we passed.

Father lifted the flap and let us enter the tent first. The tanned leather walls stretched up so high we could stand up right even at the rim. A hole at the top let out the smoke from the fire in the center of the floor. Everyone sat around the center on the rocky floor until my father stepped inside and they all stood at once, bowing to him.

"Sit my children." His cool voice washed over the room. I marveled at the respect his people gave him. They tentatively sat at his command. His gaze turned to me as he took a seat at the head of the circle of people and gestured for us to sit beside him.

Emma and I tucked our wings tight behind us as we navigated around his people. I gulped down the fear of all their eyes on us and sat beside my father.

"My family," his voice rang out. "This is my son. He may look fae, but he is mine, I assure you all." He looked at me, but my voice had retreated. "Tell them."

"It is true," my mate spoke for me. "I saw it for myself. Herrick had held me against my will and Brynjar came to rescue me. As we tried to escape, Herrick stopped us. He would have killed me, but..." Her words trailed off.

"I saw her in pain and I... I don't know what happened exactly, but I... I shifted and I..."

"You what?" My father asked.

"It's pretty graphic. I don't think I should go into too much detail." I gulped.

"Son, we are a clan of berserker warriors. There is no such thing as 'too graphic' for us." He laughed. "Besides, these who sit before you are the strongest of our leaders."

"Ok," I breathed out. "Well, I sorta tore his throat out with my teeth. I can still taste the blood." I swallowed hard at the memory.

"How can we trust one with wings?" a muscular man wearing a wolf skin on his head asked.

"Because I say it is true." My father's voice never rose, but his anger emanated from each word.

The crowd hushed at his words.

"Please, my son, tell us why you came to us?" he asked me in a softer tone. "Then we can discus other things in private."

"Emma's father was King Herrick of Svartalfheim. He poisoned Yggdrasil with iron ash beetles in hopes to destroy it and bring about Ragnarök. After what I saw in his dungeon, I think you can help us." I tried to hide the desperation in my voice.

"And how's that?" my father asked.

"Well, I noticed something unusual, and I think I need to confirm my suspicions first."

"Go on," father said.

"When I was imprisoned by Herrick, I was in a cage with iron bars. If I were just fae, it would have killed me, but instead it..."

"Made you stronger," my father answered.

"Yes. I have always known I wasn't pure fae, but I never knew what I was. My mother told me that the fae side was stronger." I looked at my mate. "I guess she was wrong. The longer I stayed trapped in that cage, the more I sensed the unfamiliar magic. My blood was no longer pure white. The bear was waking. It was as if the iron fed him. And then when Emma... It just burst forth and I had little control over him."

"The beast usually only shows itself in great need. You needed to save her, and he gave you that chance."

I nodded at my father.

"So, what is your plan?" my father asked.

"I... we... I think it's best if my mate explains."

Emma shifted her weight, tucking her legs under her. She rolled her sleeves up to reveal her angel vine tattoos.

"My mother told me they were from Jörð. After my father killed her, he took control of me. I did some awful things. But when I got home, I healed my friend when no one else could. I believe I can pull the iron and the beetles out of the tree, but it would kill any one of the fae to deal with it, but not you. You could use the iron to strengthen yourselves." She lowered her sleeves.

My father licked his lips and looked to the man on his right. They leaned in, whispering to each other before father turned back to us.

"We have no use for Yggdrasil, yet if it falls, it will affect us all. We will need to discuss our options, son. I hope you understand."

I bowed my head slightly.

Father beckoned to a man standing by the flap who approached but halted just before he reached us.

"You've had a long journey getting to us. Why don't you rest? Dion will take you to my dwelling and bring you some food. I will come to you when we are finished here."

I bowed again and stood, offering Emma a hand up. We followed Dion out of the building and down the natural path between the structures. We veered into the nearest circle of homes. A large fire sat in the middle of the ring. Several women tended to various meats cooking on a spit. My stomach growled at the aroma.

Dion stopped and raised his hand for us to stay where we stood. He walked over to the women and spoke to them, pointing back to us. Her eyes widened, but she nodded.

He approached us again and gestured to a hut like all the others only with a large red paw print over the opening flap. "Elder Espen's house is this first one. Please." He walked inside without looking back.

The room was pitch black. Dion snapped his fingers and torches flickered to life. I paused at the use of magic. I had never seen anyone other than the fae use magic.

Dion noticed my surprise then scoffed at me. "You are not the only creatures with magic, little one. Your race is not as special as they like to believe."

I shook my head and looked around. The space was as barren as the rocks on the surface. Furs lined the floor in one corner and a wooden ladder led up to a small loft.

"We are not used to visitors, so our homes tend to support only our needs." His words were cold. "There is a bed in the loft, though. Jewel will bring you some food."

"Does everyone hate us?" I heard Emma ask before I could stop her.

Dion turned on her. "Hate wouldn't be the correct word. More fear." He dropped his glare. "Our ancestors were slaughtered by your kind. We are so few today because of it. To further expand the wound, your father chose to breed with a fae and not one of his own kind. Ever since then, he has not taken another."

"So, I'm an abomination in both my mother's realm and my father's," I said under my breath, but Emma's arm wrapped around mine told me she at least heard me.

"You're not an abomination... just an anomaly... There are other half-breeds," Dion said as if it were common knowledge. My heart leapt at the thought that I wasn't the only one.

A knock at the door bolted me out of my thoughts.

"Enter," Dion said.

"I brought you some food." The woman bowed her head low, handing the plates to me.

"Thank you," I said, taking them from her. She turned and scurried out of the room without another word.

"Eat, rest. Once the elders are through speaking, your father will return. I'd suggest waiting here until he comes back, though." The man gave a slight bow before exiting.

I took the steaming plate and sat on the fur, staring past the food. Emma's warmth brushed my side, and I looked over to where she sat.

"I'm not the only half-breed." I smiled at my mate.

CHaPTer 35

Emma

It was late into the night when Espen's soft footsteps finally returned home. Or at least, I thought it was night. Being inside the cave, I couldn't tell day from night. The only comfort was being in his loft reminded me of Brynjar's treehouse. I remained on the pile of furs, curled against Brynjar, and listened to Espen's quiet preparations for sleep. Brynjar had laid silently on the floor next to me for the longest time before my body gave into exhaustion.

When I woke to the sounds of footsteps below us, I turned to Brynjar and found his eyes open and alert. I doubted he got any sleep. At the sound of Espen climbing the ladder, I sat up.

"You're awake? Good. We have much to talk about. Please, come join me," he said before descending again.

I turned to Brynjar. "Did you sleep at all?"

"My mind is racing. So much has happened. I'm sorry, my love. I will sleep after we talk. I promise." He kissed the top of my head before crawling toward the ladder and down to the lower level.

Exhaustion dragged be down as I forced my feet to follow.

Downstairs, Brynjar and his father were already sitting cross-legged on the furs, simply watching each other.

I took a seat next to my mate and when I put a hand on his shoulder, he jolted at my touch.

"I'm sorry." I pulled my hand back quickly.

The two of them laughed.

"No, it is I that should apologize, Miss Emma." Espen looked to me. "We were chatting."

My jaw dropped. "You didn't look like you were talking..."

"We were speaking mind to mind. Much in the same way you two are able to communicate."

My mate clarified. "When I was locked up in Herrick's dungeon and things were getting worse, I heard him. I could feel my bear fighting for control and was lost. He helped show me the way. Now that we are here, I can hear him as clearly as I can you."

"That's... great." I tried to smile. Now was not the time to be jealous. "So, what have you been talking about?"

"He asked about my mother." Brynjar swallowed hard before he continued. "She's... she died several years ago. I was left with the guard to be raised when I was twelve."

I wrapped my arm around his back, squeezing him. Bile rose in my throat as I digested his words. He knew just about every piece of my past and secret, yet I knew little of his. I had been too wrapped up in my own problems to ask him these things.

'It's not your fault, my Kompis. I don't think less of you for not asking. I've never been that easy to open up about my childhood. You are my mate, my world, and that is all that matters.'

His voice was like a cool breeze in my mind, and I loved him even more for it. I rested my head on his shoulder, kissing his neck.

His father smiled but his eyes were full of sadness. "I am pleased you found a love like I had, son. Your mother used to visit me. The last time I saw either of you was the day she took you away."

"I'm sorry no one told you. We didn't..."

Espen waved his hand. "We have lived apart for so long. It is as much my fault as anyone's. She begged me to come home with her, but my people needed me."

"And what about now? Will you come home with me?" Brynjar asked nervously.

Espen blew out a long breath. "We as a people have lived in hiding for so long that it was a difficult decision to make. We have been hunted by human and fae alike. My people are afraid." He rested his head in his hands for a long moment before he spoke again. "But even we understand the importance of Yggdrasil. It is the only thing that stands in the way of Ragnarök, and not even the Berserker's here on the island could survive that. My warriors are gathering as we speak. They will take the day to prepare and say their goodbyes and we will leave at dusk."

"Thank you, Father!" Pride swelled in my mate's voice. "But... How? How will we get there? Emma and I have traveled far to get to you and you don't have wings like we do."

"My son, I think it is time you learn that more than fae magic runs through those veins of yours." He stood, offering Brynjar a hand up. "Come, let me show you who you truly are."

Brynjar

My father led us back out into the early morning light on the rocky surface of the island, Emma's arm entwined with mine. Her warmth enveloped me and blocked the chill from the air. It was only now that the twinge of her magic surrounded me.

'Are you shielding me?' I asked her.

'I wouldn't want you to freeze to death.'

'And why didn't you do this on the walk here?' I asked her, remembering how she laughed at me.

'I might have been coming down from a mild panic attack and wasn't thinking clearly. I'm sorry.' She looked down at her feet.

I lifted her chin. My grin spread ear to ear and I jabbed a finger into her ribs just to watch her squirm.

'You know I love you, right?'

'I know,' she said.

My father finally stopped walking, turned around, and gestured for us to stand next to him. The cave's entrance was far off, hidden within the mountain, and the distant sound of the ocean was barely audible.

"Here is a good spot," Father announced.

"For what?" I asked tentatively.

"You were raised and trained in only one source of magic, but you are more than fae. I will show you my magic." He took a few steps forward and the wild electrical buzz filled the air. He stood with his legs apart and bent at the knees and a fist in his palm before he lowered his head. He moved his hands, palms toward the earth, and spun them around him in wide circles. The air seemed to move with his hands, kicking up dust with his movement.

He finally raised his head and thrust his hands forward toward us. The burst of wind nearly knocked me over. He lowered his hands to his side and walked past us. We turned to see a huge spinning circle of darkness several feet behind us.

"What the Hel is that?" I heard Emma ask.

"That, Miss Emma, is a portal." He stepped through it and vanished. I stepped behind it to find nothing, and back to the side where my mate still stood, stunned. And then my father stepped back through the hole of darkness, grinning. He offered Emma his hand and pulled her through. I was quick on their heels.

This was nothing to the cold pull of Yggdrasil. Stepping through this portal was easier than walking through a doorway. We now stood in front of the cave's entrance. I looked from the portal to my father. He smiled and retreated back into the portal. Emma laughed and grabbed my wrist, pulling me back through with her.

Once we joined him, my father clapped his hands and the portal dissipated.

"That is how we will travel. Much easier than the spiriting of the fae. You have the ability to do such magic as well, but portals are harder to make. I will teach you someday, though. For now, we need to control your beast." He nodded his head toward me. I looked down and saw the black fur creeping up my arms. I jumped away from Emma, trying to rein in my emotions.

"Our magic tends to awaken the beasts if we aren't trained for it. And you are far older than most who are trained in shifting," My father explained.

Emma's laugh broke the fear in my chest. My eyes snapped at her. "What?" I demanded.

She took a few steps backward and sat on the rocks. "Now it's my turn to watch you learn. It's an interesting twist of events. I wish I had some popcorn." My father and I both looked at my mate as she fell into a fit of laughter. "You two are definitely related! You look more like twins than Aric and I." She was gasping for air and ignored my glare. "Sorry." She finally slowed her breathing and tried to straighten herself. "Go on."

I turned back to my Herrick. "You'll have to forgive her. She was raised human and not quite right sometimes."

My Herrick grinned. "Very well. Now, I want you to think back to that first shift. Tell me in as much detail what happened and what you experienced."

I closed my eyes and thought back.

"Emma was on the ground screaming in pain. Her father had done something to her. He was inside her mind, hurting her. Then... rage... that's all I could feel. Rage for Herrick. I... I couldn't even see anything. I blocked out her screaming and even her image. All I could see was his blood. The burning pain came next. It started at my feet and worked its way up until every inch of me felt like it was on fire. And then everything changed, and I charged him. I can't even remember killing him. The next thing I can remember is Emma telling me how amazing I was. It was the most painful thing I've ever felt. I... I don't think I can do that again." I looked up at my father, who only nodded, and pulled the fur coat off his back, standing naked before us.

Fur crawled up his flesh with ease. His body turned and bent in odd angles until he stood on all fours. His beast was even more massive than I'd expected with fur as dark as mine, and paws nearly as wide as my chest. Then he shifted just as easily back into his human form.

"When you shift out of rage and necessity, it can be painful... especially for the first time, but I promise it will get easier." He bent and picked up his fur, wrapping it around him again. "Can you still feel your bear?"

I cocked my head, searching for him. A low humming, almost purr like sound filled my ears. "Yes. He's strong." I laughed at the image of a massive bear rolling around the ground. "And a little goofy."

Just like my mate.' Emma's voice spoke to only me.

My father smiled. "As he should be. There is no one to rival my bear, so yours will be a force as well once you both are trained. Call to him. Invite him to come forth. Let him know it is safe and that no harm will come to anyone. If you show fear, he will burst through with rage like before and it will be painful, but if you are calm, he will walk right in."

I took a deep breath, pushing the panic down. I stripped out of my new clothes, knowing my mate would be pissed if I tore them up and I called to him. Tried to coax him out, but my mind slipped and I felt Emma's pain all over again. That burning fire ripped through me and I collapsed to the ground, gasping.

'Calm, my Kompis, I'm right here and we're safe.' Her voice slammed into me like a wave extinguishing the flames.

My bear stepped closer at the presence of her voice. When I opened my eyes again, I stood above both of them. I looked down and saw paws where once there were feet. I scrambled from my father and mate.

'Calm.' I heard her say again. *'You're safe.'*

'Do not let your fear control you, my son.' My father voice joined with my mate's to still my heart. I sat on my haunches and watched them. The concern faded from their faces.

'Good. Now shift back. Tell your bear it is time to sleep again.' My father instructed me.

I told my bear what to do and slowly—and far less painful—he retreated, leaving me gasping on the rocks. Emma was by my side in a flash. I sat up to meet her touch, and she fell into my lap. Her lips on mine woke every part of me as I pulled her tighter.

"Umm..." My father's voice broke us apart. "I really am sorry to break this up, but I think we should get ready to leave." He raised his hands, creating his portal again, and stepped through it.

Emma's face flushed, and she buried it in my neck and laughed.

"That wasn't at all awkward. And I'm afraid to stand up right now," I said, making her laugh even harder. I hugged her tighter to my chest. "I could always snap my fingers and remove your clothes and make this quick?"

She pulled her face away from my neck with a grin doing exactly what I had just threatened to do. She moved on my lap, reaching between her thighs grasping my hardened shaft, guiding it to her entrance before pushing herself onto me. I moaned as she wrapped her legs around my waist sheathing me deeper into her. I wouldn't last long with the heat of her passion. She ground her hips against me in rapid movements.

I buried my head in her bare chest, kissing the skin between her breasts. She tightened around me with a gasp.

"Fuck, Bryn, I'm going to come so hard after watching you shift," she breathed into my ear. She moved faster and faster against me, moaning with every movement until I shattered into her with a groan. Her climax erupted from her a moment later.

Emma sighed, laying her head on my shoulder. "I could do that all day with you, but we should get dressed and head back before your dad comes looking for us."

I grunted my agreement before stealing a few more kisses. She pushed off me and snapped her fingers. Reluctantly, I stood and walked through the portal with my mate.

CHAPTER 36

Damion

My muscles burned and body weakened as I laid in bed for what had to be days, unable to do anything else. Thoughts of Yggdrasil and Emma flashed in my mind. I tried to remove the covers, but even the weight of the blanket was too much.

The dark fae who'd freed me from my cage slouched in the corner of the room, sleeping. My mind only now was clear enough to wonder his name. We were all on the brink of death, and I was worrying about one creature's name? My father would have cared.

My thoughts froze at the last images I saw of my father. What I remembered of him was he'd been kind, always. My heart swelled at the memories of him flooding from where they'd been hiding. I'd swim around my room giving speeches to my toys, pretending to be him. If I could do one last thing with my life, it would be to make him proud.

I grunted as I forced my body to sit upright. A fresh wave of coughing from my already exhausted body woke the fae in the chair. I slumped back against the wall as he stood and walked to me.

"Sire, you should be resting." His gentle eyes watched me. He pulled a rag from the table and dabbed the corner of my lips. Green blood tinged the rag as he set it aside.

"There's nothing left for me. The one thing I can do with what's left of my life is save yours." My words came out slow and pained. I rubbed at my chest. "Water?" I choked out.

He flicked his wrist and produced a glass and handed it to me. I gulped it down in a single breath not caring that the sooty liquid tasted awful, it wet my dry throat.

"What's your name?" I asked him as I handed back the now empty glass.

"Evander." He bowed low.

"Evander, I need your help." I waited for him to rise. "Please, sit." The small fae hesitated before he pulled his chair over and sat next to the bed. "Herrick has destroyed Yggdrasil, and I fear nothing can save it. The man trusted me with every secret he had. I think... I think I can help protect the realms but not from this bed."

"You are too weak, m'lord. You can't leave until you heal."

"I won't get better." My heart skipped at the truth of my words. Ever since the cell, an eerie presence watched over me, waiting for me. I couldn't shake it, even in sleep. "I think... maybe the siren leached a toxin as she was dying. Everything I try to eat and even that water tastes like ash in my mouth. Just sitting here talking to you weakens me."

Evander's eyes glossed over but his words were strong. "Then, if I may be so bold," he cocked his head, "what can you do to save the Tree?"

"I think I may know of a way to protect the realms. But... I don't know who to trust anymore." I rubbed at my temples. "Images of my life before Herrick cloud my mind." A few stray tears dripped down my nose as I hung my head.

The fae sat in silence for a long minute, letting me clear my thoughts. When I finally looked back up at him, his cheeks were wet as well. I wiped my face before I spoke. "I need to get to Alfheim. Emma is the only one I will speak to."

"Sire? You can hardly sit up. How do you intend to get to Alfheim?"

"I... I need to borrow some strength. Just enough to help me get to the gateway and then it's up to the gods if they believe me worthy." I watched the wheels slowly turn in his eyes.

"The dark fae have been under the rule of Herrick for so long we forgot what freedom feels like. You could have easily taken over after his death and continued the rein of torment. You may not have personally dispatched the man, but you freed us. I believe there are enough of us that would be willing to lend you our strength to do what you need to do, but..." Evander stood and placed his hand on my shoulder. "You will be missed, Sire." He wiped his eyes before rushing out the door.

I must have fallen asleep the moment Evander departed because the next thing I knew, at least thirty dark fae surrounded my bed. I startled slightly at the sight until my eyes found Evander's. He worked his way through the crowd and stood beside me.

He bowed slightly before he spoke. "We've all come to give you the strength you need." He smiled.

"Wh-what do I need to do?"

"Nothing, Sire. We will transfer a bit of our power to you and that will allow you to feel more like yourself for a time. It will be temporary, but it should last long enough to help you on your journey." He turned and nodded to the others. They all placed both hands on the shoulders in front of them. Evander on one side of the bed and another fae on the other both placed their hands on me.

The fae all bowed their heads and whispered a spell in their native tongue. Their words danced off their lips and poured into my soul. Tears fell from every eye.

A rush of magic flowed over me, pushing me back against the headboard. I gasped for breath. Their gifts scattered to every cell of my body, igniting the darkness with a warm glow. My limbs lightened, more so than when I was floating in the water back home. Every trace of the sickness I'd been battling vanished.

The two fae beside me dropped their hands and wobbled on their feet. Evander looked to the others and one by one they departed until I was again alone with him.

"Feel better, Sire?"

"Yes, thank you." I threw the covers off and stood tentatively, even though I thought I could run through a stone wall. I raised my fingers to snap, but Evander clasped my hand.

"Careful. Any magic use will drain you quicker. I recommend only using what you absolutely need."

I sighed. Stripping off my stiff and dirtied clothes, I walked to the bathroom and took a quick shower under the hot water before dressing while Evander waited in my room.

"Last chance to change your mind," he said.

"If Yggdrasil dies, then we all die. My life is not worth the rest of the realms."

"Very well. Would you like some assistance getting to the gateway?"

I thought for a moment. Walking would take too long and spiriting would be taxing, yet I couldn't take any more from the fae. I took a deep breath and looked around before looking back at him.

"No. This is something I need to do for myself. You and your people have done enough for me. When I get to Alfheim, I will let them know you are no longer an enemy." I bowed low to Evander.

He bowed in return. When we rose, tears rimmed both our eyes. "Thank you," I breathed out.

"No, thank you." He turned and walked out without another word.

I stood alone in the room I had called home for most of my life. It was as cold as Herrick had been. Not one single item held any personal value to me. I had been his tool and nothing more.

I shut my eyes, imagining the water from my childhood surrounded me once again. My room when I was little held drawings of my family and toys and instruments. I loved music. The melodies of my favorite song washed over me. My father had taught me how to play. He had loved me before his people. Mother had been wrong.

With great effort I pulled myself into spirit, willing my body to move through space to the gateway. The icy chill stabbed at my flesh, threatening to pull me out, but when I opened my eyes again, I was in front of a massive wooden gate that stood tall. My words were still etched among the vines.

My knees buckled, and I collapsed into the hard earth. I gulped in as much air as my lungs could handle.

"I am so sorry for the pain I have caused you." I pleaded with the tree.

I braced myself on its trunk and forced my legs to stand. My hand reached out to the gateway, hovering just above the spot that would take me into Emma's realm.

"Please, let me pass," I begged the twins that resided inside the Great Tree. "I need to save you. To save Emma. Please." My fingers grazed the spot, and I waited... prayed I'd feel the pull.

CHAPTER 37

Aric

My smile grew the longer I laid next to her naked form, her warmth spreading a joy I had never known before. As I trailed my fingers down her spine, Thyra rolled over to her side and cracked her eyes open.

"Morning," she sighed.

I captured her mouth with mine in response. Even after a night's sleep, her lips tasted sweet on mine. I breathed her in, freezing everything about this moment in my memory. She was my queen in every way, and I wanted to worship her all day, kiss every inch of her.

She let out a soft moan as my lips caressed her neck, then rolled over to her back, exposing her breasts. My palms massaged them with gentle passion.

She arched her back and sighed deeply. I moved to rest on her hips and laid my body on top of hers. Her eyes snapped open wide, and she shoved me off her.

"What?" I asked, landing beside her.

"I... sorry." She averted her gaze.

"What's the matter, Thyra?" Panic tightened my chest. Why did my mate not want me? I started to get out of bed when her hand grasped my wrist and I turned to see her smile and glistening eyes looking back at me. She pulled me closer, laying my hand on her stomach. She didn't say anything, just sat there like that for a long while.

I broke the silence. "What's going on, Kompis? You're acting strangely."

My hand jiggled with her belly as she laughed.

"I'm trying to tell you something monumental." Her eyes traveled from mine to our hands on her stomach and back again. She stared at me like she was trying to mentally talk to me, but no words were uttered. Her hand moved mine in circles on her belly before it finally clicked into place.

I froze.

My jaw dropped and my voice caught in my throat. "Are you...?"

She nodded.

"Are you certain? There hasn't been a child in Alfheim in..." I cocked my head and laughed. "Well, since Emma and I were born, I suppose."

Her smile widened, and I knew it was true. "Yes, I'm positive."

"How? How do you know already? We've only... only once?"

"Magic," she said. "I sensed it the moment it happened. I've heard it's an old magic meant to protect the child. Since there's so few babies here, our bodies alert us the moment it happens." She grinned at me.

I laid my head on her chest, listening to the thrumming of her heart as I stroked her belly. Mountains of gold weren't as precious as this woman. I gently lowered my face to her stomach and kissed her.

"I can't wait to meet you, my child," I whispered to the unborn baby she held within her.

My eyes found hers again, and I thought I'd burst with joy. I moved back to her face, leaving a trail of kisses as I went.

"I love you." I laid beside her, wrapping my arms around her.

"Really? You're not angry?" she asked so quietly I hardly heard her.

I sat up on an elbow and looked at her. "Why in the Nine Realms would I be angry?" I asked.

"Well... It took you nearly two years to accept me as your Kompis and getting me pregnant our first time I figured would scare the daylights out of you."

I laid my hand back on her stomach and watched the rise and fall of her breathing before I responded. "Thyra, when I saw you jump in front of that trident, my world came crashing down. I'm not the same man I was even earlier that day. Having you here in my bed, as my mate and not just another woman, is everything to me. This baby is the greatest gift you could ever give to me." I lowered my head, kissing her belly again. "I'll do anything to keep the two of you safe. I love you both."

She ran her hands through my hair, pulling me back to her face. My hand slid up and down her.

"Can I? Can we still?" I asked shyly.

She smiled. "I'm pregnant, not broken."

I let my hand travel lower as she opened for me.

A quick rap at our door had me pulling my hand away and the covers back up. Thyra groaned in disappointment. I kissed her cheek and tried to give her an apologetic smile. She shrugged.

"Enter." I didn't bother to hide the irritation in my voice.

The door swung open and in stepped Mayank. He averted his gaze when he saw me laying naked on top of the covers.

"Sorry, Sire." His eyes widened, and he looked at Thyra and back at me, and my smile grew. "Aric? Is she...?" He stammered for the words.

With his abilities to feel other's emotions, it was no wonder Mayank was able to pick up on it so quickly. "She is," I said simply. Our emotions radiated off us as if it were a beam of light.

"Sire, we will need to add more guards to her. She should never be alone. She will need to be protected at all costs."

"*She* is sitting right here and is also one of the most powerful magic users of our people. *She* is fully capable of protecting herself." Thyra spoke, looking from Mayank back to me with fire in her eyes.

I swallowed hard. "How about a compromise?" Her eyebrows lifted at my question. "One guard?"

Her face slacked, and a small grin formed. "One guard," she relented. "But let's not make a huge deal about this just yet. I need to see a midwife first and give it some time before we tell everyone. I don't want to jinx anything." She rubbed her belly.

"Agreed," I told her and turned back to my High Commander. "Why did you come here in the first place?"

Mayank turned ashen before me. "Sorry, I was surprised by her condition. You need to get dressed. Damion is here."

My blood froze at his words and it took the movement of my mate to snap me back to reality. She threw the covers off and snapped her fingers then turned and pulled me off the bed.

"Aric?" Her voice was steady but far away as the world blurred around me. "Aric, my love. We need you."

I shook my head, clearing my thoughts. "Where is he?" My voice didn't sound like my own.

"He came through Yggdrasil. He is still there, surrounded by the Guard. He hasn't made any move against us, but still."

How had he come through Yggdrasil? No enemy could have crossed through the gateway. Maybe in its weakened state the twins within weren't able to regulate the flow like before.

I nodded to Mayank and Thyra, and we spirited on the spot. The cold nothingness of travel was nothing compared to the emptiness I felt within my core. We reemerged in front of the Great Tree. A tall, slender fae clad in black stood in the center of my guard, hands raised high.

My men parted for me as I walked up to the man I assumed to be Damion. He didn't look like much but my sister had feared him, so he had to be stronger than he appeared. I looked at his arms, still raised above his head. He wore long sleeves but had pushed them up, exposing the flesh beneath.

His scars reminded me of Emma's. Hers had faded but Damion's ran deep. There wasn't a spot of virgin skin over his arms. I wanted to feel sympathy for him but couldn't find room in my heart for Herrick's apprentice.

I unsheathed my sword and raised it to his throat.

"What are you doing here?" I demanded.

He grinned. "I have seen the errors of my ways and I beg your humble forgiveness." His words thick with spite.

"Try again." I pressed my blade against his flesh.

Slowly, he knelt before me and bowed his head. "I speak the truth, Sire. I have spent far too long under Herrick's thumb and I only ask for redemption."

I lowered my sword but gripped it tight. This creature has caused such chaos in our world. Even after Herrick's death. I looked around at my guard. Every one of them still held their blades high, ready to strike. Herrick had been highly skilled at mind manipulation. How much had he taught Damion?

I took a step back, bumping into my mate. She brushed past me before I could stop her. "Thyra, no!" I shouted, but she continued forward, hands out in front of her. The presence of her magic swirled in the air and settled on Damion.

She worked in silence for a long moment before she returned, wrapped her arm around my waist, and leaned into me. I laid my arm around her shoulder and hugged her tight to my chest.

Thyra spoke. "He can't do what Herrick did. In fact, his magic is very weak. In his state, I doubt he could harm anyone."

'You shouldn't have done that. I chided her. *You need to save your energy for that baby.'*

'I know what I can handle, my love. We are safe.'

I called for my High Commander without looking away from Damion.

Mayank stepped up beside me. "Yes, Sire?"

"Make sure he is bound and settled into the darkest corner of our dungeons, will you?"

"Yes, sir," he said with an air of enjoyment.

"Aric?" Thyra whispered as she sagged into me.

I pulled my mate closer to me as I spirited us back to our room. She sank gratefully onto the edge of the bed and laid her head down.

"Maybe you have a point. I will ease up on the magic use," she said before sleep overtook her.

I brushed the hair from her face and tucked her under the covers, promising myself I'd call for a midwife the moment she woke.

CHAPTER 38

Emma

We followed Brynjar's father back through the village where every eye watched us pass. The villager's emotions poured into me making me ill. I clutched at my stomach as we walked, praying I could hold it all in. The moment we reached his father's circle, I broke into a run toward the small washroom at the back where a basin of water sat on a table in the corner. I submerged a little cup, leaned over, then poured the water over the back of my neck, letting it drip into the vessel.

A rap on the door broke my silence and Brynjar's raspy voice came from the other side.

"Are you all right, Emma?"

"Better now." I smiled, grateful for the calm the sound of his voice brought.

He opened the door and stepped inside. "What happened?"

I looked up at him. "They're all so stirred up. I couldn't shut them off."

He tilted his head at me.

"Your father's people. They're so full of emotions and I can feel them all. It was a bit overwhelming. They're terrified of us." I sagged into him. Brynjar's strong arms wrapped around me, pulling me to his chest. "Some are angry with us, while others are afraid of what our presence means for their people."

"Not all of my people are scared of you." Espen spoke from the hallway. Brynjar turned around to face his father, never letting go of me. "Some are just as curious about your people as I am." He looked at Bryn. "Even though your mother is gone, I am looking forward to seeing her world. She told me many wonderful things. My people are simply worried about their partners. It has been far too long since any of us have left this island." Espen's attention turned back to me. "Please don't blame them for their fears."

"I... I don't blame them, it's just... Well... I'm an empath so I can feel what they feel. There's a lot of emotions flying around out there and it's overwhelming." I loosened my grip on Brynjar and straightened. "I'm not used to feeling everyone's emotions. I'm better now."

Espen nodded. "Let's eat something before we head out." We followed him back outside to the firepit and sat on the hard rocks as he spoke with one of the women before joining us and said, "Jewel said she'll bring us some fish when it's done."

I settled back in Brynjar's arms, still queasy. I'd been able to sense other emotions and brush them off but this lingered.

'Bryn,' I spoke mind to mind with him. *'Something's wrong. I can feel it but... I don't understand what it is. I need to amplify my ability to reach Aric.'*

He wrapped his fingers around mine, pressing our palms together. *'Take what you need from me and find it.'* He kissed the top of my head and held me tight.

I pulled on his magic until it mixed with mine. My mind reached out for anything that felt off.

I found it in my brother's mind.

"You won't get away with everything you've done no matter what you say," I heard Aric say to someone.

I strained to see what he saw until he came into sharp focus. Damion's slender form sat in a corner of a darkened room. Thick branches caged him in. Dark circles ringed his eyes, his cheeks shallower than the last time I saw him. He was broken. My heart ached to see him that way.

"I've spoken my truth." His voice came out as shattered as his body was. "If you choose not to believe me, that is on you."

"That's not good enough," Aric boomed. "You were Herrick's apprentice. You must have a darker plan. Tell me what it is and I will spare you the same fate that befell him."

Damion's gruff laugh was anything but lighthearted. "His fate? I saw what remained of Herrick. I suppose at least it was quick. And why should I believe that you don't wish me dead? I saw the scar on Yggdrasil. I know what I have done. I'm honestly surprised that I still draw breath."

"You hurt my sister and her mate," Aric said coldly. "I'll leave your fate up to them."

"Ah, and where is the happy couple?"

"Bringing back someone that can save the tree."

"I already told you. There's no hope to save Yggdrasil. It is dying and not even Emma can heal it."

Aric pulled his sword from its scabbard and thrust it through the branches of the cell towards Damion. "And I told you I don't believe you."

Damion didn't move. He didn't even look up at the sword inches from his face. "I don't care what you believe. The truth cannot be changed." He stretched out on the cold floor, resting his head on his arms. "Now, either kill me or let me sleep. Call on me when Emma gets home. She'll believe me."

Aric growled but left his prisoner in the cell. Anger and frustration poured out of him.

'Hold on, brother. We'll be home soon.' I tried to project my thoughts to him. If he felt me, he made no indication of it.

I pulled out of his mind back to where my mate and his father sat staring at me. At some point, Brynjar had slid out from behind me, but his hand still held mine.

"What?" I asked my mate.

"How long do you think you've been sitting there?" Brynjar asked.

I thought it had only been a few minutes, but my joints ached. I shrugged.

"Well, let's just say now that you're back with us, we are all ready to head out," Espen said.

Brynjar pulled me into his lap and hugged me tight before he spoke again. "You've been gone for hours. We tried to wake you, but you didn't respond. I was so worried about you." He kissed my cheek. "What happened?"

"I... I..." My whole body stiffened at what I had seen. "Aric..." I jumped off my mate's lap and pulled him to his feet. "We have to get home! Damion is in Alfheim!"

Brynjar's feet didn't move with mine. "What? How?"

Panic rose in my throat. "I don't know. But Aric will torture him to find out. We have to stop Aric!"

"Stop him?" my mate questioned. "I'll help Aric. Don't you remember what Damion did to me?" Brynjar rubbed his chest as he spoke. "What he did to us?"

"I... I know but..."

Brynjar dropped my hand. "But what? Do you...."

I turned to my mate, tears welling up in his eyes. My hand wrapped around his middle and I buried my head in his chest. '*Never, my Kompis.*' I burned my feelings into him. '*No matter what, it is always you.*'

When his body relaxed, I released him and said, "It is nothing like that. Damion is speaking the truth but Aric is blinded by his anger. If we let him murder Damion in cold blood, Aric will be lost to us. Killing in battle is one thing but Damion's locked in a cell for gods' sake!" I was shouting as I looked at Espen. "Do we have everything we need? How are we going to do this?"

"We are ready if you two are. Let's get outside and we will show you." He turned to Jewel at the fire and rested his forehead on hers a moment before heading toward the cave entrance.

We followed him, stopping just before the tunnel, watching as more and more of his people said their goodbyes and joined us.

I had to shield my eyes from the brightness of the sun as we stepped outside. Espen beckoned us to join him, and he and his warriors formed a circle.

"We cannot create a portal directly into your world, but we can get to Yggdrasil. We just need to see your memories of where the gateway you came through is." He offered a hand to each of us. The moment we took his hand, the gateway in Denmark flooded into my mind. The stone wall and large vine gates came into view, then vanished.

"Thank you. Now, I'd stand back a bit. We haven't tried to create a portal to fit us all through in a while."

Brynjar tucked me in close as we took a few steps back and watched.

The Berserkers lifted their hands parallel to the ground and waved them around like Espen had. Electricity buzzed all around me, causing the hairs on my arms to stand on end. When the Berserkers pushed their magic to the center of the circle, one giant, swirling pit of darkness formed.

Espen turned back to us. "This will take us to the gateway, but you must help us into your world."

Stepping up to the portal, I nodded before Brynjar and I walked through hand in hand. It was like before. One moment we stood on the island and the next we had returned to the woods in front of the gateway. Espen and his warriors joined us a moment later.

Brynjar spoke, "Emma will go through the Yggdrasil first and I'll stay here to see you all get through and join us on the other side. This will not feel like your portals. There is a darkness and cold that comes with stepping into another realm. It will feel like you're being dragged through. Don't fight it. Watch where Emma puts her hand and do the same. As long as you are worthy, you will be allowed through."

Finished with his instructions, Brynjar nodded toward me.

I approached the ancient gate, laid my hand on the upper right side, and waited for the pull. It was weaker than it had before, but still the cold nothingness between the realms pulled me in. A moment later and I was home. The crisp air wrapped around me like a jacket. I inhaled deeply, taking it all in.

The flash of light of Yggdrasil behind me forced my feet to turn around. I watched as Espen stepped into our world. I ignored his wide-eyed stare and stepped up to the dying tree behind him. Bark had fallen off and cracks tore through the meat of the tree.

I touched it gently. Its lifeforce fading away nearly cleaved me in two. We had only been gone a week, but it had been too long.

Tears fell from my face freely. I didn't even turn when I smelled the lilac of my mate.

He wiped the moisture from my face before he spoke. "We're home now. My father's clan can help save it, but we must stop Aric and save Damion first."

I nodded and nearly spirited before remembering we had to walk because of our entourage. My first walk through town felt like a lifetime ago and how my body had ached when we finally reached the castle. But now, after the strengthening of my body by fae magic, it was an easy trek. If not for the urgency building in my gut, I'd have taken my time.

The stares we got walking these men—who wore nothing but animal hides—through town were a mixture of horror and awe. They all bowed tentatively to Bryn and I, afraid to take their eyes off our companions. Not even the guards at the gates to the castle fully bowed to Brynjar and I. I didn't care. I hated the bowing anyway.

My feet practically sprinted to the throne room the moment we stepped inside. I flung myself at my brother, knocking him to the floor in a fit of laughter.

"I'm happy to see you too, Sister! There is much to tell you."

CHAPTER 39

Emma

"**W**hat the Hel, Aric?" I snapped at my brother the moment I released him. "Damion waltzes into our realm and you don't tell me?" I punched him in the shoulder. "And you had to go and threaten him? Aric, that's not how we do things now, is it?"

I may have been new to this world, but I couldn't stand by and watch another creature being treated the way Herrick had treated me.

"I... You're right." Aric hung his head low. "I'm sorry. It's been a stressful week. Come, let's talk."

Brynjar stepped next to me, clasping Aric on the shoulder.

"Good to see you too, Brother. I could have used you both by my side." My brother gave a half-hearted smile.

The moment I saw his mate and my best friend, I knew. I don't know if it was the way she glowed or my empath abilities, but I just knew. I whirled around on my brother, pulling him into another hug. "Why didn't you start with this? Where you not going to tell me?" I pulled away from him and ran to Thyra, hugging her as well, only more gently than I had my brother. "I am so happy for you both!"

I looked back at Brynjar, who looked lost. I laughed and exclaimed, "She's pregnant!"

"You're what?" he stammered out.

Thyra smiled. "I am pregnant, Brynjar. You know... a baby?"

When Brynjar made no sound or movement, Aric wrapped his arm around him. "That was my thoughts exactly. And this one," he pointed to Thyra, "thought I'd be angry."

"I... I'm... Congratulations!" My mate's smile didn't quite meet his eyes.

"Thank you, brother. But we are keeping it quiet for the time being. Now, let's talk. Much has happened since you left." Aric pulled away from my mate and back to Thyra. He stood behind her and laid his hands on her belly. She leaned back into him and smiled. He looked happy. Tired, but happy, and that made me smile.

I walked back over to Brynjar's father and his warriors and stood next to Espen. "Aric, this is the Berserkers and Brynjar's father, Espen."

Aric pulled away from his mate and bowed low to our guests. "Welcome. Our home is yours. You may join us if you wish. We have an area in the north that might suit the climate you are used to. I'm sure your exhausted from your journey."

Espen returned the bow. "I think, if it is alright with you, my warriors could retreat to this area you speak of and set up a camp, but I would like to join you. They are not comfortable being so far from home, but we have information you need to hear first."

Aric motioned for one of his guards to step forward. "I feel the same way when I visit Midgard. My guard will show your warriors the way and we can head to the dining hall. I'm sure you're hungry."

Espen bowed to his second.

Once food was arranged, we shared our stories. I thought we had a rough week until I heard everything Aric had gone through. I wrapped my arms around Thyra again and gave her a reassuring hug. What she had done was difficult, but necessary.

"I'm sorry for everything you had to handle on your own, Aric," I stepped away from Thyra and glared at my brother. "But that's no excuse to treat Damion the way you did. I, more than anyone, know what he is capable of, but did you really expect torturing him to work or was it just for you?"

"He walked right into our realm. I had to know why. What would you have done?" His tone told me he didn't believe his own lie. He was trying to justify his actions and failing.

"I would have asked! Talked to him like a normal... well, not human... Like any sane creature would have. Now, where is he?"

"He's in the dungeon." He led the way out of the throne room and down toward the magic training room. "By the way... I wasn't alone. Thyra was there with me the whole time. Even after the bonds fell away. She was amazing." He wrapped his arm around her waist and pulled her closer as they walked.

My heart lightened just a bit at the sight of the pair of them. I wouldn't have guessed it when we first met, but now... He'll make a good father.

We walked past the room where my magic had been unlocked and found another doorway where a sentry stood guard. The man bowed as we approached, but said nothing.

"He's down there," Aric said.

He started to descend the stairs before I stopped him. "No, not you." I turned to my mate, who stepped forward. "And not you. I'm sorry, my love, but I can't trust either of you not to kill him. He'll talk to me, but only if I go alone."

"Like Hel am I going to let you go down there by yourself!" Brynjar snapped.

Anger coursed through my veins. "Excuse me? Let me? I am your partner, not your submissive."

Brynjar took a step back and hung his head. "You're right. I'm sorry. I'm just worried about you. I know what Herrick did to you and I have to wonder what Damion's plans are. Why would he come so willingly to our realm knowing he'd be captured?"

"That is what I intend on finding out."

"I'll go with her," Thyra's soft voice spoke.

"But you're..." Aric started before both Thyra and I shot him a look.

"He won't hurt me... he... he loves me, I think. And Thyra will be safe *because* she's pregnant. He'd never hurt a child."

"I... Fine." Aric clenched his jaw and gave Thyra a quick kiss.

Brynjar kissed me deeply before releasing me. "Be safe, my love. We will be right here if you need anything."

The musty, moldy air choked my throat the further we descended. The cold stone walls bit at my skin as I braced against it, taking one step at a time. Dried mud caked between the stones and dripped onto the dirt floor in echoing thumps. We walked as softly as our feet would let us, sidestepping spiderwebs the size of my face, and pools of water. I grabbed a wooden torch off the wall and lit it with my palm as we continued to walk.

We finally reached the spot where Damion sat in the corner huddled in a ball. The wooden cell bars stretched from the ceiling to the floor. They twisted in perfectly natural ways. I followed the branches up. *They were the roots of a tree outside. I* gawked at the beauty of them before his cough brought me back to their purpose. There were so many roots entangled that I barely saw him through them.

"Your Majesties." Damion bowed low before us.

"Why are you here?" I demanded, not letting his tone throw me off. "How did you even get here?"

He shook as he spoke. "I wanted to see your gorgeous face one more time." I only now noticed that his once handsome face was hollow and ashen. His clothes hung loose on his gaunt body. He was dying. My heart stopped, if for just a moment.

I tried to hide the emotion from my voice. "Tell me the truth. What are you planning?"

"No plan." He coughed then leaned against the rock wall behind him. "I just needed to be near the only person who showed me an ounce of kindness."

I reached out and the moment my hand touched the dark wood bars, they parted to let me pass. I stepped closer to the man I wished to save from Herrick.

"What happened?" I asked him.

"I know he's dead. I knew it the moment it happened. Don't worry. I am not angry at you or your mate for killing Herrick. If I would have gotten ahold of him, I wouldn't have made it easy but..." He rubbed his chest as he slid across the dirt floor edging closer. "Something's happened to me. I've been poisoned and no one can heal me. It... It scares me." His eyes glistened in the firelight.

"What does?"

His once strong voice broke. "Death... I... I wanted to be with you when it happens..."

I tentatively placed my hand on his shoulder as he cried genuine tears. He was not here for revenge or some other darker plan. He was here to die. I wiped my own tears away before I spoke again.

"I'm sorry, Damion. Herrick was an awful man but... I never thought he was capable of such cruelty."

I turned my head at the pop from behind me to see Thyra joining me in his cell. She knelt beside me, laying her hand on his arm for a moment before looking back at me and shook her head before she spirited out of the cell.

Damion tried to stand and fell back down again before he spoke. "I don't blame your brother for what he did to me... He doesn't understand the depths of spite Herrick had. He would—and did—do anything to achieve his goals. Too bad for him he never saw them come to light."

"Do you know how to save Yggdrasil?" I asked.

He shook his head. "It can't be saved... but... When the time comes, I will help you, Emma." His cold hand cupped my face. A deep ache for this pitiful man broke my heart and I let my tears flow. "But for now I need to rest." He let his hand drop to his lap with a heavy thunk.

I stood, twirling my hands, and conjured a soft mattress. He was no threat to us. He could hardly hold his head up, let alone use his magic against anyone. Why not let him have some comfort?

I backed out of his cell, watching him crawl onto the mattress. Thyra's kind arms wrapped around me and led me out of the dungeon. I shielded my eyes from the light as we reached the top of the stairs. I fell into my mate's waiting arms and sobbed.

"What happened? I'll kill him myself," I heard Brynjar say.

Aric gripped the hilt of his sword.

"No," Thyra said softly. "He didn't hurt her. We're in no danger with him here. I don't want either of you going down there, but we need to try to get him to eat something. I'll send one of my apprentices down there later with food."

"But—" Aric said.

"Don't start, Aric. It'll be fine. Leave it be and I will take care of Damion."

I smiled at the strength of my friend's words. I lifted my head to mouth, "thank you," as Brynjar and I turned and headed back to our room.

CHAPTER 40

Brynjar

I shifted in a chair at the front of the war room, wiping my clammy hands on my pants. If not for my mate, I wouldn't be there. Emma sat to my left and her brother next to her. I sat on the end next to my mate, feeling out of place. Emma and Aric were born royal, yet I was given a title because of my mate.

Emma's cool hand grasped mine. *'Nervous?'*

'I don't belong here.' I gripped her hand tight.

'You belong here as much as I do. We are in this together. No matter what, remember?'

'Yes, my Kompis.' My shoulders relaxed slightly.

The doors opened and everyone that called us friends entered the room. Emma rushed to Surt. I didn't even feel the slightest bit of jealousy as he wrapped her in a big hug. I stood and greeted him as well. His massive hand clasped my forearm.

"Good to see you, Surt," I said as I returned the gesture.

"I'm glad you two made it back safely from Midgard. It's always a bit tricky navigating that realm." He shook as if a ghost passed through him. "Humans."

"I'd say I take offense to that, but I'm not quite human, am I now?" My father's voice rang out behind the giant god.

"Father." I released Surt's arm and gave a quick hug to my father. "Did your people get settled all right?"

"They are a little weary of being here, but they are strong and brave. They will adjust."

I led my father to the chair next to mine as the rest of our allies gathered around the table.

"Thank you all for coming here this morning," Aric spoke when we were all seated. "My sister and Brynjar traveled far to bring new allies home in an attempt to save Yggdrasil." He gestured toward us. "Emma, can you tell the others the plan?"

She nodded and stood. "When I first got home from Helheim and learned of Thyra's condition, I went to her. Because of my abilities, I was able to draw on the magic of others and healed her. I think I can do the same for Yggdrasil. Herrick has been poisoning Yggdrasil for some time now by releasing iron ash beetles to infest the tree. I know in Midgard, the ash beetle is dangerous to the ash tree and from what I saw from Herrick's memories, the iron ash beetle leaves traces of iron wherever they go. That leaves us with little options to remove them. But we have hope. When Brynjar was imprisoned, the iron brought him strength. Once we learned what he is, we made a plan." She turned to look at me and offered her hand.

I stood, smoothing my pants before I spoke. "I'm part Berserker. I have always known I was different but until very recently did I learn how different," I gripped Emma's hand. "When I saw my mate dying, something snapped. We believe that Emma can use her magic to pull out the beetles. Emma is even more connected to nature than anyone in our history and that gives her the ability to control lower intelligent animals. Once they are out of the tree, my father's clan can handle them from there."

"A bug?" Njörðr asked. "Are you saying that all our lives are at risk over a fucking bug?"

I couldn't blame him for his anger. I went to agree with him, but it was Emma that responded first.

"Herrick might have been a horrid father, but he was also a brilliant strategist. He knew that he couldn't send his fae to destroy Yggdrasil, but he knew no one would look for something as small as an insect."

"Bastard. We didn't think to ward from something as small as a beetle," Surt sighed.

"So, when shall we do this?" a man I didn't recognize spoke. From the way he was dressed—In a fur-lined coat and thick boots—I could only assume he was now in charge of Niflheim, the ice realm, after Sigrid's death.

I sank back in my chair, rubbing my face. "Emma and I are both exhausted. I can hardly even think, let alone have her pull on my magic. If we aren't careful, it could kill us."

The man surged to his feet. "Yggdrasil is dying and you want to take a nap?"

"I see the temper is a Niflheim trait. Or are you blood to Sigrid and Skadi?" I asked casually.

He slammed down his fists against the table.

"I don't want any trouble," Aric interrupted. "The point Brynjar is trying to make is that if we do this now, and it's too much for any of us to handle and someone dies, then the tree will die. No good will come from using magic when you are drained. Can we at least agree to wait out the night and meet at Yggdrasil in the morning?" He scanned past everyone, who all nodded their agreements. He turned to Emma. "What will you need?"

"For tomorrow?"

Aric nodded at her question.

"I'll need as many magic users as we can gather as well as the warriors Espen brought. Herrick had been at this for a while and

I can't honestly say what these bugs are or what they will do." She turned to me. "But as for the rest of the day and night, I need rest. And food..." She grinned.

"Very well." Aric turned to the others. "Go and prepare your men and I'll do the same. Emma and Brynjar, rest up. I'll have food brought up to you."

I helped Emma to her feet, nodding to Aric. My father clasped me on the shoulder as we walked past and I wrapped my arm around Emma's waist as I guided her into the hallway.

She leaned against me as we walked. I kissed the top of her head. "Have I told you lately how much I love you?" I asked.

"Nope."

I halted in the middle of the hall, pulling her face to mine and kissed the tender skin behind her ear, then pulled away to look at her face.

"Emma, from the moment I saw you walk into the garden, I knew. I knew my life would never be the same. You've made me the happiest being of all time. Not even the gods are as lucky as I." I smiled.

She wrapped her arms around my neck, pulling me fully against her chest. Her lips gently brushed mine. "Take me to our room, my king," she whispered into my ear. A shiver ran down my spine. I pulled her closer and spirited us directly to our room.

The moment we were alone, her lips resumed their exploration. Her hands reached around my back, pulling off the bands that held my vest to my chest. I sluffed off the thin cloth quickly before pulling her back into me. Her fingers grazed my spine. My wings spread out behind me and her hands found their edges. I stiffened instantly at her touch.

"You kill me, Emmy," I growled into her mouth. Her hands reached between our bodies, stroking the length of me. She lowered her body, sliding my pants to the floor with her as her lips gently kissed every inch of me. I threw my head back and groaned when her mouth enclosed me. "Emmy," I breathed out.

I pulled her to her feet, undid her dress slowly and slid it to the floor as my hands traced down her sides. I took her all in, studying her, memorizing this moment.

My arms folded around her, pulling her close and running my fingers through her hair, down to her wing edges. She sighed.

"I love you more than I could ever show you. You're remarkable." I pressed my lips into hers. Her feet moved back, dragging me with her. She spun me around, sitting me on the edge of the mattress.

"Bryn, I don't even know how to show you how much I love you." She kissed my jaw. "But I'll try." She grinned as she straddled my lap, lowering herself onto me.

My face buried in her chest. "Emmy." Our wings curled into one another, feathers brushing together.

We took our time loving each other. The future wasn't set in stone. Tomorrow, we would either save Yggdrasil and the Nine Realms, or we would die trying. Today, I only wanted to love my mate and be loved in return.

CHAPTER 41

Emma

I woke early the next morning in my mate's arms. I lay there, watching him as he slept. All the worry and fear had fled his face and he was simply my mate. My finger traced down the bridge of his nose and over his lips. He twitched. I smiled and did it again.

"Good morning, Emmy," he breathed out, eyes still closed.

"Morning Bryn."

He pulled me closer and buried his face in my chest as his warm lips pressed into the top of my breasts.

"Bryn," I sighed and arched into him. I felt his need beneath my hips. I forced air between us, pulled his face up to look at me, my cheeks wet with tears.

"What if we fail?" My voice broke as I spoke.

"Shh, Emmy. I got you." He brought my face to his shoulder and stroked my hair. "We won't. We have a good plan and an army... Hel, we have five armies to back us up."

"But..." I pushed off him. "We need to talk about if we fail. If Yggdrasil dies... If the current Vörður die, it is up to Aric and I to save the realms. If... If... I will never see you again," I sobbed.

He pulled my left arm up, gripping my hand with his right. His other hand traced the vine tattoos on my arm up to the mating X on my hand and over to his own hand that had the same markings.

"The gods bound us together. That means forever. They can't break us apart now. I'm far from done being your mate and I refuse to give you up. If we fail and you have to sacrifice yourself, I'll go to Asgard myself and demand the gods release you." He kissed me fiercely. "You're not leaving me. Do you understand me!" His face now wet with tears.

"If I'm trapped inside Yggdrasil, I won't allow you through to Asgard." I smiled.

He chuckled, pulled me tighter and kissed the top of my head. "That's my Emmy."

I let him hold me longer than I knew I should have. Time was not on our side, but I wanted to make this moment last for the rest of our lives. His lilac sent washed over me. The way his wings twitched when I stroked his back. The warmth of his body pressed against mine. The way I knew I'd always be safe if he were near. I wanted to ingrain it all in my mind.

"We should get dressed," I said once the sun peaked into the windows, yet I never let go of my mate.

"We should." I knew he was etching this moment in his mind, too.

We held each other longer. It wasn't until a soft rap at the door startled us before we moved.

"Em... Brynjar... It's time." My brother's voice was full of grief and sorrow.

"Coming." My voice was weak.

Slowly, Brynjar and I stood and dressed before stepping out into the hall where Aric and Thyra clung to one another as closely as my mate and I did. Together, we strode out of the castle and toward the dying ancient tree.

Hundreds of fae awaited us as we walked closer. The whole town lined the streets, watching. I gulped hard and hugged my mate tighter. The armies parted, letting us walk right up to Yggdrasil where Espen, Surt, Njörðr, and the new leader of Niflheim stood. They all gave a slight bow to us.

"Surt." I nodded.

"Where would you like us, queen?" the giant god asked.

I wiped my palms on my skirt. My heart thrummed so loud all other noise drown out. I closed my eyes and tried to slow the world down.

"I... I..." Everything spun. Brynjar's arm wrapped around my middle, holding me upright. A year ago, I was just Emma, the crazy girl that saw faeries. Now I was the Queen of the fae and expected to save them all.

'You got this, and I got you. You hear me. No matter what!' Bryn's voice in my head gave me strength.

I straightened, opened my eyes, and looked at the other leaders watching me with concern on their faces.

"We need to circle Yggdrasil in layers. Have your fire and ice users alternate on the outside and build a wall of fae together." I looked at Njörðr next. "I have no idea what to expect of these creatures, so have your flygeblad on the outside ready for anything." Brynjar's father stood stone solid, watching me as I addressed him. "Have your people wait closer to the tree. If they'd feel more comfortable, have them shift."

Espen nodded and walked toward the group of Berserkers huddled together in the distance.

Mayank stepped up to me and bowed low. "What of our people, my queen?"

"I'll need some fae to draw power from. This will weaken them, so we will need others to protect them. Anyone else that isn't a magic user needs to be outside the wall."

He nodded and walked off.

I turned to Thyra. "I want you to go home." I couldn't stop the tears from falling. She shook her head. "No, I mean it. I've watched you nearly die twice and I can't watch you die again... not now..." I looked down to her stomach where my tiny niece or nephew grew. "I refuse to watch either of you come to harm. Go now or I will order someone to take you." I wrapped her in a hug and kissed her cheek. "If we fail, I need you safe," I whispered in her ear.

She pulled away and nodded then glanced to her mate. Tears filled both of their eyes. He moved toward her, but she shook her head, stretched her hand out, and took a step back.

"I love you," she said, and before he could respond, Thyra pulled herself into spirit and vanished.

Aric stood there speechless. I hooked my arms under his and hugged him tightly. "I'm sorry, Aric," I sobbed. "I had to make her go. They're the future of our realm."

"I know." He sank into my arms. "Thank you, sister. She wouldn't have listened to me."

I pulled out of his arms and grasped his hand, then Brynjar's, and turned to face the tree. All the fae we'd gathered circled around the tree and the Berserkers strode toward us in various predator forms. My jaw dropped. Fae scattered to let them pass. I had expected to see only bears.

Massive black bears walked alongside giant timber wolves, Amur tigers, and snow leopards and several bald eagles flew high above. I shivered as they passed me. The lead bear—Espen, I assumed—nodded to us. The circle closed back up and magic surged all around us.

Brynjar kissed my cheek and held me close. Our warriors stood all around us. They placed their hands gently on my back, pouring their magic into me. I breathed deep and focused my energy.

I closed my eyes and pictured the great tree, Yggdrasil, in my mind. The thread of life within it was weak. In my mind, I saw the twins clinging to one another. The sisters' tears streamed down their cheeks. I sucked in a breath as their pain radiated throughout me.

'Hold fast, Emmy.' Brynjar's voice in my head solidified my resolve and I pushed past the dying women and dug into the roots of the tree. The deep, earthy scent washed over me. Death and rot intermixed with the smell as I dug deeper. The *click, click, click* of the metallic creatures scurrying about drew me closer.

"Almost," I whispered to no one.

I called the bugs to me like a beloved pet. My voice cooed to them of the promise of a better meal. One by one they followed as I pulled my mind out of the tree. They scampered around the twins, who clung tighter to each other as the ash beetles crawled over them, and up and out through cracks in the bark.

Shielding my face, I opened my eyes in the bright morning sun. The bugs numbered in the thousands. My heart stopped as the Berserkers growled in unison.

My mind was still connected with that of the bugs and I felt them move before they did. Pushing past my warriors, I cried, "No, no, no..." My body shook. I gripped the hair at my temples.

"Emma!" Aric's voice sounded like he was under water.

Brynjar joined Aric at my side. "What is it, Emma?"

I looked at my mate and brother. "Move," I whispered. "Everyone needs to move." They stared at me. "MOVE BACK!" Tears streamed down my face when no one listened to me. "Please," I begged my brother.

He straightened and cleared his throat before he ordered the others. "Do as she says!"

The bugs moved before our people did. They swarmed, towering in the sky over the fae below. The beetles combined, forming one massive creature. Branches the size of my core snapped and fell to the ground.

The monstrous bug creature stood to its full height, nearly as tall as the tree itself. It opened its maw and screamed. I dropped to the ground, covering my ears at the sound of the high-pitched, metallic screeching. Blood seeped through my fingers. I peered up, watching the others writhing in pain as well.

I reached out with my mind, trying to calm the creature, but nothing I did broke its hold. When it finally silenced, I heard the muffled sounds of swords being drawn and the roar of the Berserkers. I reached out to the hand in front of my face and stood. Brynjar held me close. My feet froze to the earth.

'Remember, we are stronger together, Em.'

'Stay with us.' Brynjar and Aric spoke in my mind in unison.

With my brother and mate at my side, I slowed my breathing and nodded. I twirled my wrist, conjuring my obsidian sword. Brynjar stripped out of his pants and stepped away, shifting into his bear. I watched as his father's clan charged the beast.

The creature swiped out, knocking them to the side like flies. I nodded to my mate, who sprinted to his father's side. Gripping my brother's hand, we shot to the sky. Every winged fae joined our side, and together we attacked the beast's face, blocking his view below.

Aric issued orders for some to attack its arms while others its face. I hovered above the fight, watching. I was frozen with fear. Never in all the thoughts I had of this moment had I ever expected the beetles to form one creature. Our fire and ice wall held strong, but the fae warriors on the ground stood back.

Berserkers circled the creature, biting and slashing out with their claws. They danced around its stomping feet. Anger burned through me as more of my people were flung off than got through.

Our flyers dropped to the ground the moment they made contact with the beast. My eyes frantically looked for my mate.

'Bryn! I can't....'

'You can. You're stronger than you believe.'

'I... I need you!'

I felt him shift back to his fae form and in a flash, he was at my side in the air, his twin blades the only thing he held.

"Together," he said with a grin.

I focused my energy on my sword, igniting it. Raising my flaming blade, I nodded. We flew straight for the beast's face, swords out. Fae flew around us, slashing at the creature. Bugs fell and reformed.

We closed in. I looked at my mate. He smiled and flew higher before landing on the top of the monster's head, stabbing down. I charged straight for his eyes. I stabbed relentlessly. Aric joined my side, swiping away at the creature.

'It's useless. I thought to myself. *'It just keeps reforming.'*

Damion's voice echoed in my head. *'You have the power to stop it.'*

'H-how? How are you talking to me?' I stumbled to find the words.

'Herrick taught me some tricks. Now you can stop the creature.' His voice was weak. *'Fire will destroy it.'* He trailed off and was gone.

I looked at my sword. The bugs ran from it.

'Bryn... Aric... Pull back.' Aric issued new commands and together we landed toward the outer wall of fae. The beast straightened, the fallen bugs crawling back to it.

My eyes didn't need to scan the crowd. Surt had reverted to his fire god form and stood above all else. His horns and flame hair stood out like a beacon. I sprinted through my people toward him with the sound of my mate and brother following.

"Fire," I breathed out the moment I stopped in front of Surt. "Fire will kill it."

Surt nodded and called his fire users to him. Every other fae backed out behind us. Flames ignited in the hands of the users and Surt himself became a giant flame.

I looked at my mate. "Can we... ride the Berserkers? We still can't touch it, but you can get closer without causing harm."

Brynjar cocked his head for a moment before he spoke. "Yes," he said simply as he shifted back to his bear form.

Espen and his clan stepped up to our group and lowered to the ground. I nodded to the bear before turning to my mate. I smiled, gripped his fur, and climbed over his back. Everyone but Surt climbed upon a shifter.

"At your lead." I nodded to Surt, who raised his sword and charged. We ran toward the creature's feet, shooting flames at the monster. It screeched and swiped at us. Aric and the other flyers took to the sky to distract it while we set it ablaze. The air reeked of burning exoskeleton as the beast finally caught fire. Flames stretched skyward. The creature flailed at the flames, but it's cool movements only fueled the blaze.

The flyers landed, and the Berserkers backed away. We stood, watching the dying creature stomp around in a panic before it finally tipped over. I jumped off my mate's back and ran for Yggdrasil. Aric's arm wrapped around me, halting me. I watched in horror as the beast fell backward, smashing into the already fragile tree.

I dropped to my knees. My heart sank as I watched the bug creature shatter into a thousand pieces as it hit the ground and stilled. Time slowed down. A deafening crack echoed throughout the realm. I didn't dare breathe. I watched in disbelief as Yggdrasil split in two, crashing to the ground, exposing the Vörður inside. They looked at me for a split second but in that moment a lifetime had passed. When they broke eye contact, they too fell.

CHAPTER 42

Aric

I ce flooded my veins and I froze, watching the Great Tree crumble and fall away. Everyone watched. No one noticed Emma move, not even me until her hand rested on my upper arm, pulling me back to this world.

She and I wove silently through the crowd. My eyes glanced back to the spot the tree once stood. Reality finally settled and everyone wept. Tears fell from my own face.

Emma tugged at my arm, urging me forward. I turned my back and walked with her in a haze. This wasn't how it was supposed to be. My family. My mate. My unborn child. Only my sister's arm around me kept me from shattering completely. I glanced over at her. Her face was set in stone. Dry eyes and tight lips.

'How can you not feel this?' I couldn't speak the words out loud.

'I'm feeling more than you know.' Her voice broke slightly. *'It's just... If I allow myself to feel, I can't do what I must.'*

Flicking my eyes back to the tree, I saw that the crowd refused to depart, they stood in silent defeat. We skirted around the town and toward the training field. I dug my feet into the dirt when I saw Emma's tree. My heart echoed in my throat.

"No," I whispered.

She tightened her grip around my arm and looked me in the eye.

"I'm sorry, Brother." She pulled us into spirit, forcing me to follow. When I opened my eyes, we were standing in the middle of the field in front of the large ash tree. Emma had grown this tree in an instant out of fear of losing me and no it' would be my tomb.

My chest ached. I looked away from the tree and over my shoulder toward the castle where I knew the two loves of my life were. One had only just returned to my life and the other I had yet to meet. I was losing them, and I'd never get to say goodbye.

Images flashed into my mind. The gates of Hel opened up, releasing demons and monsters into the Realms. Floods, volcanoes, earthquakes. Jörð herself tore through Midgard, destroying everything she touched. The very ground we stood on blackened beyond recognition. Bodies of my people littered the earth, staring up at me with blank stares.

My lungs constricted. I shook the images from my head and looked at my sister. Tears filled her eyes. She reached out a hand. I took it and stepped closer.

"What was that?" I asked.

"The twins showed me what would happen if we don't do this. I... I don't want to do this anymore than you do but... They were so weak. I don't know if the healers can save them and the longer we wait, the harder this will be."

I looked back at the castle. "Thyra," I whispered.

"Will understand. And she will teach that baby that her daddy saved all the Nine Realms."

I nodded but couldn't look away, knowing my mate and unborn child stood in our room, not knowing what was about to happen. My heart shattered and I prayed to the gods for the strength to move my feet. My head knew without our sacrifice, my child would not live to see the sunlight, but my heart ached to see that day.

"The twins told me what to do." Emma's voice echoed in my ears as if from a distance. She pulled me closer to her tree and away from my mate.

My gaze remained on the castle. "Can I... can I say goodbye at least?"

"It'll only make it harder... Aric... I wish... I..." My sister's voice trailed off as she too looked toward where her mate stood.

She released my arm and I dropped to the ground, my body so heavy I could no longer hold it upright. Silent tears streamed down my face. Emma knelt beside me, placing her hand over mine.

"Let me try something," she said.

The tingle of her magic surrounded me. Images flooded my mind. A swing hung from the branches of the tree. Squeals of delight filled my ears as a tiny fae girl with brilliantly red hair flew high in the sky.

"Faster mommy faster," she cried.

My gorgeous mate stood behind her, pushing. The little girl flung herself from the swing, flapping her small wings, and landed gracefully. She bounced up to the tree, smiling ear to ear.

"Did you see that, daddy? I flew! Just like you!" The little girl threw her arms wide, hugging the tree before skipping off toward a blanket. She and Thyra sat and ate their lunch. Thyra looked at the tree and smiled. My heart fragmented as the images faded.

"You'll get to watch her grow up but If we don't do this, you'll never get to see her face." Emma wrapped her arm around my shoulder in a half hug. I leaned into her, letting more tears fall.

'When did you become the strong one?' I asked her.

'I've always been stronger.' Her smugness made me laugh.

"What do we need to do?" I asked.

She stood, offering me a hand. I dragged myself to my feet, dusting my pants off.

"First, you need to push aside your sorrow. It won't work if you hold on too tight to Alfheim."

Swallowing hard, I wiped the tears from my face and held onto the images Emma gave me. Iresigned myself to the knowledge that I'd never hold her. Finally, I nodded.

"Then we have to pray to Jörð to help us. I can hollow out the tree, but we need her to help us pass through and connect the tree to the other realms." Emma dropped my hand and laid hers on the trunk of her tree.

I watched as she scrunched up her face in concentration. Her magic swirled around me, sending a chill down my spine. I stood for a long moment in silence, watching her. Sweat beaded on her forehead.

She gasped for air when she finally pulled away and I wrapped my arms around her just in time. She sagged into me.

"Em, you okay?"

"Just took more than I anticipated." She straightened. "Ready?"

"Not really, but I'll do what I must to protect my family."

Emma smiled, but her eyes were sad. "I'm sorry, Aric."

I shrugged. "Besides you, they mean the world to me."

She turned to the tree and knelt before it. Her hands rested gently on the bark. She bowed her head and whispered prayers. I knelt beside her.

I kept my voice low so only I and the goddess could hear me. "Jörð, I will protect my family with my life. My mate and child are my universe. If I must sacrifice my life for theirs, I give it freely. My people must survive and carry on. I swear my fealty to you and to the Nine Realms. I give my life to save those of all the realms. Take my soul and use it to protect others."

The bark beneath my palms vibrated. I opened my eyes and watched as an arch formed in the tree just wide enough for Emma and I to step through.

We stood. She trembled in my grasp as I wrapped my hand in hers. I had to hold her tighter to stop my own shaking.

Without a second thought, we stepped inside. My sister turned in my hold so we faced each other. Her lips quivered. I brushed a tear from her cheek and pulled her tighter.

Two small pops called our attention back out to the field. Brynjar and Thyra stood before us, just out of my reach. Their faces white as a ghost and eyes glistened with tears.

Brynjar moved his hand in a gesture I knew meant to show his love. Thyra rubbed at her belly as her tears hit the grass. I mouthed the words, "I love you" as my own tears fell. She nodded. Brynjar wrapped his arm around Thyra, who sank into his chest.

"I will find a way... no matter what," he said to my sister. "Until then I'll keep our family safe." He looked at me.

"Thank you, Brother."

Brynjar nodded in response.

Emma and I watched our mates as the tree closed in around us.

CHAPTER 43

Damion

The sadness and grief reached me even in the dungeons. I didn't need to be there to know Yggdrasil had fallen. I didn't even have to be told that Emma and her brother had given their lives to protect their people and the Realms from Ragnarök. I couldn't feel her presence like I once had.

The weight of her loss crushed me. I hit my knees and rubbed at the throbbing in my chest. The one person who showed me an ounce of kindness gave her life for us all. She was the only one who I had ever loved. And now she was gone.

My eyes searched for something... anything sharp enough to cut through skin. I didn't want to live in a world where I couldn't see her face. But only twigs and dirt surrounded me.

I lay on the earth, sobbing, for what felt like hours. When the tears dried up, I lay there longer. My body, already weak from the siren's toxin, drained even further. Too weak to lift my hand, I lay there twirling my finger in a circle.

Herrick's cold eyes flashed in my mind. I dragged my body to the wall and leaned against it. But it wasn't the walls of Alfheim's dungeon on my back. It was the hard rock of Svartalfheim. My room came into focus around me. I sat on my bed and leaned against the cold, hard stone, Herrick watching me. I replayed the long-forgotten memory back in my mind.

"Are you alright?" he asked me.

"Yes..." I rubbed at my temples. "What happened?"

"You tried to go after him yourself. Very foolish, my son."

"I'm sorry, Sire, but you said he must die before we can complete our plans. I saw an opportunity."

He crossed his arms and frowned at me. "I admire the initiative, but did you not listen to a word I said?"

I hung my head. "I thought they were just stories to scare children. I didn't believe him to be that powerful. He's just a mage."

Shame and guilt invaded me all over again. I had once again let my anger and pride force me to act. My mind tried to piece the memory back together. Who was it we were talking about? Why had Herrick wanted him dead? I couldn't remember. I rubbed at my eyes, trying to force my brain to focus.

"And now? Do you still believe them to be stories?" Herrick had asked me.

I shook my head.

I had tracked the mage down in Midgard and I thought I'd had him cornered. We were alone down an alley. I hadn't made a move when total darkness surrounded me. The moonlight had been blocked out, and the air grew cold. It was so dark I couldn't even see the outline of the man. I dared to step closer to where I thought he was, but a strong force flung me backwards slamming me into something hard and unforgiving. The next thing I remembered was waking up in my room. But who was the man?

"But who... what is he?" I remembered asking Herrick.

He flicked his wrist and produced a chair. He sat, crossing one leg over the other. We looked at each other for a long moment before he spoke again.

"He is the oldest living creature known to man or fae. There are stories told about him from before they were written. Legends say he was the first magic user. If the stories are to be believed, he was also the first necromancer. He would perform tricks for the king by cutting the heads off animals and reattaching them and reanimating them. The king asked him to do it to a prisoner, but he refused. That's not to say he couldn't, though. That is why he must die. He can bring back the twins within Yggdrasil if he is to stay in Alfheim."

I clutched at my chest at hearing his history. This one man could ruin the plans we had worked so hard at creating. I threw the blankets off me and tried to stand, only to fall back down into the bed. My legs had given out on me. I looked at Herrick in concern.

"Don't worry. You will return to yourself soon. Just rest."

I dragged myself back to bed and pulled the blankets back over my body. My breathing labored at the slight effort. One man had nearly killed me with a single action.

"Does he... does he have a name?" I asked.

Herrick leaned closer and raised his hands to my temples. "His true name has been lost to time. Most just call him the Mystic. But you shouldn't know all this... not yet." I pulled away from his hands, eyes wide. "Don't worry... It won't hurt." His fingers touched my head. "I'm not removing the memories. Just blocking them for now. If the time comes where there is no other option, they will resurface."

I stood abruptly in my cell. My head was spinning. The answer to all the Nine Realms problems had been trapped inside my head this whole time. I stumbled forward and gripped the wooden bars. I needed to speak to someone.

"Hello!" I tried to shout but my voice came out horse. How long had it been since someone had been down here? Hours? Days? Time was a blur. "Please, someone... anyone..." I pleaded for someone to hear me.

I sank back down to the earth and continued calling to no one. With my body slowly slipping away each passing moment, I begged the gods to answer my prayers before it was too late.

"Please."

CHAPTER 44

Thyra

I woke with a start. The screaming and the nightmares wouldn't leave me alone. It had been a week since my mate and his sister had sacrificed themselves for us. I rubbed my belly as I tried to calm my nerves. The moonlight still shone in through my window as I dragged my feet from the bed and stood.

My body was weak even though my pregnancy was still young. My stomach only now started to swell. I hadn't slept a full night since that day. I paced the room I had shared with my mate for a short time. My mind raced for a way to save them.

The dreams that haunted me flashed through my mind. The voice echoed in my head. A hoarse screech sounded in my ears, as if it were in the room with me. His face was a blur. I sat in a chair in the corner of the room and focused on the figure. I let my magic flow to him. Slowly, it took shape.

I leaned against the wall, gasping. "Damion!"

Damion's face had been haunting my dreams. He had been trying to communicate with me and in my grief, I had forgotten he sat in our dungeon. I stood and snapped my fingers, dressing myself before I stormed out of my room, and toward the dungeons. My guards followed. Mayank stood in front of the doors leading to the lowest part of the castle.

"Your Majesty." He bowed. "What are you thinking? You won't get any clear answers from him."

I glared at my high commander. "I need to speak to him. He's been... something is wrong. Let me pass."

He raised an eyebrow. "In your condition?"

"If he can help me save my mate, you're damn right I'll do whatever it takes to save him." I hardened my stare. "Besides, I am your queen, and you will do as commanded."

He stared back before he relaxed and sighed. "Very well, but I'm going with you."

"Fine," I snapped, reaching behind him for the handle. He stepped aside and let me open the door.

The stench hit me all at once. It was even worse than before. Sickly sweet smells mixed with rotten eggs had me gagging before we reached the bottom of the stairs. Mayank snapped his fingers, surrounding us both in a bubble. I clutched at my stomach as I continued to descend toward the foul odor.

"Thank you," I whispered as my feet found solid ground. The smell lingered, but I was able to bare it.

I flicked on candlelight as we walked closer to Damion's cell. As we reached him, I spun around and hid my face in Mayank's chest.

"Damion?" Mayank whispered.

He grunted from behind me. Steadying my breath, I faced him. Damion gripped the bars with boney fingers. His ashen skin hung loose from his frame and dark circles ringed his eyes.

Kneeling in front of him, I gently touching his shoulder. His skin was ice. I slipped healing magic into his frail body. It wouldn't cure him, but maybe give him a little bit of strength.

"Damion?" I asked.

He lifted his head slightly. "Water?" he croaked out.

I snapped, producing a glass, and pressed it to his lips. He drank slowly and I waited a long moment for him to drink his fill.

"Took you long enough to hear me," he finally said.

"I heard you, I just... didn't understand. I'm sorry." I told him.

"It's not too late..."

"For what?"

"To save them."

"How?"

"Mystic..." He closed his eyes and slumped over.

I stood and looked at Mayank. "Get him to the infirmary, find Brynjar, and meet me at the Mystic's room."

He nodded and opened the cage. As he lifted Damion, a sound popped and the two vanished.

I took a deep breath before walking out of the dungeons and headed to the wing where the Mystic was in.

Two guards stood on either side of the double doors. They nodded at me as I arrived. Not a moment later, Mayank and Brynjar spirited beside me. Mayank shook his head as he stepped closer.

"Damion doesn't look good," he said.

"Hopefully, the Mystic will cooperate," I said. I flicked my attention to Brynjar as he approached. His eyes were dark and puffy like he had as much sleep as I had. His normal sparkle had dulled. He simply nodded. I closed the gap between us and gripped his hand. "We can still save them. We have to believe that."

He gave a halfhearted smile before pulling away.

I turned back to the guards and nodded. They opened the doors and let us pass. The room was even larger than my own and decorated with gold embellished furniture. He sat in the lap of luxury as my world had shattered. I suppressed the rage that swelled within me. We needed his help and getting angry with him for his nonchalant attitude would do us no good.

The tall, slender man standing in the open double doors overlooking the massive balcony didn't even flinch when we walked in. I watched him. The suit he wore could have fed an entire family for a year. I steadied my breathing before I stepped closer.

"Mystic."

He turned, grinned, and bowed low. "Your Majesty. I do apologize... I didn't hear you approach."

I wanted to smack the grin from his face and as I spoke, my voice shook. "Don't lie. I know you know how to save them."

He relaxed into a chair, resting his head on the back and closed his eyes. "What makes you think I possibly know?"

"I don't have time for your foolish games." I screamed through gritted teeth.

I lifted my hand and with a single thought, yanked him from the chair and slammed him backward through the balcony door into the wooden railing. I knew I caught him off guard, but I couldn't let up or he would kill me in an instant, so I slammed his head into the railing over and over again until blood dripped from the impact.

"Queen," Mayank's voice penetrated my thoughts but I held the Mystic just over the edge of the railing.

The Mystics smug smile finally faded into fear as he gripped the railing tight. I knew when my anger subsided the guilt would settle in, but I wanted my mate. I placed a hand on my stomach. *We* needed our mate.

"Queen Astrid warned you... My mate warned you... You're out of warnings. Tell me what you know or we will see if you really are immortal."

Brynjar's hand on my shoulder pulled me back to the room.

"He's no good to us dead." His voice was soft.

I eased up on my magic slightly.

The Mystic swallowed hard. "Yes... I know... Please, let me sit..." His words broke as he spoke.

I snapped my fingers and raised a shield around the room so he couldn't escape before I released my hold on him. He straightened, brushing his shirt down. I backed up, allowing him back inside the room, and shut the doors behind him.

He made his way to the oversized chair and sat. Every movement he made was in slow motion. He exaggerated everything, like he had no care for time. He brushed his pants and rested an ankle on his knee. I was fuming when he finally looked back at me.

"Well?" I huffed out.

"What's the rush? Everyone is safe. Why are you fretting?"

I shut my eyes and took a breath.

Brynjar answered him. "Because they are our mates. Our life is nothing without them."

The Mystic scoffed. "I've had many lovers in my lifetime... You'll learn to live with their absence."

Brynjar huffed.

"They are the rightful rulers of Alfheim," I explained. "Your King and Queen, and it is your duty to save them."

Mystic laughed. "They are not my King and Queen. I'm under no one's rule."

Brynjar gripped my shoulders and pulled me behind him. "If you don't tell us, I can't guarantee that I can control my bear at this point," he growled.

The Mystic's calm demeanor slipped and his eyes widened as he sunk further into his chair. He gulped hard before he spoke. "Fine... I am... Older than most... Older than even Surt..."

"Who are you?" Mayank asked from behind us.

"I've had many names... But the one my father gave me was Dedi. I was born thousands of years before Christ himself. He was not the first to raise souls from the dead."

CHAPTER 45

Brynjar

"Wait... What?" I stumbled over the words.

The Mystic cocked his head and crossed his arms as his grin widened and a small chuckle escaped his lips. The blood from his face vanished, leaving no trace of injury.

He was still toying with us. I stood tall and crossed my arms as well. Stepping closer to the man, I tried to push aside my emotions even though my heart raced.

"Explain," I stated.

The Mystic sighed and uncrossed his arms. "I am a necromancer.... I am the original necromancer, in fact. I used to perform tricks for the king long ago using animals."

"But can you do this to fae?" Thyra asked in almost a whisper from behind me.

He nodded. "It's not as simple as it is with animals. Higher order beings are far more complex."

Mayank stepped up next to us, eyes wide with a slight smile. "How so?"

Thyra's light steps crept closer until she was standing next to me. Her body lacked the tension from a moment ago and she looked on, intrigued.

The Mystic sat lightly in his chair, face pallid and eyes locked on the floor. The sudden shift in his mood cooled the air around me and I softened my stance, stepping closer.

"Please, tell us," I encouraged.

He straightened. "Higher order beings have souls. In order to bring a soul creature back to life, it requires another soul."

My heart sank. "You mean..."

"Yes, a soul for a soul. In order to bring the twins back to life, two must willingly sacrifice their lives for them."

I paused my pacing to watch Thyra. She sat quietly upon Aric's throne on the dais, rubbing her belly. Her eyes stared off vacantly. I shook my head and continued walking. The lush grass beneath my feet felt foreign. Fate had stolen my mate from me, yet there was a way to save her. I could free her from an eternity of nothing, but... could I ask another to give their lives for hers?

Thyra's voice broke me out of my trance. "We need to talk."

"I... I'm not sure what to say... I can't believe these words are leaving my mouth but... I wish Aric were here." I huffed. "Out of all of us, he's the true leader. How can I possibly ask this of our people? I never wanted this responsibility."

Thyra rose from her seat and glided toward me. She rested her hand on my upper arm. "I know, but we are what is left, and it is our decision to make."

"But how? How can we choose? Do we ask someone to sacrifice themselves for our own selfish purposes? Do we force them? Or... do we live with the heartbreak?"

"Like you said... Aric's the true leader... And Emma... Together, those two are a force to be reckoned with. I'm not sure this world could survive their absence." She wiped at her eyes. "I think we need to take it to the people. Let it be their choice."

I sighed, knowing she was right, but the thought of requesting something so grave of the people sent shivers down my spine. "What about the others? Surt? Njörðr? The new leader of Niflheim, Ragna? They are all still here. What do we tell them?"

"This decision effects them as well. We should include them and their people in this discussion."

I nodded and walked over to a guard standing by the door. "Bring me Mayank and Rajnish." The guard bowed and left.

I resumed my pacing while I waited.

It took most of the day to gather a crowd in front of the castle. Every last soul within our realm stood before us. Red ringed eyes stared up at me. Faces streaked with tears littered the crowd. Others, however, stood locked jawed. I didn't have Mayank's abilities to feel emotions, but still they rang out as clearly as if they were all screaming.

Acid churned in my gut. I looked to Thyra. Her face was tight and tears welled in her eyes. It was up to me now. I stepped up to the edge of the hastily made platform that rose above the crowd and cleared my throat.

I gulped. "As you all know, Yggdrasil fell and our fearless King and Queen sacrificed themselves to save us from the fate of Ragnarök. The original twins lay cold in the morgue. But there is a way to save all four of them still." I rose my hand to the Mystic who stood beside Thyra. "We have a skilled necromancer at our disposal and he's informed us that he can bring them back and pull Aric and Emma from the new Yggdrasil." The faces of the people turned hopeful. "But... there is a catch..."

I paused to gather the courage to speak the truth. Everyone waited. I took half a step back. My arms shook. *Just tell them, my love.'* I jumped at Emma's voice in my head. I hadn't felt her since the moment the tree wrapped around her. I don't know why I heard her now, but I didn't question it. She gave me the strength I needed.

"A life is required to restore a life."

Gasps and cries rang out through the crowd. Some buried their heads in their mates' chests, while others glared at me.

"We decided that this was not a choice we could make for anyone... not even those of the other realms." I nodded to the other rulers. "If saving our King and Queen is your wish, then I ask for two souls to volunteer. If you oppose this option, we will respect your wishes. You may leave and no one will stop you, but if anyone wishes to volunteer, please come forth now."

I stepped back and stood next to Thyra. We waited. The crowd parted silently for those that chose to walk away but more stayed than left. My chest ached with the force of my heartbeat. I gripped my arms behind my back to hide the shaking and prayed silently to the gods that someone would step up.

The crowd parted again and one fae moved forward. The ragged man had dark circles under his eyes and his filthy clothes hung loosely around his frame. The once powerful fae stood before us, a broken man. His now rounded ears distinguished him from the rest.

Lord Racnid knelt before us and placed his fist to his chest. "Your Majesties, my life is yours to do with as you wish. For my crimes against the crown, I forfeit my life to save theirs."

No tears streaked his face. His features were void of emotions. He spoke in earnest, without malice. He truly was prepared to give his life to save the man he tried to overthrow. I opened my wings, glided off the platform, and touched his shoulder.

"Rise," I said.

He stood and looked me in the eye. "I was jealous and greedy. I tried to take what was never mine. Before..." He instinctively reached around for where his wings once were before dropping his hand. "I never would have done what he did to save us all... I now see that our people need him. I freely give my life for his." He placed his fist to his chest again and bowed.

"Thank you," I spoke low, so only he could hear. I gripped him around the shoulders and flew us back up to the platform. He stood next to the Mystic.

When no one else moved I looked at Thyra. Tears overflowed my eyes. I knew what I needed to do. I opened my mouth to speak but she stopped me.

"Emma would never forgive either of us if you do this," Thyra's voice broke as she spoke. "Besides, if it doesn't work, I need you here. I won't allow you to sacrifice yourself."

My chest tightened. I knew she was right. I wiped the tears from my face and turned back to the people. "Anyone else?" I asked.

"Me," a weak voice sounded from behind us. I turned to watch Damion hobble across the bridge toward us. "I told Emma I would protect her and if this is what I must do to keep her safe, I will..." He coughed and fell to his knees.

Thyra spirited to his side and helped him stand.

"How did you get out of your cell?" I demanded feeling the heat rise in my throat.

He shrugged. "I asked the trees to help." He straightened in Thyra's grip. "Please, let me do this... for her." He begged me.

I hated this man for everything he had done to us, but I couldn't fight the empathy in the pit of my stomach. He was dying and he was willing to give his life for my mate. In this moment, I loved the man. I nodded. I turned to face the crowd. A figure pushed through the people. Her eyes were wide with fear. I cocked my head as I watched her step closer. Her features looked so familiar, yet I didn't understand why. She was shaking her head as she walked. She dropped to the ground before the platform and sobbed.

"No... no... please, not him!" She shouted. I stepped to the edge and looked down at her. Her whole body trembled. "Please... not my boy."

Damion now stepped up beside me. "Mother?" he croaked out.

I looked from the old woman to the frail man at my side. My jaw dropped. He looked just like her. Thyra was quicker to respond, and she spirited the woman to the platform. The old woman wrapped Damion in her arms the moment she landed.

"I'm sorry, my son, for all I have done," she sobbed. "I put my faith in the wrong man."

"But how..." Damion asked, not returning her hug. "How are you here?"

She pulled away from her son. "Herrick had hidden you from me. Once he died, all his spells broke, and I felt you. I knew I had to find you and help you."

I caught him as he started to slump. "What's the point? I'm dying anyway." He rubbed his chest. "Your siren poisoned me and the healers can't stop it."

The old woman smiled. "That's because you aren't fae... You are a water nymph." I cocked my head at this news, but Damion didn't react. "Fae magic cannot heal you. Only our magic will heal you. I can do it, but it will require you to be in your nymph form."

"We have a large lake. Will that do?" Thyra asked.

The old woman smiled at her son and nodded.

Thyra continued. "And you will give your life for his? For our King and Queen?"

She turned to face Thyra. "Like him," she nodded to Racnid. "For my crimes against the realms, I gladly give my life to save them. I helped Herrick rise in strength and power. It is the least I can do."

"But Mother..." Damion started.

My chest ached for the man who tried to steal my mate away.

His mother touched his cheek. "For the years Herrick stole from you... from us... I will give you your life back, my child."

Damion flung his arms around her and held on tight. I turned to the Mystic. He bowed slightly in agreement. Looking back to my people, I rose my hands and spoke. "We have all suffered greatly in the past months. Go... be with family now. We will celebrate the lives lost and saved in time." I bowed to our people. The crowd departed, leaving the six of us and the other rulers the only ones that remained. I nodded my thanks to them.

Damion sagged under his own weight and collapsed to the floor and shook. His mother's eyes went wide, and she clasped her hands over her mouth. Thyra knelt beside him.

Thyra spoke in a rush. "He doesn't have much time left. If we're to save him, we need to do this now."

His mother nodded. Thyra and Damion vanished with a small pop. I gripped his mother and took flight.

CHAPTER 46

Damion

Thyra had spirited us directly into the lake and guided me to the rocky shore. The cool water lapped at my sides, stilling my body and the aching. I sat on the sandy beach as the waves washed over my legs, waiting, half expecting to see a tail, but my feet remained. My breathing slowed as I laid down on the sandy beach and inhaled.

I watched the clouds dance. My limps and body grew lighter than I had in years. My fears fled one by one. If I were to die, I'd die happy laying there in the water. A gust of wind brought me back to my surroundings. I lifted my head up, looking backward to see my mother and Brynjar land. Mother rushed to my side and knelt.

"My boy," she said. "I'll fix this. I swear to you."

"But how? How do I change forms? I hardly remember a tail."

She walked into the lake until she was waist deep. Her hands lowered into the water for a moment before she tossed her skirt onto the beach. She turned and dove headfirst into the water, her tail flipping into the air. Not long after, Mother shot back up, splashing water everywhere. She smiled as she swam closer and motioned for me to join her.

"You need to come deeper first. It's been a long time since you transformed, so it'll be harder. You need to picture your tail and drop the glamour surrounding you. Once the glamour is gone, it'll come naturally." She smiled.

I didn't trust my legs to stand, so I scooted on my butt across the shallow lake floor until I couldn't feel the bottom anymore. My mother's hands caught me as my weakened body sunk. Floating, I let water take me over. Strength flooded into me the longer I lay there. My legs straightened, and I kicked them to stay afloat. I pulled my pants off and threw them toward the beach. The water flowed between my legs, freeing the chains that held me back.

I shut my eyes and dipped below the water. My mind wandered back to my dreams. My memories. Searching for the way my tail moved. The weight of it. The muscles tightening and loosening. I reached for it now. Begging it to come back.

"Drop your glamour," I heard my mother say.

I had grown so used to my legs that I didn't realize I was still holding onto them in my mind. The burning in my thighs as I ran and climbed. Emma's hand on my leg. *No... She is not mine. I* loved her, but I had to let her go. If I wanted to be free, I had to leave her behind. I opened my eyes and looked at my mother.

"Are there others? Like me?" I asked.

"Yes. All water is connected for the nymphs. We can travel from lake to lake, ocean to ocean, and river to river. You only have to find the portals. There is even a village here in this lake. Reach out with your mind. I sensed them the moment my skin touched the water. You can have a full life as your true self."

My heart lightened. I could let Emma be. Reaching out my mind, I tried to find the others. An image of a town similar to that in my memories flashed behind my eyes. Nymphs swam far below me. Waiting. I smiled. Pain seared down my legs and I cried out.

"Easy." My mother gripped my arm. "It's been a long time, so it hurts, but it'll pass."

As she said it, the pain lessened. I looked down. The green tail from my past flipped in the water. I lifted my hands to see the same color fins on the side of my arms. Fear and excitement raced through me. I wanted to swim. I wanted to run. Pain stabbed my chest, and I clutched my throat for air.

"Slow down, son. I need to draw the toxin from your body and heal the damage."

Relaxing my body, I let her place a hand on my chest and closed her eyes. Hot tendrils crawled up my tail and arms, heading through my veins and straight for my chest. I clamped my jaw shut to keep from screaming.

Mother's face contorted as she pulled away from me. White streaks emanated from my chest into her hand. In one swift motion, she ripped them away from my body. I watched in horror as they soaked into her skin. She coughed and spit up blood.

"Mother!" I shouted.

"I'm fine. Don't worry." She waved her hand as she wiped the blood from her chin. "You're safe now. That is all that matters." I reached out and wrapped her in a hug, she squeezed me tight. "I must go now." She pulled away and looked me in the eye. "I am so proud of you, my son. There is still goodness inside you despite all that you have been through." Her hand lingered on my cheek for a long moment before she looked away.

I knew the truth now. My mother had killed my father and let Herrick steal me away. I hated her for that. But she was giving me my life back and for that, I could find the strength to forgive her. "I love you, Mother."

"I love you too, son." She turned and swam to the beach. Her tail vanished, and she kicked with her feet. Thyra tossed her the skirt before she reemerged from the water. Once she reached Thyra and Brynjar standing on the beach, she turned back to me.

"You're not alone, my son. Go, be happy." She smiled and pointed behind me.

I cocked my head. She twirled her finger and pointed again. I turned in the water and saw a group of nymphs waiting in the distance. They all smiled at me. I knew that they were what was left of my family. I swam off toward them without looking back. My heart broke at the family I'd lost, but rejoiced at the one I found.

CHAPTER 47

Emma

Silence overwhelmed me. My heart broke. I couldn't even speak to my brother, the only living soul I'd ever see again. Sorrow took hold of me, leaving me blank.

The darkness engulfed us as if this tree were our own tomb. I rubbed my arms at the thought. The chill reached my bones.

I leaned against the wood of the hollow tree as far away from Aric as I could, which was but a few inches. It wasn't his fault, I knew. I wasn't trying to hide from him, but from myself. He'd never get to hold his child and that... that was my fault. Guilt overwhelmed me. I hadn't found a way to save the twins and forced Aric to make this choice. To leave her alone. I turned my head as the tear fell.

Aric's hand wiped it away. "Don't... don't cry."

"H-how? How did you even know? I can't even see my own hands."

"How have I always known when you were sad? I just knew. This is not your fault any more than it is mine. We did what we must for our people. I'll still get to watch her grow and that will do." He pulled me into a hug.

We stood there for a long moment in silence. Time passed differently within the tree. Maybe it was the darkness or maybe it was the magic of the tree, but I had no idea if we'd been there an hour or a lifetime. Everything slowed down somehow.

I hadn't been able to sense Brynjar since the moment the tree encased us, and I was certain Aric hadn't felt Thyra either, but somewhere in the back of my mind, I heard something... like a whisper, just out of reach. I closed my eyes and grasped for it.

It was faint, but it was my Bryn. My body relaxed at the sound of his voice. I took a deep breath and smiled. I might never be able to touch his face again, but I could still feel him. He was speaking to our people, asking for their help. He was afraid... Genuinely scared. His panic raced my own heart.

'Calm, my love.' I projected my thoughts and prayed he heard them. I lent him my strength and caressed his mind gently.

I felt him relax a bit and pulled out of his mind. It took more to hold on to him than I had strength. I would hold tight to him all of my life if I could. I sighed and leaned into Aric a little more.

"They're trying to save us," I breathed out before my body gave into sleep.

I expected to be sore when I woke, but I felt oddly renewed. It was as if the tree gave us strength. I looked at Aric. My eyes, finally adjusting to the darkness, could make out his features. His eyes were closed in a deep sleep. I leaned back against the tree and pictured what they could do to save us.

A crack brought me out of my thoughts, and Aric jumped instinctively, reaching for his sword. I moved my hand to his, gripping his hilt.

"Don't draw that thing!" I shouted at him. "You'll slice me in half in here!"

He blinked rapidly, shook his head, and relaxed. "Sorry. Habit." I let go of his hand and he dropped it to his side. "What was that sound?"

"I don't know. It sounded like the tree cracked."

"This one's not dying too, is it?"

My chest tightened and cut off air to my lungs. Thoughts raced through my mind. '*What if we didn't get all the beetles? What if Herrick set me up?*'

"Breathe, Em!" Aric rubbed at my arms, calming me.

"Sorry... but what if..."

"No. You can't think of that. We are fine."

Another crack.

I hugged tight to my brother and buried my face in his neck. A bright light blinded me. '*This is it... We're dead...*'

'*Don't you dare. Not after what we've been through to save you.*' Brynjar's voice sounded in my head. My heart leapt in my chest. '*Turn around,*' he told me.

Slowly, I turned my head. Through slitted eyes, I saw his silhouette. He stood with four other figures. The light burned my eyes.

"Your eyes will readjust to the light," a monotone voice spoke.

"Now, if you will come out, we will take your place," the same—but not the same—voice spoke.

I looked at Aric. He smiled through tears. Only Thyra could make him feel that way. I looked back at my mate. I now saw the figure of Thyra beside him. Brynjar held up a hand for me to take. I gripped Aric's forearm and together, we stepped out into the light, into our mates' arms.

The voices that spoke were the twin sisters standing next to Brynjar. They were much smaller than Aric and I. Smaller even than Thyra. Like children. Their pale skin shone in the light and their long hair was drained of all color. Even their white eyes stared off in the distance.

They took a step forward. I gripped one of their arms, stopping them.

"Are you sure you want to do this? I mean, you had your freedom."

They cocked their heads at me.

"We were created solely for this purpose, Your Majesty. The gods made us for this. It is our duty," the one on the left said with no emotions.

"But don't you have dreams of your own?" I asked.

"We have no names. No dreams. No thoughts other than to protect the Realms. Now," she ripped her arm from my grasp, "I believe your work here is done. Thank you for protecting the people when we could not."

"What... what happened? How are you healed?" I asked them.

"Dedi took the lifeforce of those who willingly gave their lives and placed their energy into us, giving us life," the other one said as if it were the simplest thing in the world.

"So... two died for you?"

The twins bowed their heads slightly and stepped forward into the new Yggdrasil. The tree enclosed them the moment they stepped inside.

"Who?" Aric asked before I could.

"Racnid and Damion's mother," Thyra answered.

I looked from her to the tree to my mate. I reached out toward him. My hands roamed over his body. He was solid, not a dream. We were really out and he was really there before me. My fingers traced his face. His cheeks were damp.

"I'm really here, my Kompis," he whispered.

I collapsed into his chest and breathed him in. Lilacs penetrated every pore. Every emotion I'd been holding back hit me all at once. Tears streamed down my cheeks and a laugh burst out of me. His chest rumbled with joy as he held me tighter.

Aric and Thyra laughs joined ours, and not long after, their arms wrapped around me. We laughed and cried until I thought I'd fall to the ground.

I was home.

EPILOGUE

Emma

One Year Later

T he warm mid-day sun shone down on the festivities. The fae stopped their activities and bowed as we strolled by their shops. Hardly a moment passed when Brynjar wasn't at my side, and I couldn't have been happier. After everything I had gone through in the past year, being alone frightened me. I hugged his arm tighter as we weaved through the crowd.

We stepped into the former training grounds where the new Yggdrasil stood even taller than before. The twin sisters' magic helped it grow strong. Since they entered it, the space became hallowed ground. I visited often when the weight of the crown became too much to reflect on what could have been. I shivered at the thought.

"Are you all right?" Brynjar asked, moving his hand from my arm to my waist.

"Yeah... I'm just..." I looked into the face I loved so much and smiled, "thankful to be here with you." I leaned in, kissing his lips softly.

He drew me closer, deepening the kiss. The squeals of a tiny fae pulled us out of our embrace. I turned to see Aric, Thyra, and baby

Armina walking into the field. Thyra held her baby tight, despite her flailing arms stretching out, not toward me, but to my mate.

His deep rumble of a laugh warmed my heart. He stepped closer and took the bundle from Thyra. Armina settled the moment she was in his arms. He shifted just his hand into the furry paw of his bear and gently set it on the baby's stomach. Her hands laid upon his. She cooed and fell asleep almost instantly.

"I don't know how you do that, Brynjar," Aric laughed. "We've had several sleepless nights as of late and you seem to be the only one that can get her to sleep so fast."

My mate prodded my brother. "Oh, we know you've had sleepless nights... You know we're still right next door. You could always ask for help.... Unless it's beneath you."

"Boys!" I scolded them.

"Sorry," they said in unison.

I stepped up beside Thyra and wrapped my arm around her back. She rested her head against me.

"How are you doing, momma?" I asked.

"Exhausted," she sighed. "Everything hurts and I just want to sleep."

"Bryn and I can take the baby a night or two if you need. You and Aric could even sneak back to his treehouse if you need to rest." I hugged her tighter. "Don't worry. We will help you through this phase, sis."

She stepped out of the hug and turned to look at me. "Thank you."

"You're welcome."

"No... I mean it. You've always been kind to me, even when I was lying to you about who I was, and even after you found out. You're the only one that I'm proud to call sister and I just want to thank you for that."

I smiled. The kind of smile that radiated all over. "I'm proud to call you sister as well."

She returned the smile before moving back to my side. We stood together watching two of the strongest men in the realm staring with goofy grins and wide eyed at the sleeping baby, and if I wasn't mistaken, Brynjar's arm was wrapped around my brother.

'Maybe you do like him after all.' I projected the thought to my mate. He pulled his arm off Aric and grinned, but didn't say anything back.

"It's almost time. You think I could have my baby back?" Thyra asked.

Brynjar nodded and handed the baby back. We walked closer to the tree. No platform had been created. No fancy decorations. No adornments. Just the massive ash tree stood in a field of lush green grass.

As we continued to walk, more joined us. By the time we reached our spot in front of the tree, the field was full. I stood with my back to the tree and scanned the swarm of fae. Our allies had joined us. Surt and his fire demons stood peacefully next to Njörðr and his Flygeblad. Ragna and her shadow warriors sat on the other side of Surt. The new leader of Svartelfheim, Evander, had accepted our invitation and he and his dark fae stood reverently beside the rest. Even Espen's entire clan of Berserkers had joined us for this festivity. The leaders of the other realms stood with us and faced their people as they sat on the ground before the new Yggdrasil.

My heart stopped to see Damion and the woman on his arm—I assumed to be his mate—stride up to us. I hadn't seen him since he'd joined the nymphs. He was still weak and pale, but now that he stood before me, he looked happier than he ever had. He wore loose green pants and she a long green skirt, her long brown hair pulled in front of her to cover her exposed chest. More beings dressed similarly walked close behind them. I stepped up to greet them.

They bowed. I only now noticed the small crowns on their heads and bowed back.

"Thank you for the invite," Damion's mate spoke. "Our people have not been on land in a long time." Damion coughed at her words and she bowed again. "Apologies Your Majesty, but under your mother's reign there were many restrictions forced upon us."

"I apologize for my mother's laws. Under our rule, you won't have to worry about that. We want peace and equality among all fae."

"Thank you," she said. Her smile was genuine.

I looked from her to Damion and back. Damion's eyes didn't meet mine. His mate nodded for me to continue. "Damion?"

He finally looked up with tears in his eyes. "I am so sorry for all I did to you and your people." He dropped his head the moment he finished speaking.

I stepped closer and hugged him. He relaxed and hugged me back.

"You more than made up for it when you were willing to give your life for mine." I stepped back and looked him in the eyes. "And congratulations," I said, looking back at his mate.

He wrapped his arm around her, and the two of them beamed. They nodded and took their spots. I returned to my mate's side. We waited until everyone was seated in the large field before anyone spoke.

My Kompis spoke low and reverently. "We gather here today one year after Queen Emma and King Aric were pulled from the tree and the twins took their place. We are here not to shout our joy or sing our praise but to simply be." He knelt low, letting his fingers comb through the grass. His voice was low as if he only spoke to me but magically it echoed as he continued speaking to the masses. "We are fae. We come in all shapes and sizes, but we are fae. Today, every elemental is represented. Today, nature is one with fae and the fae are one with her. Instead of the boisterous parties we have grown accustomed to, in the future, this festival will be known as The Day of Silence."

All work will stop and only the sounds of nature will be heard. Take the time to appreciate Her a little more than we normally do. Even the fae can forget where we come from and it's good that we never forget how quickly things can change and our world can be torn apart." He wrapped his arm around me and pulled me closer, then nodded to the people. "Go and enjoy the day in whatever way you see fit."

The fae of Alfheim departed first, heading back to their homes. We bowed and parted to let those of the other realms pass one by one through Yggdrasil. There would be other days of celebration to catch up with old friends. Damion and the water nymphs were the last to leave. I smiled as they headed toward the large lake.

Aric and Thyra—still cradling the baby—stood beside us. "Well spoken, brother," Aric said to Brynjar as he rocked his daughter. "Thank you for addressing the people. I know public speaking isn't your favorite, but we have been a little preoccupied as of late."

"You look exhausted," Bryn replied. "I'm happy to help whenever you need it. If you need us to take Armina for a night or if you want me to handle the council meeting in the morning."

"I think Armina's alright for now but I'd happily let you take over the meeting." My brother winked at my mate.

My Kompis nodded as Aric and Thyra turned and headed back to the castle.

Bryn reached for me and I leaned into him, sighing in my mate's arms. It was a day to be joyful, yet a sadness intertwined my soul. I felt a deep loneliness in my stomach. I tried to shake the feeling, but I couldn't hide it.

"What's wrong, Emmy?" Brynjar asked.

I shrugged. "I... I don't know... I am happy for Aric but..."

He laughed. The pain stabbed through me and I twirled in his grasp, ready to yell at him, but his grin stopped me.

"What?" I asked.

"I think I know what's wrong. Here," he stepped back and lifted his hands to my temples. "Let me show you something."

"A dream?" I asked, but he didn't respond.

The moment his hands touched my skin, we were no longer in the field but in the great hall of the castle. The four of us sat upon the dais at the far end, watching a handful of children playing. One I recognized instantly as Armina floating on clouds above the rest. Another tried to match her height with his dark wings.

But what lifted me were the three tiny bear cubs wrestling with a white-winged little girl.

Afterword

If you enjoyed this book chech out my other books!
If you are interested in keeping up with my writing journey, please follow me on TikTok or find me on my website and sign up for my newsletter.

One of the best ways to support Indie Authors is by reviews so if you enjoyed this story, Please leave a review everywhere Books are Sold or on Goodreads or StoryGraph!

Check out my website for my other books and other cool stuff!

kari robins.com

Acknowledgements

This book is dedicated to the four friends that kept me going, Julia, Lianona, Amanda, & Marissa. Without their help Damion would have been pure evil and would have dies in a firey ending and Emma and Aric would have been trapped in Yggdrasil forever. Words cannot express how much you all mean to me and maybe someday we will have our writers retreat.

I also want to thank my family for having patience and understanding and for giving me the time I needed to write.

I had an amazing set of editors that helped me rework this story and bring it to light. Lianona West and Destany Booth, thank you from the bottom of my heart for all your hard work!

ABOUT THE AUTHOR

Kari Robins has always preferred the written word to the spoken word. She has been writing flash fiction since she was in middle school. She would write stories instead of taking notes in class.

Kari is a working mom and wife.

A high school teacher encouraged her to become a writer but feared her grammar wasn't good enough. But now she pays an editor for that!

She recently graduated from college to become a teacher for Technology and Engineering but the COVID-19 pandemic changed her plans and she started writing again.

She started off writing new adult paranormal romance but has recently discovered the paranormal woman's fiction genre and has fallen in love with older main characters.